David Thomas is a journalist and writer, who already has an ongoing thriller franchise under the name of Tom Cain, published in the UK by Transworld. *Blood Relative* is the first book under his real name.

BLOOD
RELATIVE
DAVID THOMAS

Quercus

First published in Great Britain in 2011 by

Quercus
55 Baker Street
7th Floor, South Block
London
W1U 8EW

A CIP catalogue reference for this book is available
from the British Library

ISBN 978 0 85738 797 4

10 9 8 7 6 5 4 3 2 1

Typeset in Swift by Ellipsis Digital Limited, Glasgow

Printed and bound in Great Britain by
Clays Ltd, St Ives plc

FRANKFURT, WEST GERMANY: 1978

Out on the tiny, circular dance floor a blonde and a brunette were dancing to the Bee Gees, giving it their best moves. All they needed now was some male attention. But Hans-Peter Tretow wasn't about to oblige.

'Well then, here I am. What do you want?' Tretow said, turning his back on the girls. He was in his midtwenties, dressed in a double-breasted suit and a silk kipper tie. His voice still had the brash, even cocky, selfconfidence of youth. He leaned against the bar, a glass of beer in his hand, looking at a second man, who was sitting down, his tall, thin, pipe-cleaner body folded onto a stool.

The thin man said nothing. He had rocker sideburns and black hair slicked back. A caramel leather jacket with flared lapels hung from his bony shoulders and the deep shadows in his sallow cheeks darkened still further as he held a hand to his mouth and sucked on the last few usable millimetres of his cigarette.

'Get on with it,' Tretow insisted. 'I've got business to do tonight.'

Now the thin man spoke. 'No, you haven't.' He stubbed out his cigarette into a plastic ashtray on the bar. 'You've got to get out. You were followed. They've got you nailed.'

Tretow looked angry, as though this were all somehow the other man's fault. 'Not possible. I'd have noticed if someone was watching me.'

'Evidently you did not.'

'Well then, call Günther, get him to pull some strings. He can make this go away.'

'No chance: the investigation is too far advanced. Anyone steps in now, people will start wondering why. You'll have to disappear.'

'I know a place in Bavaria, right up in the mountains. I could take a break there. Take the wife and kids.'

The thin man tapped another cigarette against the bar, beating out time as he said, 'You don't get it, do you? This isn't about taking a holiday. You've got to disappear . . . completely . . . now.'

'Don't tell me what to do!'

'All right then, go to the mountains. Then wait to see who finds you first – the cops, or whoever Günther sends to silence you. You'll never make it to the inside of an interview room. You know too much. He won't let it happen.'

'He wouldn't dare!' Tretow's voice was still assertive, but there was more bluster than certainty in it now.

The thin man reached out and gripped Tretow's lower arm hard. 'Listen to me, you arrogant sack of crap. You must have known this could happen. You've got an escape plan, right?'

Tretow nodded.

'Well then,' said the thin man. 'Use it.'

On leaving the club, Tretow did not return home to his wife Judith and their two infant children. Instead, he drove his smart new Mercedes 250C coupé to a grimy, run-down side street lined with lock-up garages. He opened one of them up and drove in, parking next to another car, an unwashed ten-year-old Volkswagen Beetle, painted beige: as anonymous and nondescript as any vehicle in Germany.

At the back of the unit a door led to a small, dirty, foul-smelling toilet. Tretow reached behind the low-level cistern. He pulled at two strips of black masking tape and released a clear plastic bag no more than twenty centimetres square and then tucked it inside the Beetle's spare wheel. From a storage cupboard covered in flaking green paint Tretow removed a workman's boiler suit, boots and donkey jacket. He put these on in place of his smart suit and tie. Then he drove the Volkswagen out of the unit, locked the doors behind him and started driving.

When Tretow reached the outskirts of the city, following the signs to the A45 autobahn, north towards Marburg, it was twenty-seven minutes past one in the morning.

He drove for two and a half hours. For three hours after that he slept in the car park of a service area beside the autobahn. When he woke, he set off again, heading east.

It was now seven in the morning. In Frankfurt, a detective coming to the end of a fruitless surveillance shift was reporting back to his boss that Tretow had not come home all night. Voices were raised, increasingly agitated phone calls were made and police across the state of Hesse were told that Hans-Peter Tretow was now, officially, a fugitive from justice. Local railway stations and airports were also informed. It would, however, take a little time to coordinate a wider, nationwide alert.

In all the fourteen hundred kilometres of border between West and East Germany, there were just three points at which motorists could pass from one country to the other. One of them was at Herleshausen, eighty kilometres west of the city of Erfurt. Tretow's VW joined the long line of cars and trucks waiting to enter the communist dictatorship. All the drivers, passengers and vehicles were inspected by East German border control officers from Directorate VI of the Ministry of State Security, otherwise known as the Stasi. Tretow was ready. He had both his passport and Federal Identity Card. He explained that he was travelling to West Berlin where he hoped to get work on a construction site.

In order to get to there, however, first he had to cross 370 kilometres of East Germany. For this he needed a visa, which was issued not by the day or month but by the hour and minute. The East German authorities did not want anyone stopping by the side of their autobahns to pick up clandestine passengers who might wish to escape to the West. Drivers were therefore ordered to proceed down the road at a continuous eighty kilometres per hour. At this rate, the journey was calculated to take no more than four hours and forty minutes. That was, therefore, the amount of time for which Tretow's visa would be valid. Should he arrive at the Drewitz-Dreilinden checkpoint on the south-west outskirts of Berlin any later than this, the Stasi would want to know why.

Tretow waited his turn in the interminable queue before he was finally issued with his visa and set off again. It was now nineteen minutes past ten. In Frankfurt a formal alert was being sent to West Germany's Federal Border Guard, requesting Tretow's immediate apprehension and arrest. The checkpoints on the western side of the Berlin Wall were included in this alert. If Tretow attempted to enter West Berlin he would be caught and returned to Frankfurt by air.

But Tretow had other plans. When he reached Drewitz-Dreilinden he joined one of several lines of vehicles backing up along the autobahn. Each line crawled towards a raised platform. On each platform stood six white wooden passport control booths, one per car, occupied by uniformed personnel.

Up ahead of the checkpoint the Berlin Wall was clearly visible, topped by barbed wire and supplemented at intervals by guard towers filled with machine-gun-toting soldiers. Beyond the wall lay an open killing field strewn with anti-personnel mines and tank-traps, and patrolled by guards with attack dogs. Beyond that space stood a second wall. Many civilizations in history, from the Chinese to the Romans, had built mighty walls to keep their enemies out. None had ever gone to such lengths to keep their own people in.

Tretow inched forward until the Beetle was lined up alongside one of the booths. As he handed over his papers he said, 'I wish to defect.'

The passport control officer frowned, wondering whether this shabbily dressed worker in his beat-up car was playing some kind of a joke. Before he could respond, Tretow spoke again. 'I am seeking political asylum,' he said. 'In the East.'

1

TUESDAY

York, England: now

My wife Mariana was the most beautiful woman I'd ever laid eyes on and yet she was so bright, so complex, so constantly capable of surprising me that her beauty was almost the least interesting thing about her. Six years we'd been together and I still couldn't believe my luck.

That morning, when it all began, I'd told her that my brother Andy was coming to stay for the night. I said we were planning to go out for a quick pint before supper.

'It's Mum. Andy's going over to see her today. He's bothered about the way she's being treated. He just wanted to talk about it with me and he knows you never got on with her, so . . . hope you don't mind.'

I must have had a particularly sheepish look on my face because Mariana laughed in that wonderful way of hers, so carefree and full of life, but always with that tantalizing hint underneath it that she knew something I didn't: 'That's fine. You guys go and have your brother-talk,' she said, just the faintest of accents and oddities of grammar betraying her German origins. 'I will stay home and cook, like a good little hausfrau.'

Mariana giggled again at the absurd idea that she, of all people, could ever be the meek, submissive wife. I just stood there in the kitchen grinning like a fool: but a very happy fool.

My name's Peter Crookham, I'm an architect and I'm forty-two years old. If I have a distinguishing feature it's my height. I'm tall, six-three in my stockinged feet. I played rugby at school and did a bit of rowing at university: nothing serious, just my college eight. These days, I'm like every other middle-aged guy in the world trying to get his act together to go to the gym or stagger off on a run, wondering why his trousers keep getting tighter. Those love-handles: where did they come from? I have pale-blue eyes and mousey-brown hair, just starting to thin. Last summer for the first time I got a small patch of sunburn on my scalp, the size of a fifty-pence piece. 'Poor bald baby,' teased Mariana as she massaged the after-sun cream into my bright pink skin.

As for my face, well, when women wanted to say nice things about me they never used to describe me as hunky or handsome. They told me I had a kind smile.

I was never anyone's dirty weekend. I was the nice, reliable, unthreatening type of guy that a woman didn't feel embarrassed to be seen with at a party. But she wouldn't be worrying herself sick that some other girl was going to make a beeline for me, either.

Basically, I'm Mr Average. Or at least I was. Then Mariana came into my life.

Twelve hours had passed since I'd told her about Andy and now the pint would have to wait. I'd been held up on a site visit in Alderley Edge, Cheshire, eighty-odd miles from our place outside York. Heading home along the M62 I called her on the hands-free. A combination of snow-flurries, roadworks and speedcams had slowed the traffic to a crawl: an all-too familiar story for a Tuesday night in February. 'I'm definitely going to be late,' I said. 'Looks like I'll have to scrap that drink with Andy. Is he there yet?'

'Yes, he is here,' Mariana said. There was something strange about her voice: a flatness that I'd never heard before. Or maybe it was just a bad connection.

'Can I have a word with him?'

'No,' she said, 'he cannot talk.'

'That doesn't sound like Andy,' I said, smiling to myself. The hard part was usually getting him to stop talking, particularly if he had a chance to take the mick out of me. 'What's he up to?'

'He is . . . he is on his own phone, I think. Maybe he will call you back when he has finished. I must go now. The dinner is cooking.'

Then she hung up. And that was odd, too, because Mariana always said, 'I love you', or sent me what she called a 'sweet kiss' at the end of a telephone call. When she was feeling particularly naughty she'd say something in German and then cut the connection, laughing, before I could work out just how filthy she was being. But she never just hung up.

I wondered whether Andy had been standing nearby and made her too embarrassed to say anything. But Mariana didn't do embarrassment. I'd learned that from the first moment I'd met her.

Maybe Andy had pissed her off. God love him, my kid brother could be an irritating little tit sometimes. A newspaper reporter has to be persistent even if that infuriates some of the people he deals with, so never knowing when to stop must have come in handy when Andy was investigating a story. But it could be a seriously annoying characteristic in a social context. That might explain Mariana's tone of voice, though, if the flatness were just suppressed anger.

It took me about another hour to get home. Along the way I ran through a bunch of possible scenarios in my mind, working out various ways of pacifying two people who'd always got on perfectly well until now.

Then I put that to one side and turned on the radio. I was the senior partner in a practice called Crookham Church and Partners – Mariana worked there too – and we got a lot of business from footballers. In our part of the world, they were just about the only people still making enough money to pay for fancy new houses. One of our clients was playing in a Champions League game that was about to kick off at Old Trafford. I might as well find out how he had got on.

Shortly before the game reached half-time, I pulled into our drive and parked the car in the triple garage. As the door automatically shut behind me I walked across the gravel towards the front door, my shoulders hunched against the freezing wind. I was just about to put my key in the lock when it swung open.

Mariana was standing there.

Her long, honey-coloured hair was tangled and matted with something liquid that had started to dry in thick, rubbery clumps, as though someone had poured paint over her head.

The stuff was on her face, too, fully dried by the warmth of her skin and then cracked by the movement of her mouth and forehead.

In the half-light of the porch it was hard to see what colour it was. But as I got closer I saw that her dress had been patterned by wild spatters of the stuff.

'Darling?' I didn't know what else to say.

Then she stepped away from me, back into the house and the light, and I could see that the colour was a deep crimson, darkening in places to a purple black.

And now I knew what it was that had sprayed her entire body; that had drenched her hair and her dress; that clung to her face, her arms and her hands; that had been smeared across the flagstones behind her as she walked.

Mariana was covered from head to toe in blood.

2

We stood there silently, motionless, maybe four feet apart. Mariana looked at me but seemed to see nothing. Her tawny, tiger eyes, flecked with gold and green, had always sparkled with intelligence and life. Now they were blank and her face lacked any expression. She seemed entirely indifferent to the state she was in. She just said, '*Hereingekommen*', the German for, 'Come in', turned and walked back into the house.

From the back she looked almost normal. She was clean.

Our house was a barn conversion. The way we had designed it, the garage and main entrance were at the rear of the building. A hallway served as a repository for coats, umbrellas and boots. At the far end an internal door led you beneath the sinuous glass and metal curves of the staircase to the showpiece heart of the house, a huge, open-plan living space, open to the full height of the building.

The kitchen area was to the right. The units were 'Modern Purism' by Poggenpohl: Mariana's choice and another one of her surprises. I'd expected something warm and natural, but their sleek, unsentimental efficiency made the kitchen look less like the heart of a family home than an office for cooking in.

Maybe she'd been trying to tell me something. We were so busy perfecting other people's homes, there'd been no time to give our own place the love and attention we lavished on our clients'. For them we were obsessive about detail. We'd go to any lengths, take any amount of trouble to source the perfect tile, tap, door handle or work surface. When we worked for ourselves, though, it was more a case of getting the basics in fast, and adding all the personal touches later. To make life simpler and quicker we'd bought most of the furniture from the Conran Shop, everything chosen in a single Saturday afternoon. Three Naviglio leather sofas formed a square whose fourth side was a massive fireplace. The dining table was walnut, as were the matching chairs.

All but one of the walls were painted in Casablanca by John Oliver: a soft, dusty, soothing and completely inimitable white emulsion. The far wall, however, was almost entirely glass, with spectacular views across the North Yorkshire countryside. At night the glass became a shining black backdrop against which we played out our lives.

Or a death, as it was in this case.

Mariana turned right into the kitchen. '*Ich muss die Nudeln retten bevor sie überkochen,*' she said.

Apart from the odd dirty joke, we'd always spoken English. Mariana used to say she preferred it to German, which she only half-jokingly called 'Hitler's language'. But out of embarrassment at my own incompetence and just wanting to do something for her I'd spent a few months playing a Speak German course in the car. I'd picked up enough to get the gist of what she was saying. She was worried that the pasta was about to boil over.

I didn't reply. It wasn't that I didn't know the right words. I was simply incapable of speech.

Andy was lying almost directly in front of where I stood, about halfway to the far wall. His face was frozen in an expression of fear and bafflement. His pale-blue, button-down shirt was punctured with stabs, though they were nothing compared to the terrible open wound that had cut his left thigh open almost to the bone.

Andy had died at the centre of a spreading, swirling eruption of blood. It lay on the floor in puddles and smears whose patterns showed the thrashings and spasms of his dying limbs as clearly as angel wings in the snow.

The blood was not confined to the floor. It had been flung across the canvas-white walls like the first scarlet spraying of a Jackson Pollock painting. It was dripping from the fancy leather sofas – one of them in particular was doused in it – and the wheeled bookcases that stood on either side of the fireplace. It soiled our creamy rugs. There was even a single scarlet handprint on the glass opposite me. The floor beneath it was a messy confusion of bloody footprints. Andrew must have reached out for support. Or perhaps it had been Mariana. Maybe she had gone to help him. Maybe that was why she was covered in blood. I mean she couldn't have . . . no, that wasn't possible. Not Mariana.

Up to now I had been numb, as though my brain had been overwhelmed, unable to process the torrent of sensory and emotional information with which it had been flooded. I'd never in my life seen a dead body before. Our father died when I was twelve and Andy was five, but Mum wouldn't let us see him. She said it would be too upsetting. So I had no idea until then how utterly changed the human form is by the absence of life, how absolute the difference between existence and its termination can be. A corpse bears no resemblance whatever to an actor lying still and trying not to breathe. A corpse that has bled out is doubly emptied: the stuff of life has left it as well as the spirit.

Finally, the reality of Andy's death seemed to register, like a website that takes an age to upload but then flashes all at once on the screen. I actually reeled back a couple of paces, as though I'd received a physical blow, and that was probably just as well because it took me away from the corpse and the blood. So when I threw up all over the floor in front of me none of the vomit corrupted the evidence.

I straightened up, wiping the spit and puke from my mouth, and walked over to the kitchen sink. I turned on the tap, caught some water in my cupped hands and used it to rinse out my mouth. A second handful was splashed over my face.

Mariana was almost close enough to touch, standing by the hob, ladling spaghetti out of a giant pan into three white bowls. '*Viel von Nudeln für jeder*,' she said in a cheery, almost singsong, voice: plenty of pasta for everyone. And then, more to herself, '*Die Männer haben Hunger. Sie müssen genug haben, zum zu essen*': the men will be hungry, they must have enough to eat.

Her bloodied fingers had left red smears on the white china crockery and the aluminium pan. I had a terrible vision of blood in the cooking water, like squid-ink, and as the pasta came out of the water I half-expected it to be pink. Mariana was working like an automaton, oblivious to the fact that the bowls were piled to overflowing and that the pasta spoon she was dipping into the pan was coming up with nothing but water.

I didn't know how to react. I didn't know what to feel. Grief for Andy and anger at his death; fear and concern for Mariana, mixed with love, a kind of pity and an instinctive desire to protect her; above all a total bafflement at what was confronting me. All those emotions swirled inside me, colliding and cancelling one another out until all I was left with was numbness.

Mariana's mood suddenly changed. Her head darted from side to side. She was obviously looking for something. *'Wo setzte ich der carbonara Soße?'* She was wondering what she'd done with the carbonara sauce. The hob had nothing on it apart from the pan that had held the pasta. For a second, I too looked about me for the sauce, as though it could be magicked into being, that normality could somehow be restored.

That was when I saw the knife.

Mariana had bought a set of Japanese chef's knives: the Ryusen Blazen series. They featured a core of powdered tool steel, sandwiched between two layers of soft stainless steel, with cutting edges honed to the thinness of a razor blade. The biggest knife in the set had a wide blade 240 millimetres long, which tapered to a point sharp enough to draw blood if you so much as rested a finger against it. It was called a Western Deba. It was lying just the far side of the three white bowls, and the last drops of stringy, semi-coagulated blood were still falling from its blade to the pure white of the Poggenpohl work surface.

Finally, I found my voice.

'What the hell are you doing?'

'What it looks like. I serve the meal.'

Finally, Mariana had spoken English, but her accent was still more Germanic than usual. She sounded like a different person.

'But Andy's dead!'

She looked at me uncomprehendingly.

'Sorry? I don't understand. Your brother is now not coming to supper?'

3

I dialled 999. When the woman on the other end of the line asked me which service I wanted, my mind seemed to scramble. 'I don't know,' I blurted. 'Someone's dead at my house. He's been stabbed. Somebody killed him.'

She took my name and address and told me to stay where I was: 'The police and an ambulance will be with you soon.'

When she mentioned the police I thought of all the thrillers I'd read, the TV cop shows I'd seen: detectives always suspected the family first. What if they thought we'd done it? Somewhere inside I must have known that Mariana was the only possible suspect, but I was a long way from admitting that to myself or anyone else just yet. I speed-dialled my lawyer, Jamie Monkton. He handled all the practice's contractual work. Jamie wasn't the kind of lawyer who hung around a lot of police stations. But he was the only one I knew.

'I need your advice,' I said.

'No worries,' he replied. 'Give me a call in the morning. Can't talk right now, I'm afraid. We've got people over for dinner.'

'No, this is an emergency. My brother Andrew is dead.'

'Oh shit, I'm so sorry. When?'

'Tonight, at the house. He's lying on the living-room floor. There's an ambulance on the way. They've probably notified the police, too.'

'My God, what happened?'

'He was stabbed. He was lying there when I got home.'

'Stabbed? Jesus . . . I'm sorry, Pete, I don't know what to say . . . How's Mariana?'

'She's here. She's not doing too well. I mean, physically she's fine, but she's in a hell of a state mentally. They were the only people in the house.'

'Oh, right . . . I see.' Monkton's voice changed as he took in the implications of what I'd just said. He seemed to be casting aside his role as my friend and, for the first time, looking at the situation through lawyer's eyes. 'Look, this is a bit out of my territory. You're going to need criminal lawyers – both of you, I should think. And they're pretty hard to find these days. No money in it, you see, and you have to be specially registered to be able to take legal aid cases.'

'We don't have much time, Jamie. Would it just be quicker for me to look in Yellow Pages?'

'No, I'll find someone . . . hang on, there's someone here . . . Samira something: one of our friends brought her as his plus-one. I'm sure she said she did legal aid work. She might be able to help. Look, I expect the rozzers'll bring you both down to York nick. They might move you to the force HQ at Newby Wiske later if they think the case is important enough. But the first stop will definitely be York, so I'll meet you there, with anyone we can rustle up. In the meantime, don't touch anything that looks remotely like evidence. And when the police arrive, say nothing. Keep it to name, rank and serial number.'

'Sorry about your dinner party,' I said, still under the mistaken impression that I was living in a world in which any of the normal rules and manners of my past life still applied.

'Don't be ridiculous,' said Monkton, 'that's the least of our worries. Listen, Pete, be careful, OK? This is serious stuff . . . Right, I'd better go and get things moving. I'll see you later.'

I managed to get Mariana to a dining chair, well away from Andrew's body. I guided her with a hand in the small of her back, where there wasn't any blood. Aside from that, I didn't touch her. I didn't put my arms around her to comfort her. I told myself I was doing only what my lawyer had told me. But it was more a case of self-preservation. I didn't want to be implicated in whatever had happened here. If only I'd known what was going to happen over the next hours, days, weeks, months, I'd have let the evidence and implications look after themselves, taken Mariana in my arms and pressed her as close to me as I could, just to feel her against me. But I didn't, and I've regretted it ever since.

Mariana was settled now, still very passive, staring blankly into space. I pulled up a chair, sat down and tried to talk to her, but she didn't even seem to be hearing me. We were still there a few minutes later, as silent and still as two showroom dummies, when there was a sharp rap on the door.

The police, it turned out, had got there before the ambulance. Two cars arrived in quick succession: a pair of uniformed officers in one, two detectives in the other. When he saw Mariana, the senior of the two detectives called up his station and asked for a third car and a female PC. And that was just the start.

We were both arrested and read our rights. I imagine that for some people the words of the police caution must be part of their everyday lives, as familiar as their name and address, or the words to 'Happy Birthday'. But I'm not one of them. As the constable intoned, 'You do not have to say anything. But it may harm your defence if you do not mention when questioned something which you later rely on in court. Anything you do say may be given in evidence,' I could barely credit that he was talking to me. When I said, 'But I haven't done anything,' he didn't even try to disguise his scepticism.

Once that was done, we were asked to give our version of events. I refused to talk without a lawyer present. I also pointed out as strongly as I could that Mariana was incapable of understanding anything that was said to her, let alone responding with a coherent answer. Finally, the police realized there was nothing to be gained by trying to get any more out of us there. One of them led me down to a police car and bundled me in the back. Mariana was taken to another car, accompanied by the female constable.

By that point our house was already making the transition from a home to a police crime scene. An ambulance was parked by the door, its two-man crew chatting to one another as they waited for permission to remove Andrew's body. Inside the building, a pathologist was crouched over the corpse, while white-suited scene-of-crime officers got to work on the gory evidence.

We left them all behind as we were driven away. Mariana's police car was ahead of mine. Just as we were passing through the gates, I saw her turn her head and look back, whether towards me, the house, or something quite different, I don't know. Her face was caught wide-eyed in our headlights. Mariana's beauty, her self-confidence and her once unbreakable spirit had all deserted her. She looked strained, helpless, frightened, with the particular fear of an animal or small child that cannot comprehend what is being done to it, still less do anything to change its circumstances.

I barely recognized her.

4

Jamie Monkton was right. We were taken to York police station, a modernist seventies block hidden away behind the Victorian walls of an old army barracks. The words North Yorkshire Police were written across the front in white sans-serif capitals.

As I arrived I caught a brief glimpse of Mariana's back as she was led away by the WPC. I was booked into custody by a uniformed sergeant and told I could have someone informed that I was being detained at the station. I gave him the name of my business partner Nick Church. The sergeant then offered me a copy of the Code of Practices governing police treatment of suspects under the Police and Criminal Evidence Act and informed me of my right to consult a solicitor, free of charge.

'My lawyer should be getting here any minute,' I said.

'Very well,' he said. 'Now we need to fill in a risk-assessment form.' Even in the nick you can't get away from health and safety.

He asked me whether I was currently taking medication of any kind, would need to see a doctor, or suffered from any form of psychiatric illness. Then he told me to take off all my clothes except my socks and underpants. He also asked for my watch and mobile phone. They would all, he said, be needed for forensic examination. I didn't bother to protest or plead my innocence. But I remember, very clearly, a sudden pang of fear that somehow some of Andy's blood might have got onto me and that this would then be used to claim that I was there at the time of the murder. That was immediately followed by a spasm of guilt that my first thought was to save my own skin, rather than think of the far greater trouble that Mariana was in.

I was given a rough, grey blanket to wrap myself in and led away to a cell. I am not someone who normally suffers from claustrophobia, but when the steel door was closed and locked, imprisoning me, it was all I could do to slow my breathing and force myself to overcome the near hysterical surge of fear and panic. I lay down on the solid, padded bench that ran along one wall, closed my eyes and tried to relax. My confinement, though, was a brief one. Within minutes the door was reopened and Jamie Monkton walked in. He frowned as he saw me shifting into a sitting position, swathed in my blanket.

'What happened to your clothes?'

'Taken away as evidence.'

'Well, they're not leaving you like that.'

I wasn't interested in my clothing, or lack of it. All I wanted to know was, 'Have you seen Mariana? What are they doing with her?'

He shook his head, 'They're keeping her under close watch, making sure she doesn't hurt herself or anything until they can rustle up a police doctor to examine her. But they'll need a shrink, too, if they want to section her.'

'Section her? But that's for loonies, isn't it?'

Monkton sat down next to me on the bench. 'Listen, Pete, you've got to face facts. I don't know what's happened to Mariana, but she's acting, well ... unusually, to put it mildly. And if they do charge her, some kind of insanity plea may just be her best line of defence.'

'Why does she need a line of defence?'

'You know the answer to that question.'

'No I don't! She hasn't done anything. She can't have. I was with her in the office all morning and she was fine. I spoke to her mid-afternoon and it was a perfectly normal conversation. How could she go from that to ... ?'

'I don't know, Pete. Better leave that to the experts to decide. I just wanted you to know, though, I was right about the girl at the party. She does do crime.

You and Mariana are each going to need a lawyer, so she's gone to get her boss. They'll be here soon. Meanwhile, I think they want to get you sorted for a photograph, DNA swab, all that kind of thing, OK?'

'I suppose. I mean, it's not like I have any choice in the matter, right?'

'Afraid not. But I will insist they get you something to wear.'

'Just make sure Mariana's all right.'

'I'll try,' Monkton said. 'You OK?'

'I'll live.'

He stood up, gave me a quick, almost embarrassed pat on the shoulder and asked to be let out. Ten or fifteen minutes later, I was given a pair of jeans intended for someone considerably shorter and fatter than me, and denied a belt to hold them up. They also found me a white shirt, made from some sort of synthetic fibre that made me feel as if I were wrapped in a plastic bag. I was asked to fill in a form giving my consent to being photographed and swabbed, then I was taken away to have the procedures done. I spent another twenty minutes back in the cell, and then I was taken away again.

5

The interview room was featureless, just a box painted an indeterminate pale grey with darker grey carpets; a rectangular table with a voice recorder and a couple of microphones; two metal-framed plastic chairs placed by each of the long sides of the table; a camera on the far wall pointing down into the room.

I was sitting on one side of the table, facing the camera. A uniformed cop stood on the far side of the room, watching me, saying nothing. Then the door of the room opened and a woman came in. She was Asian, with huge brown eyes emphasized by dramatic make-up and lips painted a glossy, almost liquid crimson. She wore a short, close-fitting, sleeveless dress, with sheer tights and teetering heels, all black, and as she walked up to the table, the room was filled with a heady, spicy scent.

'I'm Samira Khan,' she said. 'And in case you're wondering, no, I don't normally dress like this for work.

I was at the Monktons' dinner party. Jamie said you might need some help.'

'What about Mariana? Is someone looking after her?'

'My senior partner, Mr Iqbal,' said Khan. 'He insisted.'

She looked at the policeman. 'You can go now,' she said, like a young duchess dismissing a footman. 'I need some time alone with my client.'

Once we were alone, Khan sat down in the chair next to mine.

'Right,' she said, 'we don't have much time, so pay attention. You are about to be interviewed by Detective Chief Inspector Simon Yeats. He's good and he knows it, but remember: you don't have to tell him anything. If there's a question you don't like, don't answer it. Don't let him put words into your mouth. Words can easily be twisted. You say something one way now, it sounds very different when it's being read out in court.'

'But I don't have anything to hide. I haven't done anything,' I said, thinking that she at least would believe me.

She gave me a smile like a mother indulging a foolish child.

'You think that would make a difference?'

I was about to reply when footsteps sounded just outside the door. Samira Khan raised a finger to silence me as Yeats entered the room. He was about my age, early forties, wearing a dark-blue suit with a white shirt unbuttoned at the neck, tie loosely knotted. He was shorter than me, but fit-looking: the kind of man who plays squash three times a week and doesn't let the younger guys at the club knock him down the ladder.

'Good evening, Ms Khan,' he said, draping his jacket over the back of his chair.

'Chief Inspector,' she replied, coolly, but I caught an undercurrent in her voice: whether it was hostility, something sexual or a bit of both, I couldn't tell. They knew each other pretty well, though, that was for sure.

Yeats sat down, placed a notebook on the table in front of him and smiled. 'Ms Khan has a very low opinion of our working methods,' he said. He had a voice like mine: middle-class, educated, but with an unmistakable trace of Yorkshire. 'But I can assure you, Mr Crookham, at the risk of stating the obvious, that we take cases of murder very seriously. We play them by the book. So let's proceed.'

He pressed a button on the recorder and stated the names of all the people in the room as well as the date and time. Then he repeated the words of the caution. Before he could ask a question I said, 'I want to speak to my wife.'

'I'm afraid that won't be possible, Mr Crookham,' said Yeats, his tone more formal now that the tape was running. 'She's currently being examined by a doctor.'

'Is the lawyer with her?'

'She has the proper legal representation, yes.'

'Is she all right?'

'That's not a question I can answer. Nor would I tell you, even if I could. You are a potential suspect in a murder case, Mr Crookham. I think we should concentrate on that. So perhaps you could start by telling me exactly what you were doing in the hours leading up to the arrival of the first officers at your house, shortly before nine o'clock this evening.'

I looked at Khan. She gave me a nod.

'Where do you want me to start?' I asked.

Yeats gave me another smile, more like a friendly GP asking a patient to describe his symptoms than a copper trying to nail a murderer. 'Just talk me through the day, why don't you?' he said.

'All right. Well . . .' I stopped for a second to gather my thoughts. All the normal, everyday things that had happened earlier in the day seemed to belong to another lifetime, lived by a different person. 'Mariana and I left for work at about half past eight this morning. We work together, at our architectural practice Crookham Church. Our office is in Archbishop's Row.'

'Very nice area,' said Yeats. 'Business must be good then.'

'It's holding up OK, yes.'

'So you drove to work . . . Together?'

'No, separate cars. We knew we'd be coming home separately.'

'Could you tell me exactly what cars you were both driving?'

'Certainly: I drive a Range Rover Sport, Mariana has a Mini Cooper S.'

'And these vehicles are currently at your house?'

'Yes, in the garage.'

'And your brother, did he have a car?'

'He has . . . had, an old Alfa, the one parked in our drive.'

Yeats made a note, then looked up and said, 'So, how long were you at your office?'

'Till about one. I had lunch early, at my desk. Then I had to leave for a 3.30 site visit in Alderley Edge: just a routine meeting with my clients and the contractor.'

'Can you give me the names of these clients?'

'Mr and Mrs Norris . . . Joey Norris.'

'Like the footballer?'

'No. The actual footballer, and his wife Michelle.'

Yeats raised his eyebrows, pursed his lips and went, 'Humph.' He was impressed. People always were. I wondered, a little bitterly, whether he was tempted to stop the interview and ask me the same question everyone else did: 'What are they really like?'

Instead, Yeats just asked, 'They can confirm you were there?'

'They could, but I'm sure they'd much rather not get involved with all this. I can give you Joey's agent's number, or the contractor. His name's Mick Horton; he can tell you everything you need to know. And you can work out where people have been from the location of their mobile phones, isn't that right?'

Khan frowned. She didn't look happy that I might be about to volunteer information.

'We're already checking that,' said Yeats.

'Good. Then you'll find that I called Mariana at about 4.30, from Alderley Edge. She was still at the office then. She said she was planning to head home at five to make sure she was there when Andy, my brother, arrived.'

'What was the purpose of your brother's visit?'

'He'd come up north to visit our mother. She's in a nursing home near Harrogate and Andy lives down near Ashford, in Kent. It made sense for him to spend the night at our place.'

'So your brother went alone to see your mother? You didn't think you should go too ...'

'I visit my mother regularly, Chief Inspector. But she suffers from dementia – Alzheimer's – so she easily gets confused. It's better if we go one at a time.'

That wasn't the truth: not the whole truth, anyway. But it seemed to satisfy Yeats.

'I see. And what was the purpose of the call you made to your wife at 4.30?'

'I told her the meeting looked like it was running late.'

'Why was that?'

'That's not relevant,' Khan intruded. 'My client has already told you that you can confirm his movements.'

'So he says, yes,' Yeats agreed. 'But the more detailed Mr Crookham's account is, and the more it tallies with the accounts given by other possible inter-viewees, the more I'll be inclined to believe what he says.'

'It's all right,' I said to Khan, then I looked across the table at Yeats: 'If you must know, Michelle Norris wasn't happy with the stone tiles in the front hall. She thought they were too dark. We had to sort out getting some new ones trucked over from Italy. Anyway, I didn't leave till about half-six and I called Mariana again an hour later, from the car – hands-free, before you ask – to let her know when I was getting home.'

'I'm not interested in traffic violations, Mr Crookham. Go on . . .'

'Well, Andy and I had been planning to have a drink at the Queen's Head before dinner, but I told her we'd have to scrap that.'

'So this would be at approximately 7.30?'

'Yes.'

'You're sure about that?'

'Yes. I was listening to Five Live. They were doing the

build-up to the United game at Old Trafford. Kick-off was 7.45, so it must have been about 7.30.'

'Was this a long call?'

'No, a couple of minutes at most. Not even that, probably.'

'Because you were just informing your wife that you wouldn't be going down the pub with your brother?'

'Yes.'

'Did you speak to your brother?'

'No.'

Yeats frowned: 'That's odd. You didn't feel like saying hello, telling him yourself?'

'Actually, I wanted to talk to him.'

'So why didn't you?'

'Because ...' Suddenly it hit me why Andy had not come to the phone, but I didn't need Samira Khan to tell me to keep to that to myself. I just answered the question truthfully: 'Mariana said he couldn't talk to me. She said he was on his own phone.'

Yeats leaned forward like a hound picking up a scent. 'I see ... and how did she sound? When she said your brother couldn't talk ...'

Khan leaned across and whispered in my ear: 'You shouldn't answer this.'

Then she spoke up: 'A witness cannot be forced to incriminate their spouse, you know that Chief Inspector.'

'Really?' the detective replied. 'Show me the statute

of criminal law that says that. It's common law at best: at worst just a legal urban myth. In any case, Ms Khan, you're missing my point. We don't have a formal time of death yet, but it's clear that Andrew Crookham had been dead for at least two hours before the pathologist examined his body. If your client's alibi holds up, he cannot possibly have committed the murder. Meanwhile his wife, who almost certainly was in the house at the time of the death, is covered with blood. She appears to be in a very disturbed state of mind. A knife, also covered in blood, was recovered at the scene of the crime. It will be examined for fingerprints and DNA evidence. In the meantime it would be very helpful to be given some idea of Mrs Crookham's mental state at the time her husband arrived home.'

'If she's ever charged, maybe it would be,' said Khan, 'but not before.'

'The closer to the events described, the more powerful the evidence.'

'I'll answer your questions,' I said. I didn't care how much evidence the police said they had, it was inconceivable to me that Mariana could be guilty.

Khan glared at me: 'Well then you do so against my advice.'

Yeats looked pleased at his victory. 'So, your wife: how did she sound?'

'Odd. Flat. A little spaced-out. Like she wasn't quite with it.'

'Are you suggesting she was under the influence of alcohol, or drugs?'

'No. Mariana isn't a heavy drinker. And I've never known her to take drugs.'

'I see. So how did the conversation end?'

'She just hung up on me.'

'You didn't try to call her back?'

'No, there didn't seem any point. I was going to be home soon enough. If there was any problem, I thought I'd sort it out then.'

Out of the corner of my eye, I saw Khan give a rueful shake of the head, as if to say, 'I told you so.'

'What sort of problem did you think there might be?' asked Yeats.

'How can he answer that?' Khan interrupted. 'It's pure conjecture.'

'I don't know,' I said, ignoring her. 'I suppose I thought they might have had a row or something.'

Yeats said, 'Did they do that often, have rows?'

'No, they always got on fine.'

'So why would they start arguing now?'

'I can't think of a reason. It was just a possible explanation for her to sound the way she did.'

'Flat ... spacey?'

'Yes.'

'And now what do you think?'

'My client will not answer that question,' said Khan, as much to me as to Yeats.

The Chief Inspector changed the subject: 'So your relationship with your wife, how's that been lately?'

'Again, irrelevant,' said Khan.

'I'll be the judge of that,' Yeats insisted.

'My marriage has been fine, thank you very much.' I said. I wanted it on the record, for all the world to know.

'There's no one else involved?'

'No! My wife is the love of my life, Chief Inspector. She's the most beautiful woman I've ever seen. Why the hell would I want anyone else?'

'Plenty of men cheat on beautiful wives.'

'Not this one.'

'Has she cheated on you?'

'No, I'm sure she hasn't. Why can't you just believe me? We were happy.'

'I'm not trying to cast aspersions on your married life, Mr Crookham. I'm trying to work out why your wife would lash out with a knife and repeatedly stab your brother in a frenzied attack that led to his death. And one reason why a woman attacks a man is sex. Maybe she was defending herself. Is it possible your brother might have tried to force himself upon her?'

'What, so my wife is an adulterous murderer and my brother is a failed rapist? Has it occurred to you that they might both be victims? Why aren't you looking for someone else, an intruder? Criminals break into people's houses all the time and if there's anyone there they kill them. Or it could be some kind of loony, a schizophrenic or something. Anyone could have done it. But all you want to talk about is my family.'

'That's because one of your family's lying dead in the mortuary and the other's currently being examined by a police doctor, prior to a full psychiatric examination,' said Yeats. 'Meanwhile there is no evidence of any break-in: no forced locks, no broken windows, no footprints, nothing. So excuse me if I don't waste my time looking for people who don't exist. Now, let's get back to your story. What time did you arrive home?'

I talked him through the sequence of events from the moment I got out of the car until the arrival of the police. When I finished the Chief Inspector said, 'Thank you, Mr Crookham. I've just got two more questions.'

'Go ahead.'

'First, for the record, did you kill your brother, Andrew Crookham?'

'No, I did not.'

'And second, do you have any information that might help us to establish why your wife would have killed your brother?'

'Absolutely not.'

The Chief Inspector spoke into the microphone to state that the interview was being terminated and gave the exact time before he switched the tape recorder off. Then he got up from his chair, paused before leaving the room and said, 'Thank you for your cooperation, Mr Crookham. I'm sorry for your loss.'

Samira Khan and I were left alone in the room. She walked to the far wall, directly beneath the camera, then motioned me across to her.

'They can't see us here. The camera's supposed to be switched off at the end of the interview, but you can't be too careful. I just wanted to ask: that information you gave, about the site visit and the phone calls: it'll hold up?'

'Yes, of course.'

'You didn't touch the knife?'

'No.'

'Then they've got nothing on you. You'll be all right, I'll make sure of that. It's your wife you need to worry about.'

6

Of course I didn't sleep. How could I? Even if my mind hadn't been picking away at the events of the past twenty-four hours like a fingernail attacking a scab, police procedures demand that suspects held in cells are checked every thirty minutes to make sure they've not tried to harm or even kill themselves. The officers don't actually come into the cell. But the sound of a metal panel sliding back and forth across a hole in the door, and the sudden shaft of light from outside and the unsettling sense of being examined by an unseen eye are more than enough to stop anyone who isn't obliterated by drink or drugs from getting any rest.

So I lay on that hard slab of a bench with just a single rough blanket to cover me, trying to come to terms with what had happened. And this is where I have to make a confession. I know I ought to have been thinking about Andy. He was my brother and he was dead. I should have mourned him, grieved for him, run through scenes from our life like home movies in my head. But I didn't. All I could think about was Mariana.

I went right back to the day we met. At that point I'd been divorced from my first wife Stephanie for two years. Steph was nice, kind, sweet, modestly attractive, averagely unexciting: the perfect woman for the man I was then. She was a pharmacist. When we bought our first and only home she chose a nice little three-bedder in a new development because she preferred the cleanliness of a new build. We very rarely got angry with one another. When we split it was all very civilized. There were no children, no recriminations and the most depressing thing about it was my relief that the marriage was over.

Still, I made a poor job of being a bachelor. I told everyone I was too busy with my career to have time for a new relationship, and that was half true. The practice was still in its infancy so I had to work all the hours God gave just to keep the whole thing moving forwards. But it was also a good excuse to avoid a repetition of the kind of relationship I'd had with Stephanie. We'd stopped being individuals and become Peter-and-Stephanie, the Crookhams. Pete'n'Steffi to our friends. I'd really had it with that.

It was an unusually warm day in May when Mariana Slavik arrived at our office, looking for a summer internship. She was twenty-four years old; German, though her English was excellent; studying for her postgraduate diploma in architecture at Sheffield University. It's not a bad faculty by any means, highly regarded in fact, but I was curious about why she'd come to England at all. Germany is hardly short of first-rate places to study our profession.

Mariana tilted her head to one side, pouted very slightly as she thought for a moment and then explained with a shrug that there was nothing for her in Germany any more. Her father had left home when she was a girl and made no effort to stay in contact. Her mother had just remarried for the second time, 'And this one is even worse than the last.' She had no siblings. 'I broke up with my boyfriend,' she said. 'He was such an asshole.'

It didn't seem to bother her that she had brought her private life into a job interview, or used a mild obscenity. She just gave a dismissive, almost noiseless, 'Puh!' with such natural comic timing that it was all I could do not to burst out laughing. I tried to look very serious as I shuffled through her references, qualifications and drawings, all of which were excellent: far too good, in fact for the menial coffee-making, photocopying, errand-running work we had in mind. When I glanced up again, Mariana was sitting calmly, awaiting my next question. Behind her, however, Nick Church was grinning lewdly and giving me a massive thumbs-up. Our secretary,

Janice, was shaking her head in silent despair at male idiocy. And our two junior staff, Jake and Laurie, were staring, as goggle-eyed and slackjawed as goldfish.

Frankly, my performance had been little better than theirs. Mariana had walked into my life wearing a sleeveless orange T-shirt and jeans, with a big brown leather bag slung over one shoulder. Over the years, I'd get used to her entrances and the ripple of people's expressions as she walked down a street or across a room. But this was the first time, and its immediate effect was to make me suddenly nervous, slightly sweaty and hopelessly incoherent. I felt as though she were interviewing me, rather than the other way around.

As I would discover from being with Mariana, extreme beauty is a force of nature and a form of power. It strikes at some deep, primal, instinctual level of our animal selves. It defines its owner as an alpha-female. And Mariana was certainly that.

'That's a one-woman argument for Intelligent Design,' Nick said to me in the pub after work. 'You'd have to have God-like genius to dream up a body like hers. There's no way random genetic mutations could do the job.'

I smiled at the truth as much as the humour of the joke. Any half-decent architect knows that the measure of a building isn't in the flashiness of its exterior or the money that's been spent in tarting it up. It's all in the detail, from the craft that's gone into the joinery of a timber roof, right down to the smallest light switch. And it was the details that I came to know and love in Mariana: the parabolas described by the curves of her eyebrows; that arrow-straight nose that was almost, but not quite, too long for her face; the way the line of her lips was so precise, yet the flesh of them so full and pillowy; the arch of her back as she cat-stretched first thing in the morning, lying next to me in bed; the velvet touch of her skin beneath my fingers.

I wish, too, that you could know, as I do, how she smelled and tasted; what it felt like to have her in my arms; the combination of incredulity, ecstasy and triumph that surged through me every time we made love. That I should possess such a creature: no matter how much time went by, it never really seemed possible.

At first, of course, I never even tried. I didn't look on it as weakness or cowardice, simply a realistic appreciation of where I stood in the sexual pecking order. Nick, on the other hand, had a go within a few days of Mariana's starting work with us in August. Well, of course he did. At the time he was driving a second-hand Porsche 911, while I had a Land Rover Discovery: slower and much less impressive, perhaps, but far more practical when you have to get to a barn conversion at the far end of a Yorkshire dale. Those two cars told you all you needed to know about the difference between us.

Nick took Mariana out for a drink a couple of times, then laid on dinner at a restaurant he knew near York Castle. The owner knew Nick and appreciated his generous tips and fondness for expensive claret. He always greeted Nick with an effusive smile, gave him the quietest, most secluded table and made a fuss over the girl he was with. From then on it was up to Nick to close the deal.

'Not a chance,' he replied, when I asked him about it over bacon sandwiches and coffee in the office the following morning. In those days it was our habit to get in early once in a while to talk things over before everyone else arrived. Since Mariana was an employee, albeit unpaid, we agreed that her dinner with Nick constituted company business and thus a fit subject for discussion.

'She was very polite, very sweet, said thank you for dinner and gave me a peck on the cheek. And it was blindingly bloody obvious that was all I was ever going to get.'

'Have the dynamic duo tried their luck?' I asked.

'Jake did. He's such a chancer, that lad, he'll always have a go.'

'And?'

'Same thing: smile, peck, no dice. Young Master Laurence is still trying to find the courage to make a frontal assault. But let's be honest, it's a kamikaze mission.'

'Which just leaves me . . .' I said.

Nick laughed. I laughed. We both knew that was never going to happen.

The following day, I took Mariana on a site visit to a farmhouse renovation we were doing for a couple called the Blacks, just outside Harrogate. The main building work had all been completed. It was now just a question of fitting out the interior.

Mariana was quiet and watchful, saying nothing as I spoke to the tradesmen, checked work against the plans and had a lengthy discussion with Mrs Black about where she wanted various bits of equipment to go in the kitchen and utility room. There were seven men working on site and every single one of them found a different reason to come into the kitchen during the fifteen minutes or so that we were talking. It was painfully obvious that they were all after the same thing: a good look at Mariana.

The fuss was making Mrs Black increasingly irritated. She was a well-preserved woman in her fifties and it had obviously taken a great deal of exercise, shopping, dieting, hairdressing and make-up to keep her looking the way she did. Yet here was a girl young enough to be her daughter outshining her without any visible effort at all. It didn't help that her husband was barely able to stop himself drooling at the vision that had descended into his unfinished kitchen.

I was wondering how to ease the growing tension and persuade Mrs Black to put her hob where I had originally planned, not where she now wanted it, when Mariana spoke up.

'Excuse me, Peter,' she said, 'but I have to agree with Mrs Black. I can see, of course, that it is practical, yes, to have the hob against the wall, where you have put it. But there, whoever is cooking must look at a blank wall. If you place it on the island, as she suggests, then Mrs Black can look out and see what is happening in the house. She can talk to guests. She does not have her back to everything. So it is much better.'

Then she looked at Mrs Black and in a low, conspiratorial voice said, 'You know, Mr Crookham is a very brilliant architect, but still, he is only a man. There are some things he will never understand.'

The older woman smiled for the first time since the conversation had begun. Mariana walked over, took her arm and said, 'I think you have the most beautiful house. Everything is so perfect, so English. We have nothing like this in Germany. Please, I would love to see it all. Could you show me?'

'Of course, my dear, I'd be delighted,' said Mrs Black, all the tension and hardness now gone from her face. 'I'm so glad we've sorted out that business with the gas hob. We can leave the boys to deal with the rest of it.'

I should have been outraged. An intern had just contradicted me in front of a client and compromised the partnership's design. But how could I be angry when she had so obviously charmed our most valuable clients?

'Bloody hell, that's a right little smasher you've got there,' said Mr Black as the women left the room. 'Didn't know you had it in you, lad. Just make sure you keep me well informed if she's planning to make any more visits, eh?'

The weather had broken and the blue skies of a week earlier had given way to oppressive banks of black cloud marching in close formation over a bleak landscape of grey, brown and dull green. At lunch Mariana and I sat in the Discovery, ate sandwiches and shared a flask of coffee as the rain lashed down on the roof and ran in a single, unstinting torrent down the windscreen.

'I am sorry I was so rude,' Mariana said. 'It was wrong of me. But I could see that Mrs Black was about to become unhappy. Then her husband, he would become unhappy and then ... well, I thought I must act.'

'Don't worry about it,' I said. 'You did well.'

'You looked so sweet. I could see you were a little angry, but then I saw that you knew what I was doing, so I felt much better.'

Somehow, coming from her, 'sweet' sounded better than it had done from any other woman.

'The husband, though,' said Mariana, grimacing. 'Ugh! He is such a pig! Twice he tried to grab my ass.'

'I don't blame him,' I said, almost as a reflex, the words bursting out of my mouth before I could stop them, hanging in the air between us as the voice in my head went, 'Shit, shit, shit, shit, SHIT!'

A knowing smile spread lazily across her face.

'So you would like to grab my ass too?'

Ninety-nine times out of a hundred I would have said no, no, of course not, heaven forbid. I am, by nature, a cautious man and I was also Mariana's boss. The last thing I needed was accusations of sexual harassment from a young female employee. But there was a curl at the corner of her smile, a glint in her eye that hinted this was some kind of a test. And there was something else, too, some kind of connection, like a current flowing between us, an indefinable energy in the air. So I smiled back.

'Yes,' I said. 'I would.' And before I could lose my new-found nerve I added, 'Though I wouldn't grab it, exactly. I would caress it, or stroke it . . .'

Mariana laughed. 'And spank it maybe?'

Sod it, I thought, in for a penny . . . 'Yes, if you pull another stunt like that one in the kitchen, that's exactly what I'll do . . .'

A year later, almost to the day, we were man and wife.

7

The noise went on all night: the shouted arguments of drunks and coppers, the slamming of doors and the ringing of unanswered telephones. I tried to shut it out, keeping my eyes closed and concentrating on what was going on in my own head. As I looked back at those early days with Mariana, what struck me most was the sheer improbability. Of all the offices in all the towns in all the world, she walked into mine. What were the odds?

In retrospect, the ease with which she fell into my hands raised all sorts of questions about her true motivations that I'd never really dared to ask myself before. But how did that connect to the corpse lying on my living-room floor – the cold, ash-grey body, lying in a carmine pool that kept flashing into my mind, unbidden, like rogue frames cut into the movie of my life? I wasn't consciously thinking about Andy, but my subconscious wasn't letting go of him that easily. I opened my eyes to make the image disappear, waited a few minutes to reboot my mind, then went back to my memories of Mariana.

People treat you differently when you're married to a beautiful woman. It wasn't just the winks, the digs in the ribs and the frank expressions of envy from other men: women too changed in their attitude towards me. They were more flirtatious, but also somehow more serious, as if they really meant it. Over time, I came to realize that Mariana had given me an invisible seal of approval. She wanted me, so I must be worth having.

But why? The French have a saying: the woman chooses the man who's going to choose her. Mariana certainly chose me, and after a couple of years I plucked up the courage to ask her why. 'Well,' she said, taking a step back and looking me up and down appraisingly, 'you were the only man in the office who did not, as you would say, try it on with me. You were always very nice, very polite and respectful, the perfect English gentleman. But . . .' and here she gave a flirtatious little smile, '. . . when I gave you the chance, you took it. So then I knew that you could be a man, as well as a gentleman. And I thought, yes, he is the one.'

'Do you ever regret that choice?'

She wrapped her arms around my waist and stood on tiptoe to kiss me. 'Never,' she said. 'Not once.'

I beamed with pleasure at the sheer joy of being loved by her. Mariana laughed at the sight of me: 'And that is the other reason . . .'

'What is?'

'Your smile . . . When I first came to work, I would watch you in the office and most of the time you looked so serious, always frowning . . . the boss: always making decisions, talking to clients, arguing with suppliers. And then, just once in a while, something funny would happen and suddenly you would smile like a schoolboy, a cheeky schoolboy. I thought of how good it would feel to be the one who made you smile like that. And before you ask . . . yes, it is as good as I hoped.'

When a woman like Mariana says things like that, you feel like the king of the world. Under her influence I became more confident, started dressing a little more sharply. I swapped the Disco for a Range Rover Sport, and got that top-of-the-line convertible Mini for Mariana. We could afford the cars, along with a spectacular barn conversion of our own, because the business was going through the roof.

Part of it was just the general madness of those years as we all hurtled so merrily towards the great crash. But Crookham Church outperformed even that bull market, and the reason was not just my dogged ability to get a job in on budget and on time, nor even Nick's undoubted flair for coming up with new and original ways to adapt period buildings in a modernist style. The real reason, I'm sure of it, was Mariana.

One day, shopping for jeans at Harvey Nichols in Leeds, she got talking to another woman of about her age. After they'd bonded over trendy, absurdly expensive Swedish denim they went upstairs for coffee and girl-talk in the fourth-floor cafe. It turned out that Mariana's new best friend was an actual, real-life WAG. Her husband had played for Leeds United and then been transferred after they were relegated from the Premiership. 'How should I remember?' Mariana replied, when I asked which club he'd gone to. 'I have no interest in football. It begins with a 'B', I think.'

The 'B' club was paying the WAG's husband £50,000 a week. The couple had bought a house, torn it down and had new plans drawn up for the site, but things weren't going well. 'It looks rubbish,' the WAG had said. 'And the bloke that did them drawings is a total snob. He never listens to what we wants, just treats us like right idiots.'

Mariana mentioned that she worked at an architectural practice. 'Ooh,' said the WAG, assuming Mariana was a secretary, 'what's your boss like?'

'He's my husband,' said Mariana, laughing. 'And I am one of the architects.'

The WAG's eyes widened, she reached across the table and grasped Mariana's arm. 'Oh my God!' she squealed. 'You and your fella could help us with our house. I mean, you couldn't be worse than that other old bugger, could you?'

And so we became architects by appointment to the Premier League, installing private cinemas and games rooms for the players, and spectacular kitchens, bathrooms, master bedrooms and walk-in wardrobes for their wives. We became experts in gyms that put most health clubs to shame, and indoor pools big enough for Olympic swimming events. Our years of learning how to save money and get fancy effects at budget prices were now at an end. All our clients wanted was the best, brightest, newest and smartest, no matter what it cost.

I have to admit, I loved it. All architects dream of working for clients with bottomless pockets. When those clients can also provide free tickets to private boxes at Anfield and Old Trafford, or backstage passes to their girlfriends' concerts, or invitations to parties where half the other guests are household names . . . well, I defy anyone not to have their head turned.

I discovered, too, what a moreish substance money can be; how quickly one becomes used to it; how extravagances that once seemed unimaginable become part of one's normal, everyday expectations. My values were distorted: I admit it. But these were the boom years and there was a lot of distortion about.

As for Mariana, well, for the first year or two I worried that she would leave me for one of our fit, young, overpaid clients. Plenty of them had a go. That's what footballers do. Even the most apparently effete or nitwitted of them is a fierce competitor, a ruthless survivor who has only arrived at a professional career after a process of elimination that has seen hundreds of other young hopefuls fall by the way. Yet Mariana rejected them all, batting them away with her wit and charm, ensuring that no offence was taken on either side.

Instead, she put all her effort into winning over the women. Once they knew that she wasn't after their men, the WAGs loved being able to chat with a girl their own age. Mariana knew about fashion. One moment she could talk about the latest hot handbag and the next explain the technicalities of clients' building plans in language they could understand. Our business depends on word-of-mouth for new commissions, and the word among footballers' wives was that Mariana was a star.

And all the time, every minute of every day, I lived in the knowledge that Mariana wore my ring on her finger; that wherever she spent the working day, she spent the night with me.

*

I must have fallen asleep at some point because the next thing I remember is dreaming that I was back at the house, looking down at Andy's body. He was talking to me, but I couldn't hear what he was saying so I kept asking him to speak more clearly, then shouting at him – really angry because I was so frustrated – until Andy started trying to get up, so that he could make himself heard, and then he was sitting up and getting to his feet and . . .

I forced myself awake and there I was again, back in the cell. And for a brief moment that stark confinement felt like a place of safety.

8

WEDNESDAY

In the morning I was given breakfast. Then I stared at the wall. There was nothing else to look at. An hour after the empty plate had been taken away, when the panel slid open for the second time, I said, 'Excuse me.'

'What is it?' came a voice from outside the door.

'I'm going out of my mind with boredom here. Can I have something to read, please?'

'What do you think this is, t' bloody Hilton? You'll be wanting coffee and biscuits next . . .'

The panel shut again, leaving me embarrassed and defeated in equal measure. But a few minutes later, there was a rattling at the door and the custody sergeant came in, holding a loosely rolled-up tabloid newspaper.

'There you go,' he said, handing it to me with a smirk. 'Congratulations, you're famous.'

I found out what he meant, and why he'd been looking so pleased with himself, when I got to a double-page spread about ten pages in. 'Designers to the stars in knife-death horror,' read the headline. The paper had got hold of a picture taken at a big charity ball the previous year. It showed Mariana chatting to three football wives. Mariana was described as a 'busty blonde stunner . . . the German-born golden girl every WAG turns to when she wants the perfect home.' There was a much smaller picture of me, taken at the same event, looking smug in my dinner jacket and black tie as I shared a joke with a couple of Premiership managers. And inset into a panel, which had its own headline, 'World of Football Shocked by Slaughter', were shots of Joey and Michelle Norris and three more of the footballers we'd worked for. All, claimed the paper, were too upset by news of the tragedy to comment.

More hours went by. In the afternoon Samira Khan appeared, dressed for work this time. She saw the newspaper lying on the bench beside me, raised an eyebrow and just said, 'Ahh . . .'

'How do they know all this?' I asked, pointing at the spread.

'There's always someone in any police station who can't wait to call up a newspaper and make easy money. I would say the police leak like sieves, except that they're worse than that. A sieve has no choice in the matter. But some of these people do it deliberately.'

I put the paper down and asked, 'So what's happened to Mariana?'

'She was seen by a psychiatrist this morning. He determined she was not yet fit to be interviewed.'

'So can I see her?'

'I'm afraid the answer is no. But I am working with Mr Iqbal to see what will happen as and when you are released. It is a very delicate situation. On the one hand you are Mrs Crookham's husband, so you should be allowed supervised visits. But on the other you are potentially an important witness in the case and so it is possible that the judge may forbid any contact between the two of you.'

'But if she can't even answer police questions, how could she say anything to me that would affect the case? I just want to see her, let her know that I'm thinking of her. Give her a hug. Is that so wrong?'

Khan looked at me thoughtfully. 'I hope you don't mind me saying this,' she said, 'but I do not understand your attitude. Your wife is accused of murdering your brother. Yet all your sympathy seems to be for her. Surely your family, your blood, comes first?'

'Well, yes, I suppose . . . but . . . what can I say? Andy's gone. There's nothing anyone can do for him. Meanwhile, Mariana's being accused of killing him and no one seems to be thinking about any other possibility. But there has to be one. She couldn't have done it . . .'

'You have to face up to the facts,' Khan said, so gently that I just brushed her words aside. I was still thinking about her question, trying to work out the answer for myself as much as for her.

'I know this sounds terrible, but I maybe can live without Andy more easily than without Mariana,' I said. 'I mean, we had a pretty screwed-up family. My dad died young. My mum wasn't the easiest woman in the world to live with. Still isn't. We were, I don't know . . . complicated.'

'I think all families are pretty complicated in their different ways, don't you?'

'I suppose. But even so . . . do you know the worst thing of all? I haven't cried for Andy. I mean, my brother is dead, and the truth is, I'm just not feeling it like I should.'

'That is probably just shock,' Khan said, resting a hand on my shoulder. 'You have been through a very traumatic experience. It will take time for your mind to process everything. It's natural.'

'I hope so, because I feel pretty bloody heartless right now. All I know is, I just want to see my wife.'

Khan sat quietly, letting me know in her silence that there was nothing she could do.

'So what about me, then?' I asked.

'The police must very soon charge you, or release you. I think that, too, is about to be decided. Yeats wants to interview you again.'

Five minutes later I was led away down a corridor and into another grey room.

'I'm sorry to keep you,' said Chief Inspector Yeats, ushering us to our chairs. 'But I think you'll agree that it's been worth the wait.'

9

Yeats' attitude had changed in the fifteen hours or so since I'd last seen him. He looked tired – I doubt he'd got any more sleep than I had last night – but fundamentally relaxed. He was a man who'd done his job and got a result.

'I have good news, Mr Crookham,' he said. 'Your phone records match the account you gave me last night and the Norrises were both able to confirm your presence at their house. You can have your clothes back, too. There were a few very small traces of blood on one of the sleeves of your jacket, but that was entirely consistent with transfer from your wife's dress when you guided her across the room. Your prints are not on the kitchen knife, which appears to have been the murder weapon. There is therefore no reason to suppose you were involved in your brother's death.'

'So my client is free to go,' said Samira Khan.

'Well, I'd appreciate it if he'd answer a few more

questions first. And before Ms Khan objects, let me be frank with you, Mr Crookham.'

Yeats shifted forward, resting his elbows on the table: 'The evidence against your wife is overwhelming. You must know that.'

'No, I don't know that! And I don't know anything about any other explanation for what happened, because you've not even tried to find one.'

'For the last time, Mr Crookham, the basic facts of the case are not in dispute. To be honest with you, we've done our job as police officers: this is one more for the clear-up stats. But I will admit I'm not happy about the absence of a motive. I don't know why Mariana Crookham killed her brother-in-law, and it niggles me.'

'I'll bet it niggles. Your only suspect had no reason whatever to commit the crime. But maybe someone else did.'

'There is no "someone else", Mr Crookham. The sooner you understand that, the better. So . . .' Yeats looked down at his notes, frowned as he ran his eyes over a page and then asked, 'Your brother was a journalist, correct?'

'That's right.'

'How did that affect your relationship?'

'How do you mean?'

'You had a lot of celebrity clients. Did you ever discuss them with your brother?'

'No, absolutely not. I don't discuss my clients with anyone, nor does Mariana. When we design a home for someone, we become privy to a lot of personal secrets. I know things about the people I work for that would make instant front-page headlines. So my brother was the last person I'd tell stories to.'

'Because you didn't trust him?'

'Because it wouldn't have been fair. Stories were his business. I couldn't expect him to make an exception for me. It would be like a friend of yours confiding that he'd committed a crime. Would you keep that secret?'

Yeats shrugged: 'Point taken. So you kept things from him. Do you think he kept things from you?'

'I imagine so. He never liked talking about his work until it was safely in the paper.'

'So he might have been working on an investigation and you'd never know about it?'

'Of course. We weren't that close. It's not like we spoke every day, or even every week. I didn't know most of what he was doing.'

'I see . . .' Yeats leaned forward again. 'So he could have been investigating your wife and you wouldn't necessarily have been aware of it?'

'What?' The question had caught me totally by surprise. 'Why would he want to investigate Mariana? What is there to investigate? And who would ever want to know?'

'Quite a few people, judging by today's papers . . .'

'Only because . . . because of what's happened. There'd be no reason to investigate her, as you put it, without that. In any case, Andy wouldn't do that. He was a pretty ruthless bastard when it came to getting a good story. But he wouldn't betray his own brother.'

'What if he wasn't trying to betray his brother? What if he was trying to save him?'

'Save me from what? I'm sorry, but what on earth are you talking about?'

'How well do you know your wife, Mr Crookham?'

I had to make myself pause and take a deep breath to stop myself losing my temper. 'We've not spent more than a dozen nights apart in the past six years. We work together every day. I know everything about her.'

'So you've met her family, then?'

'She's estranged from them. Her father left home when she was very young and she doesn't speak to her mother any more.'

'That's what she told you, anyway.'

'What do you mean? Are you trying to suggest she was lying?'

The moment I said it, I was struck by the appalling possibility that he might be right. I'd spent all night creating an image of Mariana. Now the first faint cracks were appearing before my mind's eye.

'Well, where did your wife grow up?' said Yeats.

This at least I could answer: 'In East Berlin. Her mother took her to the West after the Wall came down, but she was an Ossi, an East German, for the first few years of her life. I used to tease her about it. I called her my Ossi Darling.'

'Adorable,' said Yeats drily. 'And what was her surname when you met?'

'Slavik.'

'And her date of birth?'

'Well, she was thirty on the 14th of June – you work it out.'

'There's no need. Your brother did . . . when he was trying, and failing, to find her birth certificate. It's all on his laptop, which we found in his car. Very organized, your brother. He had a special folder, just for your Mariana: internet links, research data, pictures – all carefully filed in the right place. You should take a look at it all one day. You might get quite a surprise.'

The image cracked a little more.

'What are you trying to tell me?'

'That I have reason to believe your brother uncovered information that could have caused your wife a great deal of embarrassment. He went to Berlin: did you know that?'

I couldn't keep the surprise from my face. Andy and I weren't the closest brothers on earth. But given that I was married to a German, who had been born in Berlin, you'd think he'd have told me that he was going to her home town. Unless the whole point was that he didn't want me or her to know.

I tried to bluff it out: 'Are you sure about that?'

'Absolutely,' Yeats replied. 'There are numerous references to his visit in his notes as well as confirmations of his flight and hotel bookings among his emails. We've checked them too, of course.'

'All right then: no, I don't remember him mentioning that. Maybe he was planning to tell me last night . . .'

Yeats nodded. 'Maybe he was. Maybe that's what upset your wife – that he was on to her.'

'On to her how? Don't tell me he'd got some dirt on her because I don't believe it. Not unless you can show me something specific, with evidence, written in those notes of his.'

'No, I can't do that.' Yeats admitted. 'There's a lot of stuff on there, but most of it's dead-ends and questions.'

'So he hadn't really found anything at all?'

'Nothing definitive,' Yeats agreed, 'but I think that just made him even more curious. Because he should have found something, shouldn't he? Think about it. No matter how obscure we are, we all leave a trail as we go through life. But with your wife, it's like she was invisible. He'd got one possible lead, a photograph . . . but even that didn't have a positive ID and he doesn't seem to have followed it up successfully.'

'So are you going to do that?'

This time Yeats' smile looked genuinely amused. 'Go on a wild goose chase to Germany, for a murder we've already solved? No, that wouldn't be an appropriate use of police resources. Not the way our budget's being cut. But let me put this hypothesis to you, Mr Crookham. Suppose your brother had finally discovered something big about your wife, a real breakthrough in the case. I know what that's like. It's a very exciting feeling. And suppose he hadn't had time to log it in his computer. Or it was something he was keeping private, locked away in his head. In any event, he finds himself at your house, alone with your wife, and this discovery is banging around in his brain. So he can't resist. He asks your wife a question, or he puts an allegation to her. Because that's what he does. It's his job. And this discovery, whatever it is, comes as a huge shock to your wife. It makes her feel as though her whole world, everything she's worked for, is about to fall apart. So she panics. Maybe the balance of her mind is disturbed. But anyway, she . . .'

'She launches a savage attack on my brother with the knife that just happens to be lying within easy reach. Is that it?' I asked.

'Something like that.'

'Well it's totally absurd. I just don't believe it.'

'Do you have a better explanation, Mr Crookham?'

I said nothing. Yeats looked at me.

'I didn't think so. Well, thank you for your help, anyway. You are free to go now. Your clothes and personal effects are still at the lab, but they will be returned to you in due course. Your brother's clothes will be needed as evidence, but we'll be returning his effects and his computer once we've taken a copy of the hard drive. Given the state of your mother's health, can I take it that we should send everything to you?'

'Yes, I'll be responsible for it all.'

'I thought you might. Now, I don't know how aware you are of the media interest in this case, but you won't want to be leaving through the front door. The vultures are starting to gather and you don't want to be talking to them. Far too easy to say the wrong thing.'

Samira Khan spoke up, 'Why don't I read a statement explaining that no charges have been brought against my client and respectfully requesting the media to allow him some peace and quiet at this difficult time?'

Yeats nodded: 'While you're doing that, we'll get Mr Crookham out through the back and away before anyone's got time to react. And here's my card.' He passed it across the table towards me: 'If you think of anything that might be useful to the investigation, or come across any relevant information, you can call me at any time . . . if Ms Khan has no objection.'

'I would advise my client to speak to me first,' she said. 'But no, I don't object.'

Ten minutes later I sneaked out of the police station. I was a free man again. But Mariana was still in there, still a prisoner until someone, somehow, came to set her free.

10

They gave me back my belongings when I left the police station. The moment I switched my phone on it started going crazy, pinging and beeping with a flood of incoming emails, texts and voicemails. Half a minute later, I'd switched it off again. I wasn't even close to being ready to deal with other people's reactions to all this. I was having a hard enough time making sense of my own.

A police officer drove me back to the house. He watched over me as I gingerly made my way round the edge of the living room, unable, despite myself, to take my eyes off the dark stains of Andy's blood that seemed to cover so much of the walls, floor and furniture. I filled an overnight bag, though I did not know where exactly I would be, or for how long. Then I got in the Range Rover and made my way back into town.

I'd worked out a basic 'To Do' list when I was in the nick. I wanted to sit somewhere quiet and dark and just try to deal with Andy's death, Mariana's arrest and my own inability to understand either. But there wasn't going to be any chance of that. Like it or not, the next few hours were going to be spent running errands.

First stop was the office where Samira's boss, Mr Iqbal, was based.

'I take it your wife will not be applying for legal aid, Mr Crookham,' said Iqbal, opening our conversation. He was a small, unprepossessing figure, just running to fat, with a few strands of hair stuck to his balding scalp.

'No, just send the bills to me,' I said, doing my best to sound like an important, revenue-generating client who needed to be taken seriously. 'And whatever it takes, whatever it costs, I don't care. I want her to get the best defence. I don't give a toss what the police say, I can't believe she could have done this ... Not Mariana ... It's not possible ...'

Iqbal perched his chin upon steepled fingers, examined me for a second and then said, 'I understand, Mr Crookham. Your feelings are very natural at a time like this. You have my deepest sympathy and condolences for the loss of your brother. And I am sure that we will consider every possible option when we enter a plea on your wife's behalf.'

That was not what I had wanted, or expected, to hear.

'Why do you need to consider "every possible option"? Just say she's not guilty. Job done.'

Iqbal shrugged. 'I'm afraid it's not that simple, Mr Crookham. I am sure that the police have already told you that the weight of evidence against your wife is really quite overwhelming. When this is coupled with the absence of evidence suggesting the involvement of anyone else . . .' He sighed: 'Well, let us just say that this may not be a case in which the fundamental facts of the matter are in dispute.'

'So you're just giving up?'

He frowned. 'Not at all, not at all! There are many other options we can pursue. As you know, your wife has been in a very disturbed condition since you found her. We await proper psychiatric evaluation, but there may well be mitigating circumstances that might lessen the severity of any sentence that she receives.'

'I can't believe you're talking about sentences already,' I said.

Another shrug: 'One must be realistic.'

'Well, can you at least tell me how Mariana is and when I will be able to see her? Has she asked after me at all? Maybe she can tell you what really happened in there . . . she could describe someone, perhaps . . .'

'Ah, so many questions . . .' said Iqbal, with a sigh.

'I'm sorry.'

'No, no, not at all, Mr Crookham. Your anxiety is perfectly understandable. I will therefore try to deal with your questions one by one. You asked first about your wife's current state. I have to tell you that she is now a little more responsive. She is still very delicate, very confused, but she can answer a few simple questions . . .'

'What has she said?'

Iqbal spread his hands in supplication: 'Please, Mr Crookham, I am her lawyer. I am bound by client confidentiality.'

It felt as though I was constantly being stonewalled: first Samira Khan telling me why I could not see Mariana, now Iqbal refusing to tell me what, if anything, she had said.

'But I'm her husband. I'm paying her bills,' I said, my frustration rising.

'Oh yes, Mr Crookham, that is true, but neither of those facts makes any difference to my moral and professional duty to my client. Besides which, you are a potential witness. It is a matter of some debate as to whether I should be talking to you at all, let alone describing your wife's condition. It would not do any of us any good if there were any suggestion that we had in any way prejudiced the possibility of a fair trial.'

I did my best to accept the position he was in. It wasn't easy: 'Surely you can tell me if she's talked about me, or has any message for me?'

'She has not said anything about you, or passed on any messages for you, I can tell you that much,' Iqbal replied.

I tried to mask the stab of disappointment with a businesslike approach: 'So what happens now?'

'Ah, well, the police can only hold a suspect for thirty-six hours. After that time they have to apply to the magistrate's court for an extension and we have the chance to apply for bail, or, if it is appropriate, for the accused to be moved to a medical facility. There are always complications finding a bed and getting health authority funding, but I'm sure we can find a solution, should it ever come to that.'

'If Mariana needs medical care, I'll pay for that too. Perhaps she could be looked after in a private hospital ...'

Iqbal made a note on a pad in front of him. 'To be honest, I am not sure about that. I will have to look into it. Some private hospitals do have secure facilities for those patients who have been sectioned. But whether they would be considered secure enough for someone accused of murder, I cannot tell you.'

'When will this hearing at the magistrate's court be, then?'

'Let me see ... your wife was arrested at approximately nine o'clock last night, which would mean that the hearing would naturally occur at nine tomorrow morning. I think we will know a lot more then.'

At least something was happening and decisions would be made. But once again, it was all based on the assumption that Mariana was essentially a criminal, and I wasn't ready to accept that.

'What then?' I asked. 'Is there anything I can do, anything that will help my wife?'

'The best thing you can do is simply to let the process take its course and leave the professionals to do the hard work. The criminal justice system does not move quickly. These matter can take months, even years to resolve. In the meantime, my advice to you, Mr Crookham, is to try to carry on in as normal a fashion as you can. It is not easy, I know. But it is for the best.'

11

'Well, to do the bloke justice, I can see his point,' said Nick Church.

I'd gone round to the practice out of a sense of duty. I was a senior partner. I ought to show my face at least. As I walked through the main office, trying to look purposeful and composed, I encountered for the first time something to which I was about to become very accustomed: the confused and helpless looks of people who have not got a clue what to say. I didn't blame them. I didn't know what I wanted to hear. As for Nick, I'd hoped he'd share my righteous indignation about Iqbal's apparently laid-back attitude. Yet here he was, apparently taking the lawyer's side.

'I mean, face it, there's not a lot you can do now except pay the bills and be there for Mariana. If you really think she's innocent . . .'

'What do you mean, "if" she's innocent? You know Mariana. Do you think she could kill anyone?'

I could see Nick thinking he'd have to handle me with kid gloves.

'I'm sorry,' he said. 'It's just that, you know, you've lost your brother and . . . well, no one would blame you for finding it hard to forgive her, that's all.'

'How do you know there's anything to forgive?'

A look of surprise crossed Nick's face: 'Well that's what everyone . . . I mean, it just looks bad for her, I suppose.'

'Yes, it does. And that's why I've got to stand by her. Someone has to. Look, it's bad enough losing Andy. I still half expect him to call up and say why don't we have the pint we missed last night. But if I lose Mariana as well . . . what would I have to live for?'

'Even so, Pete, you've got to trust the lawyers. I'm sure they'll do the best for her. And they're the experts. It's like when we build a house. We're constantly telling clients things they don't want to hear. This is the same, only you're the client, not the professional . . .'

Yes, I was the client and now I understood how help-less that could make one feel, paying the bills for a process that was totally out of your control.

'It's hard to take, that's all,' I said. 'I feel like I should be doing something, for Mariana's sake and Andy's.'

'Like what?'

'I don't know . . . finding out what really happened, and why?'

'Well, that's the police's job, isn't it?'

'It should be. But as far as they're concerned they've got their suspect, wrapped the whole thing up and put it to bed.'

'Well, they know what they're doing, and, frankly, you don't. You're an architect, not a detective. You can't go around playing Hercule Poirot. You don't know where to begin.'

'I can't stand this, people telling me not to worry, not to get involved, just go away and carry on as if nothing has happened.'

'Yes, but what could you actually do? Listen, you're a damn good architect, so why don't you concentrate on that? Come back to work. Like the man said, try to get some normality back in your life. It's for the best, I'm sure.'

'But it isn't normal, is it? I can't even imagine what normality would feel like right now . . .'

'OK, then, forget your imagination,' Nick snapped. 'Just concentrate on reality, and the reality is that we're in the shit. The phones have been ringing off the hook, clients wondering what the hell's going on.'

'I know. I had to turn my phone off, just to hear myself think.'

He gestured me into a meeting area that was sheltered by screens from the rest of our open-plan work-space. 'Well, here's what you're missing, then . . .' he went on, in a quieter, almost furtive voice. 'Some of them, the women mostly, have asked after Mariana. But a lot of them are really edgy. Any minute now we'll get the first email threatening to pull out of a contract. And we're going to have a bloody hard time getting any new ones, either. Not with this hanging over us. So I'm not asking you to come back just for the good of your health. I'm saying, there are twenty-odd people here with jobs on the line because of what happened last night. You owe it to them to sort this shit out.'

'OK, I get it. But I've got to go and see my mother, tell her that Andy's dead. When I've done that, I'll try to write some kind of round-robin email to all our clients. You know, expressing confidence in Mariana's innocence, having confidence in the justice system, meantime it's business as usual. All right?'

Nick gave a grudging nod. 'It's a start, I suppose.'

'Well, it's all I can do right now. Mariana's in court tomorrow. I have to sort out what's going to happen to Andy's body. I suppose there'll be a funeral to arrange at some point. Give me a couple of weeks. That should do it.'

'Two weeks?' he said, his voice rising. 'It could all fall apart by then . . .'

'Calm down. Just tell the staff and the clients that I'm taking compassionate leave. Why wouldn't I? It's a lot more natural than swanning round the place like nothing's happened.'

'And what if the clients start marching?'

'They won't. Not all of them. Look, Nick, most of the big-money jobs are footballers, right? So they're all used to media aggravation. I think we'll get more support than you think. Plus, they all like Mariana. They've no reason to think badly of her.'

'Except that the papers are basically saying that she's a murderer.'

'Yes, but we both know footballers hate the papers. Given a choice between believing in Mariana or believing in a bunch of reporters, what way do you think they're going to go?'

Nick sighed, letting some of the tension go: 'All right ... maybe ...'

'Good. I'll still have my phone and my laptop. If anyone really needs me, I'll be accessible.'

'So what are you going to do? Apart from the funeral and stuff ... ?'

'I don't know, Nick, I really don't. But I'll tell you one thing for sure. I've bloody well got to do something.'

12

The home we'd found for my mother when she could no longer fend for herself was meant to be a good one. It charged accordingly. But that didn't make it any less depressing. There were jaunty little posters on the notice-board in the front hall, announcing days out and special events; blaring televisions, volume turned up to penetrate deaf ears; a day room filled with shrivelled, snowy-haired figures, staring blankly into space. It was enough to make me want to kill myself, rather than end up anywhere like it. But this was where I'd put my own mother.

The shaming thought struck me that I'd been trying to get my own back. Mum might have lost her mind, but she hadn't lost the ability to make me feel inadequate. It wasn't really about me. I understood that as an adult, even if I hadn't as a child. To my mother, my existence was a reminder of something and someone she would much rather have forgotten: the man who got her pregnant, then left her to raise a child alone, at a time when single motherhood was still a long, shame-filled way from the acceptable, state-subsidized lifestyle choice it had since become.

You see, Andy was actually my half-brother: the child of John Crookham, the man who had married Mum, given me his name and been the only real father-figure in my life. From the moment he was born he'd been the apple of Mum's eye, the symbol of everything that was good, and after Dad's death he became the living memory of the one man she'd truly loved. I'd tried frantically to earn her approval, but my best had never been enough. My A grades would be trumped by Andy's latest poem. If I won a long-distance race, she'd say, 'But of course your brother swims like a fish.'

'You'll never be handsome, but you've got a funny face,' she said to me once, when I was fifteen, covered in spots and paralysed with self-consciousness. 'Andrew's got all the looks in this family, bless him.'

The bias was so blatant that Andy and I were able to treat it as a joke. I think that's what kept us from falling out. We just drifted into a sort of lazy, affectionate, somewhat distant acceptance of each other. We were never going to be bosom buddies. He was seven years younger than me, living at the opposite end of the country and no better at keeping in touch than I was. There didn't seem to be any need to make any big effort to be any closer. We weren't in any hurry.

And now it was too late.

As for Mum, her attitude towards us had never changed. She'd never liked Mariana, either. Just after we got engaged we invited Mum to Sunday lunch. Mariana pulled out all the stops, cooking up a storm, dressing like the perfect demure bride-to-be and doing everything she could to charm her future mother-in-law. But Mum didn't bother to disguise her instant, visceral dislike.

I called her the next day and asked her what the problem was. 'There's no problem,' she snapped. 'I just didn't take to her. She's German. That's probably what it is. I never liked Germans.'

Mariana was upset for a couple of days, but we were both so caught up with the excitement of falling in love that other people's disapproval simply drew us even closer together. Over the next couple of years, as my mother's behaviour became progressively more erratic and the rages that seem to be an inescapable part of dementia became more frequent, we looked back on that disastrous lunch as an early symptom of her problems. It seemed to demonstrate what I sincerely believed: you actually had to be mad to dislike Mariana.

But mad people can be extraordinarily perceptive, perhaps because they say what they really think, without any self-control or inhibition. And so, as I walked down the nursing home corridor towards my mother's room, I thought back to that lunch and wondered whether there was something my mother had sensed about Mariana, some intuition that had told her I'd picked a wrong'un.

I shook my head. That was ridiculous. The truth was, I'd found a beautiful wife, while her favourite son was still working his way through a random assortment of short-lived relationships and drunken one-night stands. The contrast had been more than her disintegrating brain could handle.

Mum was sitting in a chair by the window, looking out, apparently unaware that it was already dark. She didn't recognize me, of course, but that at least was nothing personal.

I got down on my haunches, took one of her bony, mottled, old-woman hands and as gently as I could I told her that her son, my brother, was dead.

She heard the news without a flicker of emotion or comprehension. I wasn't even sure whether it was worth keeping going. It felt as though I was talking to myself as I said, 'I'm sorry, Mum. It happened at our house. I came home and Andy was lying there and there was nothing I could do. I'm so, so sorry . . .'

One of the nurses passing by must have heard me because she came into the room. I could see the fight going on behind her eyes as she tried not to ask all the questions that must have been flashing across her mind.

Her professionalism won. She leaned over my mother.

'This is your son, Muriel,' she said. 'Your son . . .'

She looked at me questioningly.

'Peter,' I said.

'Your son Peter,' the nurse said. 'He's got news for you.'

My mother frowned: the first expression that had crossed her face since I'd come into her room. Then she looked at me with a depth of bafflement and confusion that I'd never encountered before, even at the darkest moments of her dementia.

'Oh no, this isn't my son. I'm sure it isn't,' she said. She seemed to be wracking her brain for information that would not come. Finally she said, 'My son is Andrew. This man isn't Andrew. This is not my son.'

Five minutes later, I was sitting in the car, in the dark, trying to tell myself that my mother didn't really mean it. Just for distraction, I switched my phone back on. It was time to face the clients and their people. But as I looked down the list of text messages, one name kept coming up in a repetitive, intensifying pattern that told its own desperate, grief-stricken story. It was Vickie Price, Andrew's girlfriend for the past couple of years.

How could I have been so stupid?

She must have been going crazy, and it had never

even occurred to me to call her. But then, I hardly knew her, either. We'd met once or twice, but only in passing. We never had family get-togethers. It wasn't our style. But what sort of excuse was that?

I made the call. And put my foot in it, right from the off.

'I'm sorry, I didn't get your messages. I had my phone off all day.'

'Did you really need a reminder to call me?' Vickie's voice sounded exhausted, tearful and just a little bit drunk. 'I've been living with your brother for the past two years. Didn't you think of me at all?'

'You're right. I should have called. It's just, the last twenty-four hours . . . well . . . it's not been easy.'

'No, well, it hasn't exactly been a walk in the park for me, either. Do you know what it's like, opening up the newspaper and discovering your boyfriend's been murdered?'

I don't know what it was that did it: maybe the acidic tone of her voice, or just the accumulated stress of the past twenty-four hours, but I snapped right back: 'No . . . do you know what it's like, walking into your own house and finding your brother dead on the floor?'

For the next several seconds the only sound was the faint, static crackle of interference on the line.

'I apologize, that was out of order,' I said.

'No, well . . . it's not easy for any of us, is it?' Vickie

replied, sighing with the effort of trying to be reasonable. 'We were going to get married, you know. That's what Andy wanted to tell you . . . the good news . . .'

'Oh, I'm sorry . . .' I repeated as she started crying again. 'That's . . . that's . . .'

What was it, exactly? What word could possibly suffice?

'And now . . . and now . . .' Vickie went on, squeezing her words out between the tears, 'the church where we were going to get married . . . well that's where I'll have to bury him . . . Oh God, it's so unfair! What did he ever do to you, or to Mariana? What did he do to deserve being . . . being cut up like that . . . it's just wrong!'

'Yes . . . yes it is . . . for everyone. But I just want you to know that I'll take care of everything . . . all Andy's things. And we'll have to work out what to do about his body . . .'

'Oh please . . .' she gasped.

'Look, I know, it's horrible, and this probably isn't a good time. But there's never going to be a good time, is there? We just have to deal with all this . . . Try to get through it as best we can.'

It suddenly struck me that I was doing precisely the same thing as Nick had done at the office: evading the heart of the issue by reducing it to sensible, unemotional practicalities. I kept doing it, too: 'So, I'll find out at this end what the deal is in terms of collecting him from the police, and what the best way is of getting him down to you. And when you feel ready, just give me the name of an undertaker and we'll take it from there.'

'How do you do that?' Vickie asked.

'Do what?'

'How do you . . . how can you just talk to me about collecting the body and arranging an undertaker just like you were, I don't know, ordering floor-tiles or something. Don't you feel anything?'

Good question. One best evaded: 'Yes of course I do. But I don't exactly have a choice, do I? There's no one else to do any of this. And I owe it to Andy and . . .'

'And who?'

'Well . . .'

'You were going to say, "and Mariana", weren't you? Weren't you . . . ?'

'Yes . . . yes I was.'

'You've got a bloody nerve, you know that? You've got a bloody nerve thinking about that woman, when she's the reason your brother, my fiancé, is lying in a sodding fridge.'

'Yes, that's right, he's in a fridge. And our dad is dead too. And our mother's so out of it she no longer even acknowledges me as her own flesh and blood. Don't you get it? All I have left is my wife. If I lose my faith in her, I've got nothing.'

No sooner had I said those words than I realized two things. First, that they must have sounded appallingly insensitive to Vickie. And second that they were, nevertheless, absolutely true.

EAST BERLIN: 1978

At the tail-end of the sixties, when an eighteen-year-old Hans-Peter Tretow had been growing his hair and protesting against the Vietnam War, his outraged father tried to persuade him that he was deluded. The real criminals, the old man maintained, were not in the White House or Pentagon, but in Hanoi, Peking, Moscow and all the other outposts of what he always described as the global communist conspiracy.

'Just look at what is happening in the East, in your own fatherland,' Tretow senior growled. 'The Stasi are animals. They torture people – proper Germans, just like you and me – in ways that make the old Gestapo lads look like a bunch of nursemaids.'

'Don't get all nostalgic with me, Dad,' Hans-Peter had replied. 'If you feel so fond about the old days, just go off and polish your old Waffen-SS dagger. Make sure it's nice and bright for your next reunion.'

'Don't you talk to me like that, boy. We fought a war

to keep this country free from communism. You should show a little gratitude sometimes.'

Hans-Peter laughed at his father's political tirades. He was a child of postwar prosperity, part of a generation that saw no contradiction between pinning Che Guevara posters on the wall one moment and lusting after the latest Porsche the next. His childhood had been scarred by the verbal and physical abuse he had suffered at his embittered, defeat-ridden father's hands, but once he'd grown big enough to retaliate, the balance of power within the family had shifted decisively in his favour. Still, as much as he felt sure that his father exaggerated the evils of the Soviet bloc, he'd seen enough spy movies to know that the KGB and their allies weren't exactly gentle with their enemies, real or imagined.

And yet now he was choosing to come to the East and place himself at the mercy of the Stasi.

This was a puzzle that intrigued Tretow's first interrogator, too. He was dressed in a field-grey military uniform, but looked bland and inoffensive, with mouse-brown hair cut into a rough crewcut that seemed more suggestive of a prisoner or a lowly conscript than a commissioned officer. His unlined face was oddly boyish and his eyes were a pale, watery blue. Now the interrogator asked himself, why had Tretow left the West? He gave no sign of any ideological commitment to the cause of socialism and its defence against Western imperialism. One look at his soft, manicured hands was enough to establish that he was not the workman that his clothes suggested. So what, then, was his game?

'We found the package in your car,' the interrogator said.

'Good,' Tretow replied. 'You were meant to.'

The interrogator frowned. The prisoner's confidence was another unexpected anomaly. The man should have been nervous, even terrified. Either he was a simpleton, or he believed he had something that would guarantee his safety.

'We examined the contents,' the interrogator continued. 'Are you aware that they provide evidence of criminal activities that would carry a minimum twenty-five year sentence at a forced labour camp?'

'Yes.'

'Do you deny that you are guilty of these crimes?'

'No.'

'Is there any good reason, then, why I should not have you committed to trial immediately, found guilty and sentenced?'

'Yes.'

'Would you care to share it with me?'

'If it is all the same to you, I would prefer to share it with someone more important.'

*

Markus Wolf was Director of the *Hauptverwaltung Aufklärung*, or HVA, the foreign intelligence directorate of the Ministry of State Security. He was the Stasi's spymaster, the second most powerful man in the entire organization, subordinate only to the Security Minister himself, Erich Mielke.

At fifty-five Wolf had the worldly, patrician face of a banker: a Rothschild of espionage. His proud, fleshy nose bisected narrowed, analytical eyes. The downturned corners of his mouth suggested a certain detached scepticism: a gentle, ironic amusement at life's rampant absurdities. He would never normally have troubled himself with anyone as insignificant as a low-level asylum seeker. But when word was brought to him of Tretow's particular circumstances, he decided to make an exception.

'You realize, of course,' Wolf told Tretow, 'that I could have all the information you possess extracted from you by interrogation whether you like it or not?'

'Of course, sir,' Tretow replied. He had no idea who Wolf was, but he knew a powerful man when he saw one. 'That is the risk I take. But the material you have seen so far is just a small sample of what I can offer. I therefore calculate that it will, in the long run, be easier and more beneficial for you to indulge my very modest requests. I mean no disrespect, sir, but I am surely more use to you as a healthy, fully functioning asset than a broken prisoner.'

Lesser men would have been outraged by Tretow's presumption, not to mention the intolerable suggestion that the DDR treated its prisoners improperly. Wolf, however, rose effortlessly above such pettiness.

'Very well,' he said, 'I am prepared to consider your proposal. If you produce information that assists the defence of democratic socialism against its capitalist enemies, then you will be suitably rewarded. But if you fail me in any way, I will make it my personal business to see that you receive the maximum punishment that your crimes merit. Are we clear?'

'Completely.'

'Good. You will, of course, be kept in solitary confinement for your own protection until we have been able to determine your value to us. Think of this as the merest hint of what awaits you if you have tried to mislead me.'

Tretow spent the next week in a Stasi cell. To his relief, conditions were not as bad as his father's horror stories had led him to expect. He had to make do with a bare wooden bench for a bed, but his cell had a window, a basin and a proper flushing lavatory. Food was terrible, but regular. After the stress of the past few days and weeks it felt good to relax. He tried hard not to think about his past, or the family he had left behind. Instead he contemplated his future. That a senior official had taken a personal interest in his case was surely a splendid sign. He would soon be able to reinvent himself as a whole new man.

And then he would start to enjoy himself once again.

13

THURSDAY

Samira Khan carried her coffee over to where I was sitting in a cafe, just a couple of minutes from York Magistrate's Court. She sat down, opened her briefcase and pulled out a few sheets of stapled A4 paper.

'They did your brother's post-mortem yesterday and we were emailed a copy of the report overnight. Do you want to hear about it? I'm afraid it's not particularly pleasant.'

'No, I don't imagine it is,' I said, glancing up at my lawyer. 'But go on, tell me . . .'

'I won't give you all the technical jargon, but he died of exsanguination, which means he bled out and—'

'I know what it means,' I interrupted sharply.

'Sorry, I wasn't sure how much—'

'It's OK, go on.'

She looked back at the papers. 'He lost roughly half of all the blood in his body, more than two and a half litres.'

'A paint can,' I said, automatically. 'Two and a half litres is a standard decorator's paint can. Imagine what it would be like to spill one of them . . . every last drop.' I drifted back to the house that night and as I spoke again, I was barely conscious of Khan's presence. 'There were puddles of it . . . splashes . . . There was blood everywhere. Even my spaghetti was stained with blood.'

She cleared her throat self-consciously: 'There were twenty-one stab wounds, some of which were inflicted after he had died. The pathologist described it as an exceptionally violent, even frenzied assault. And there were almost no defensive wounds on your brother's body, just a couple of cuts on his hands, indicating that he was taken completely by surprise. Whatever happened, it came out of the blue . . . like a tornado from a cloudless sky.'

'Jesus!'

'The point is, there's no getting away from the fact that all the evidence points at your wife. We can't base our defence on arguing that she didn't do it. We have to look at why she did it, and what state she was in at the time.'

'I'm sorry,' I said, 'I know it looks bad for her. I was the one who found her. But I can't—'

Khan tilted her head slightly to one side as a gesture of sympathy: 'Look, I think it's wonderful that you're so loyal to her. But you have to think about what's really best for her. And that means that you have to accept what she did and try to come to terms with it. There are people who can help you.'

'Thanks, but the last thing I need right now is some kind of counsellor, asking me how I feel.'

She straightened up and held my gaze for a moment. 'All right. How much did Mr Iqbal tell you about today's hearing?'

'Not much.'

'It's really just a matter of deciding what's going to happen to your wife in the immediate future. We'll be up in front of a district judge. The police have to give a good reason why they want to hold her for an additional thirty-six hours. This is a murder investigation, so it's perfectly normal for an extension to be granted. But we'll be trying to get bail, or, failing that, to have her transferred to a secure psychiatric facility on the grounds of her mental condition, as per section 35 of the Mental Health Act, 1983.'

Despite the state she'd been in on Tuesday night, it was hard to take in the fact that Mariana would probably be locked up in a loony bin. 'Is she still that bad?'

'I don't know.'

'Don't know, or can't tell me?'

'I honestly don't have a clue. It will all come down to the Forensic Medical Examiner. The judge will probably go along with whatever the FME says, unless we can give him very good grounds to the contrary.'

'Iqbal said there might be a problem with beds and funding.'

Khan took a sip of her coffee: 'Well, this is the NHS, you know. Hospital care for mental patients is expensive, particularly secure care. They can get niggly sometimes about money. We'll do everything we can to make sure she gets treated as well as possible.'

'Suppose that doesn't work?'

'We'll cross that bridge when we come to it.' Khan slipped the papers back in her briefcase. 'OK, I've got to go and help Mr Iqbal prepare for the hearing. Give me a minute or so, then walk across to the court and sneak into the public gallery. Try to keep a low profile. It's just possible the CPS might try and kick up a fuss if they see you in there, but I think they'd have a hard time arguing you're not even allowed to set eyes on your own wife. Oh, that reminds me.' She smiled at me for the first time that morning: 'We've put in a request for you to be able to visit her, either in the police station, or any other location to which she might be taken. On compassionate grounds alone, I think we've got a reasonable chance of success.'

14

The court was one of those imposing, red-brick, late-Victorian buildings that might equally well be a museum, a town hall or an old grammar school. A man wearing a pair of dirty grey tracksuit trousers and a battered leather jacket was sitting on the flight of steps that led up to the entrance. He was drinking a bottle of cider wrapped in a plastic shopping bag.

I went past an airport-style security check to a long corridor floored in a marble mosaic that ran the full width of the ground floor. Along one side bright purple padded benches were filled with young men in football shirts, cheap anoraks and the same sagging tracksuit trousers, and whey-faced women with greasy, pulled-back hair and heavy-bellied T-shirts over their stretch leggings. They looked at me with cold, flat stares as I walked by feeling unexpectedly out of place in the suit and tie I had naïvely imagined were appropriate court attire. This wasn't a place, they seemed to be saying, for the soft, spoilt, middle-class likes of me.

On the other wall were two red doors, maybe thirty feet apart. Their upper panels were glazed and the word 'SESSIONS' was etched on the glass just as 'SALOON BAR' might be in a pub of the same vintage.

Mariana's hearing was taking place in the right-hand court. I pushed on the door, slipped in as quietly as possible and sat down on one of the several curved lines of carved, graffiti-covered wooden benches at the back of the court that served as the public gallery. At the far end of the room, on a raised dais beneath a carved panel of the royal coat of arms sat the district judge, with his clerks and stenographer directly in front of him at floor level. Opposite them were the benches for the opposing teams of prosecution and defence lawyers. Between the public gallery and the lawyers, directly in line with the judge, stood the dock. It was contained within a plexiglass surround, which also enclosed the entrance to a set of stairs that led downwards, presumably to cells in the basement.

Mariana's legal process began without any grand ceremony, just a shuffling of legal personnel and a sudden flash of dull gold that caught my eye and made me turn towards the dock as she was led up the stairs to take her place behind the plexiglass. Her lank, unwashed hair was drawn back into a ponytail. Her head was down and

I only saw a glimpse of the side of her face, drawn and grey-skinned, with an expression of exhausted, drained indifference that made her look barely more alive than Andy's bloodless corpse. She had the same dull, non-responsive expression that I'd seen on the night of the killing, as though that old wives' tale had come true: the wind had changed and she'd been stuck with it. With her dead eyes and her grimy, shapeless, police-issue clothes she looked little different and certainly no better than the women sitting in the corridor outside, and I wanted to shout out to the judge and the lawyers: 'This isn't Mariana! It's not what she's really like!'

The proceedings, once they got underway, were more like a low-key planning meeting between fellow professionals than the kind of courtroom drama I'd been expecting. Iqbal didn't bother asking for bail. It seemed that the judge had already received a copy of the FME's report and was satisfied that Mariana was a suitable case for hospital treatment. There was then a brief debate about the practical issues that both Iqbal and Khan had described to me, and the Yorkshire Centre for Forensic Psychiatry was suggested and mutually agreed on.

Throughout all this Mariana said nothing and showed no signs of being aware of anything that was said about her. Her body might have been in the courtroom, but her mind was a million miles away.

Almost as an afterthought, when the secure unit issue had been settled to everyone's satisfaction, the clerk of the court asked Iqbal whether there was any indication of his client's likely plea in the event of a trial.

'Oh, she will be pleading not guilty,' he said, as if that were a matter of course.

The clerk nodded and made a note. The whole thing looked to be done and dusted and then, without the slightest warning, Mariana suddenly stood up straight and very loudly said, 'I am guilty!'

Iqbal looked in horror at Mariana, then turned at once to the judge. 'I assure you, sir, that we will not be making a guilty plea. As you can see, my client is very distressed and not at all in her right mind.'

'I am guilty!' Mariana repeated. 'It was all my fault . . . all my fault . . .' She shook her head from side to side, muttering under her breath. It was unbearable to watch, and a palpable sense of unease and embarrassment swept the chamber as the routine, complacent tone of the proceedings was ruptured by this display of raw, unedited pain.

'Is there a nurse in the court today?' the judge asked. 'I really think Mrs Crookham requires immediate medical attention.'

Mariana was led back down the stairs. As she went, she said something in German. First I caught the word '*Mädchen*' – a girl – and then '*böses*'. I didn't know what that meant. But it was the same phrase, '*böses Mädchen*', repeated again and again like a grim, tuneless refrain.

I tried to catch her eye as she was taken away, but either she had no idea that I was there, or she was simply not willing to look in my direction.

When she had gone I sat stunned for a moment, trying to come to terms with what I had seen and heard. There was no escaping the words she had used. Mariana had said, explicitly, that she was guilty.

It took a moment or two to identify the emotion churning away inside me as anger. I felt as though all my trust in Mariana had been betrayed. I had done my utmost to ignore the evidence of my own eyes, and fight the arguments of the police, the lawyers, my business partner – everyone who had tried to tell me there could be no other killer but her. And now she had come down on their side, not mine. She had admitted to killing my brother and made me feel like a fool for ever believing anything else.

In the corridor ouside the court I took out my iPhone and translated the phrase '*böses Mädchen*'.

She had been calling herself a naughty, bad or wicked little girl.

'I'm sorry you had to see all that.'

I looked up. Samira Khan was standing next to me. I shook my head in bemusement: 'I look at Mariana and I hardly recognize her any more. Part of me is furious with her. Another part feels this huge sense of pity and real sorrow for her, too. I can't deny what she did any more and that changes everything. I think I always looked on her as a sort of fantasy figure, the perfect woman. And now . . .'

'It's not easy for any woman to be someone else's fantasy,' Khan said. 'She needs to be loved for herself. Somehow you have to try and accept her as she is.'

I nodded but felt nothing. 'So, she pleaded guilty. I suppose that's game over,' I said.

'No, actually, that's one thing you needn't worry about,' Khan assured me. 'The clerk was only asking for an indication of how she might plead. It's just a guideline, really, to let the court know whether we intend to mount a defence at any actual trial. Nothing your wife said had any legal standing. The only thing it did was to confirm the fragility of her mental state. So in a funny sort of way, that actually worked for us.'

'How do you mean?'

'Well, there are two lines of argument we can pursue in a case like this. The first is that the defendant is simply not fit to stand trial. At the moment that would certainly be true of your wife, but it will be months before any trial is likely to take place, so I actually hope for her sake that she is much better by then.'

'In which case, what will you argue then?'

'That the charge of murder should be replaced by

one of manslaughter on the grounds of diminished responsibility. It's a plea in mitigation. We'll say that she had no prior intent to cause your brother any harm, and was not responsible for, or even aware of her actions when she attacked him.'

I winced.

'It's very hard, I know,' Khan said. 'But I'm sure we have a good chance of persuading the court.'

'All right, then, suppose you win. Suppose the jury says, yes, she was out of her mind, it's manslaughter not murder. What then?'

'Then it makes a huge difference to her likely sentence. In a manslaughter case like this judges have incredible latitude. They can order anything from immediate release to life imprisonment. To be honest, neither of those two extremes are very likely. I can't see a judge giving your wife a life sentence, given the state she's in, but neither do they like setting murderers free: it doesn't look good. Mitigating circumstances, however, almost always result in a much reduced sentence.'

'Reduced by how much?' I asked.

'Depends. The judge has to consider two things: the degree to which the accused was or was not responsible for their actions, and the danger, or lack of it, they pose to the public now. If we can convince the judge that this defendant suffered a single psychotic incident that will never be repeated, then she could be looking at secure hospital care, the duration of which would be very much at the discretion of the psychiatric experts. Hang on a moment . . .'

Khan's phone was ringing. She took the call and listened intently for a few seconds before asking, 'You're quite sure of that?' and, 'So that applies immediately?' Then she turned to me with a broad smile.

'At last I have some good news! The judge has decided that your rights as a husband outweigh all possible prejudice to any testimony you might give as a witness. You are free to visit Mrs Crookham.'

'Oh God, that's fantastic news.' I slumped with relief as some of the tension left my body. 'Where is she? When can I see her?'

'She's being transferred to the medium-secure facility now, so I'll give you the address and directions. I'd allow a few hours for her to be moved and settled, but I don't see why you can't go there today – mid-afternoon, four o'clock, perhaps, something like that.'

'I'm so relieved.' I gave Khan a weary smile.

'Please, don't get your hopes up too high. You saw the state your wife is in. She is a little more aware of her surroundings now, but she's hardly going to greet you with open arms and a kiss.'

'I know. Believe me, I'm very, very aware of how damaged she is. But just to see her, to hold her hand. Well, that at least would be something.'

15

The unit where they were holding Mariana was about an hour's drive away, south of Leeds. I found a complex of low, yellow-brick buildings with steeply gabled roofs. A heavy, oppressive portico, clad in black-stained wood, loomed menacingly over the main entrance like the Grim Reaper's cowl. But despite this, and the further depressive effect of a freezing drizzle seeping from leaden skies, there was actually a spring in my step as I crossed the visitors' car park. I was about to see Mariana! We would talk at last and maybe, just maybe, she'd be able to answer some of the questions that had been nagging at me day and night. But just to see her would be enough.

The reception area didn't look much different to any other hospital. The same bland, pastel-toned modernism, the same harassed receptionist. I beamed at her with what I fondly imagined was my most ingratiating grin.

'Hi, my name's Peter Crookham. My wife Mariana is a patient here and I have a judge's order authorizing me to see her.'

The receptionist did not smile back.

She consulted a computer screen and then said, 'I'm sorry. That won't be possible.'

I was not deterred. 'If I've come at the wrong time, just let me know when visiting hours are and I'll come back then.'

'No,' she repeated. 'It will not be possible. Not at all.'

'You don't understand,' I insisted. 'The judge personally said I could visit my wife. Look, I'll get my lawyer on the phone. She can confirm it.'

'I'm sorry, sir, that won't make any difference. It will not be possible for you to visit your wife, even if she is a patient here, which I cannot confirm or deny.'

After all the pent-up frustrations and horror of the past few days something inside me snapped.

'Don't be so fucking ridiculous. I know she's here and I've got a court order to prove it. I insist on seeing my wife.'

She sat up straighter in her padded office chair. 'This unit does not allow the abuse of staff members. You will have to leave. If you do not, I will call hospital security.'

'Oh for God's sake! Can't you stop reading the bloody rules and react like a human being? I'm sorry if I offended you, but I'm desperate to see my wife. There must be something you can do. Please.'

'I must ask you to leave the premises, according to hospital policy.'

'I'm begging you. Isn't there anyone I can talk to?'

Two bruisers in pale-blue uniform shirts, dark trousers and heavy-toed black shoes were striding across the foyer towards the desk.

'Please . . .' I repeated.

The first of the men had got within a few feet of me.

'You – outside!' he snarled.

This couldn't be happening. I'd finally been given my chance to see Mariana, to look into her eyes and perhaps get some tiny fragment of understanding about what was going on in her mind, and now it was being taken away by a bunch of knuckle-dragging jobsworths because I'd used a dirty word. Every animal instinct was screaming at me to lash out at them, but I fought to maintain some degree of coherence.

'If you could just wait one moment,' I said, my voice trembling with suppressed rage and grief, 'I am not a security risk, and I am not threatening anyone or anything. So, please, may I make a reasonable request to see someone in authority? And while you think about that, consider the fact that my wife and I have been all over the tabloids in the past couple of days and I'm sure the *Sun* lads would just love to get their teeth into a story about how I got thrown out of here. Believe me, those reporters will certainly want to speak to someone high up in the hospital, and I can't see that going down too well, can you?'

The security men looked at the receptionist. She looked at me. She pursed her lips, gave a heavy, 'suit yourself' sigh and dialled a number. Then she spoke with her hand over the mouthpiece so that I couldn't make out what she was saying. Finally, she put the phone down and spoke to the two security men: 'Take Mr Crookham to Dr Wray's office. He's expecting him.'

I was marched off between the two men, half a head taller than either of them, but a lot less wide. We walked down a series of corridors at right angles to one another, right into the heart of the facility. Finally, they stopped outside a door that looked indistinguishable from any of the countless others we had already passed, but for a nameplate that said, 'Dr Tony Wray'. One of them rapped twice and a voice from inside answered, 'Come in!'

'In you go,' said the guard who had knocked. 'We'll be waiting for you outside.'

He said it in a way that was almost daring me to to give him and his mate the excuse to come in and give me the beating they were so obviously longing to dole out. I ignored him and went in.

16

Dr Wray stood up, leaned across a desk covered in files, assorted scraps of paper, random bits of stationery and a mass of nondescript junk, and shook my hand. He was a small, wiry man in a tweed sports jacket and black jeans and he had a mass of greasy, steel-grey hair that looked as though it had been left the same length for the past forty years, in defiance of the large, monkish bald spot clearly visible on the top of his scalp. All the years of dealing with the criminally insane had left their mark in the deep lines on his face, but there was, nevertheless, a buzz around him. When he spoke, his words were interrupted by vocal tics: hums, hahs and ers, like little bursts of excess energy being expelled from his system.

'Sit down, sit down,' he said, pointing to a chair. 'Why don't I join you, eh?'

He came out from behind the desk and sat in a chair

opposite mine. 'Hmm . . . I gather things became a bit fraught.'

'Yes, I'm sorry about that. I'd been looking forward to seeing my wife. I was pretty upset when I heard I couldn't. Took it out on the receptionist. I shouldn't have done that, I know . . .'

'Don't worry, they're used to it,' he said. 'Happens all the time.'

'She didn't seem to understand the situation, though. I mean, I have the judge's permission. I am officially allowed to see Mariana.'

'Well, ah, it's not really the judge's decision,' said Wray. 'I mean, he can say that he has no objection to your seeing your wife. But that does not mean that you can. Or even that she's actually a patient at this hospital.'

I'd been comforted up to now by the delusion that I'd be able to talk to Wray man-to-man and sort the whole thing out. It suddenly struck me that he might be living in the same Alice-in-Wonderland world as everyone else I'd met in the psychiatric unit.

'Look, I know she's here,' I said. 'The police brought her here today. She's bloody well here . . .' I was conscious that my voice was rising. I thought of the gorillas waiting outside with their ears pressed to the door, and forced myself to lower the volume: 'Why can't you admit that she's here?'

Wray frowned to himself. He pressed his lips together, deep in thought. He ran a hand through his tangled hair. He gave another 'hmm', grimaced and then said, 'I can't admit or deny anything about your wife at all, Mr Crookham. But I can tell you about the general conditions that I, like any clinical psychiatrist, operate under. Maybe that would help.'

'I suppose . . .'

'Well then, let me explain a little about patient confidentiality,' Wray said. 'It's a matter of duty-of-care. Any psychiatrist, in any facility, is governed absolutely by the wishes of their patient. If a patient is eighteen or over their right to total confidentiality is assumed unless they choose to waive it. They may agree to limited information being made available to their spouse, or their parents. But equally, a patient may insist that they don't want anyone to know anything. And when that is the case, we are obliged to respect their wishes.'

'Are you telling me Mariana doesn't want to see me?'

'I'm not telling you anything about her.'

'She's my wife, for God's sake. Doesn't that count for anything?'

Wray sighed. His voice softened a little. 'I understand, Mr Crookham, really I do. But there's nothing I can do. I'm afraid that any kind of mental illness is incredibly hard on the patient's loved ones in many different ways, and this is just one of them . . . Ach!'

Wray's fingers made another trip through the wild greasy strands of his hair, pausing to scratch the top of his scalp. He frowned, then said, 'Look, as well as my work here, I practise at a private clinic, hmm? When they come to us, some of the patients are in a terrible state, close to death, or suicidal. Their families are often desperate for news. I've had mothers calling me, wanting to know whether their sons or daughters are alive and I've not even been able to tell them that.'

'But that's just being cruel.'

'I know . . . it's not easy for us, either. But our first and only concern as doctors has to be for our patients. And those patients own their conditions. Whatever they are going through, it is their experience, their struggle and, in the end, hopefully, their cure. You see? So they have the right to decide whether they want to share that experience with anyone else.'

'But they're ill, you said so yourself. How do they know what they really want?'

'Ha! Even patients who are psychotic or delusional in one aspect of their lives may be perfectly rational in another. And they can make reasonable decisions about the degree to which they do or do not want anyone to know about their illness. Do you understand?'

'Yes, but I still don't understand why patients wouldn't want to be with the people who love them. Wouldn't that make them feel better?'

'Not necessarily. It might make them feel ashamed. Should they see a family member, or someone they love, and that person is upset, that will only cause terrible feelings of guilt. And the deeper the love, the greater the guilt. The patient thinks, "I am doing this to someone I love. I'm hurting them. I must be such a bad person." This adds to the feelings of shame that they already possess about themselves: feelings that may very well have caused their problems in the first place. That's why they can't bear to be seen.'

'Well is there anything you can tell me? Anything at all?'

Wray looked at me with a completely flat, unresponsive expression that was somehow more infuriating, more provocative than anything he'd actually said.

'You don't get it,' I said, getting to my feet as my voice rose again. 'I mean, screw Mariana's guilt and shame! What do you think I feel like? I'm tense all the time, day and night. It never goes away.'

I started pacing up and down, desperately trying to burn off some of my nervous energy, ranting more than talking in an unbroken stream of consciousness.

'I feel nauseous. My guts are churning and I've got a choking feeling in my throat. And it hurts, physically hurts, like I'm being bruised from the inside out. My mind is racing round and round, but it never gets anywhere . . .'

'Mr Crookham, take it easy. Try to relax.'

'Relax? How the hell am I meant to relax?' I tapped a finger hard against my skull. 'In here I'm screaming. I've got a million questions and not one bloody answer ...'

I heard the door open behind me and saw Wray lift a hand as if to say, 'Don't worry I'm handling it.' The door closed again.

Somehow the hand seemed to push me away too. I slumped back down into my chair.

'I feel so guilty,' I confessed, burying my head in my hands. 'My brother's dead, my wife's locked up and it's all my fault. They'd never even have met if it wasn't for me. But I'm the one who's free. I can't take it. I'll go mad if this goes on much longer. I swear I will.'

Wray looked at me again, and now there was kindness, or more accurately, perhaps, compassion in his eyes.

'Wait,' he said, 'maybe I can help you ... just a little.'

17

Dr Tony Wray got up, walked over to his desk and scrabbled through the mess until he had found a pen and a ring-bound notepad. Then he came back and pulled his chair next to mine. He drew a small circle near the top of the page. 'This is a child,' he said. 'A very small child, maybe just a baby.'

He drew arrows pointing at the child. 'These are the hurts inflicted by its parents. Maybe they are absent and don't give the child enough love and attention. They don't respond to its need for food or comfort, for example. Maybe they are actively abusive in some way: sexually, emotionally, physically, you know the kind of thing. Or they are inappropriate and make the child feel responsible for their state, like the mother who says, "Now look what you made me do!" or, "You made me cry." I mean, we all do this to our children to some degree, no matter how hard we try not to.'

'"They fuck you up, your mum and dad . . ."'

'Exactly. So, anyway, the child assumes that if its parent, the most important, powerful person in its life, is behaving towards it in this way, then it must deserve this bad treatment. And it doesn't have to be a parent: any adult with a close relationship to the child can have the same effect. The point is, the child assumes blame, guilt and, above all, shame. It knows that it's bad, or dirty in some way. And, ah . . . it buries this shame deep inside itself, like so . . .'

Wray drew a dot inside the circle. 'Now,' he went on, 'it's obviously very important to the child that people should not know about this shame. It has to stay out of sight. So the child creates a shell around itself, like a wall, to keep the shame well hidden.'

This time he drew a black square that enclosed the circle and the dot.

Was he talking about Mariana? He can't have had time to diagnose her properly yet. But he'd have seen the case notes, maybe talked to the Forensic Medical Examiner. And in a place like this, he'd be used to people who kill.

Wray went on: 'If the growing child fears that it is not lovable, it may develop incredible charm to compensate. It may be perceived as immensely likable, attractive, even charismatic. But none of the affection that it receives ever changes its deep, inner feeling of self-loathing. The child, or the adult it becomes, simply feels like a fraud. It sincerely believes that it would not be liked or loved if anyone knew its true personality, its actual, hidden self.

'Now, when a patient goes into therapy, one of the things the therapist will try to do is expose the original shame, to let the light in on it . . .'

Wray drew lines breaking through the square like shafts of sunlight: 'You see, once the shame is exposed and admitted to and even shared with other people – a sort of coming-out – then its potency swiftly diminishes. Patients discover, more likely than not, that things aren't as bad as they feared and people don't think any the less of them.'

'I sense a great, big "but" coming on,' I said.

Wray smiled, 'Ha! Indeed you do. Let's go back to the very beginning of the process, to the creation of the shame. Sometimes this occurs as the result of a genuinely terrible event that goes far beyond the day-to-day failings of an ordinary, fallible parent.'

'Some kind of abuse, you mean?'

'Yes, or it could be the loss of a parent or family member, particularly in violent circumstances; even witnessing some terrible event. There are lots of ways any of us can become profoundly traumatized at any age, after all. Some theorists even suggest that unresolved traumas can be passed on like, ah . . . unexploded bombs through the generations, so that we may have to suffer for wrongs committed before we were ever born. In any case, this extreme trauma is buried, just as before. The patient builds a wall, just as before. But this psychic wound is much more dangerous. It may be completely forgotten by the child's conscious mind, but it sits imprinted in the unconscious like a ticking bomb, just waiting for something to set it off: a trigger, if you will.'

I asked: 'About this "bomb": you're speaking purely in general terms, I assume?'

'Of course,' Wray replied. But he would not be telling me any of this if it did not contain the key to understanding someone like Mariana. And now I realized something else. Though he could not possibly say so, he was as keen to learn from me as I was from him. After all, he was going to need information to work with, too.

'And this trigger, what might it be?' I asked.

'Oh, er . . . anything really that creates an immediate connection: an association of ideas that suddenly brings the hidden trauma from the subconscious back into the conscious mind. Suppose a child has been harmed in a room in which there is a large grandfather clock, ticking away. The sound of a ticking clock might, at a later date, trigger off an explosion of that mental bomb . . . I mean, I'm being fanciful here. I'm just trying to give you a rough idea.'

'And that reaction could be violent?'

'Possibly.'

'And it's uncontrollable, right? I mean, the bomb just goes off inside someone's head and they flip. It's not something they planned or anything. They're not even aware of what they're doing?'

'That's right,' Wray nodded.

I felt a sudden surge of hope. If I could find out what had set Mariana off, and establish a connection to her early life, then I might be able to explain why she'd lashed out at Andy and provide the evidence needed to mitigate her sentence.

'You said it can take years to get to the bottom of this kind of thing and find out what made someone act a certain way, and why.'

'Well, a psychiatrist isn't like a police detective,' Wray replied. 'We don't have any clues to work with apart from the ones in a person's head. And they can take a while to dig out.'

'But if you could actually go and investigate someone, like a detective does, that would save a lot of time, wouldn't it?'

Wray laughed. 'I really don't know! I suppose so.'

There was a chance, then. In which case, there was one more thing I needed Wray to tell me: 'These triggers you were talking about: would they include something somebody said? I mean, suppose you had been abused and I asked you, straight out, "Were you abused as a child?" would that do it?'

Wray shook his head thoughtfully: 'No . . . oddly enough, I doubt it. I mean, it's possible, I suppose. But a direct question such as that would be dealt with by the conscious mind. And the conscious mind has blanked out the truth. Chances are the person would just reply. "No, of course not", and honestly believe they were telling the truth. So it's more likely to come from something that bypasses our rational minds: a non-verbal sense experience; sight, sound, smell, taste . . .'

'And that sort of thing could unlock memories that might have a violent reaction?'

'Quite so,' Wray replied. Then he snapped into a different mood, looked at his watch and said, 'Well, I have another appointment! It's been a pleasure meeting you, Mr Crookham. I hope I've been of some help. And if you do find out anything useful . . .'

'I'll let you know.'

The two goons showed me back to the main entrance. Every time we turned a corner I prayed that somehow I'd see Mariana coming the other way. Just to catch a glimpse of her in the distance would be something. But she never appeared. My journey had, on that level, been in vain. I was as frustrated as ever about that. But on the other hand, I did now have a purpose.

The only way Mariana was going to receive a light sentence was if someone found out why she had killed Andy. As far as the police were concerned, their job was done. Dr Wray himself had said it could take years for him to find an answer. The lawyers were just going to work their way through the whole case in their usual, routine way.

So that just left me.

EAST BERLIN: 1984

Hans-Peter Tretow lifted his four-year-old daughter and threw her, shrieking with a blissful mixture of fear and excitement, up into the air. He caught her again, planted a big kiss on her forehead and put her back down on the path outside the family's apartment building.

'Me! Me!' squealed his son, a chubby-cheeked little lad of two, holding out his arms to be picked up just like his sister. Tretow obliged, laughing along with his children. His wife watched the whole scene with an indulgent, maternal smile wreathing a face as bright and pink-flushed as an apple. With her cornflower-blue eyes and golden hair – a gift she'd passed on to her daughter – she had the well-fed, docile, obedient look of the perfect German hausfrau.

Sometimes she was so dumbly, infuriatingly obliging that Tretow felt compelled to give her face a good smack, just to shake her up a little. On these occasions Frau

Tretow cried, promised to do better in future, but never complained or threatened to leave her husband. This was one of the many clues that had convinced Tretow that she was a Stasi agent, planted on him to make sure he did not stray too far from an acceptable way of life. Added evidence for his theory came from her remarkable resemblance, in both appearance and character, to Judith, the wife he'd left behind in Frankfurt. It was surely too much of a coincidence that such a *doppelgänger* could possibly be employed at the carpet factory where, thanks to Stasi influence, he had worked as a sales executive since his arrival from the West; too good to be true that she should then be so available and so willing to satisfy him in ways that totally belied her air of homely decency.

He wondered sometimes whether he would meet his Stasi spouse one day in an interrogation room, her mask torn away to reveal the hard, flinty stare of a secret policewoman, her docility replaced by cold-blooded professional savagery as she tortured a confession from him. She must surely have been longing to avenge the slaps, the betrayals and the routine, petty humiliations he had inflicted upon her. Recently he had almost been daring her to break out of her assigned character and show her true feelings towards him: he wanted to see, close up, all the hatred and anger she must feel.

And yet their lives continued in the same old settled routine. So maybe he was mistaken, and had merely imagined the whole thing. He pondered this as he wandered from the apartment block, one of the prefabricated *plattenbau* projects that had sprung up all over Berlin. Tretow and his family were housed in a top-of-the-range model, brand new and built to a Swedish design. It was located barely two hundred metres from the Wall, so close that he could see into West Berlin from his fourth-floor balcony: a constant reminder of what he had left behind. Rumour had it that the block had been erected directly above the site of Hitler's bunker, where he'd spent the final weeks of his life as the Third Reich disintegrated around him. It saddened Tretow that he could not invite his father to come and stay. He'd have loved to have seen the old bastard's face when he told him that this was the spot where his beloved Führer met his end.

A Trabant, painted in an excremental shade of brown, awaited Tretow at the kerb. The days when he drove fast, rock-solid, eternally reliable Mercedes were long gone. Now he had to stagger down the road in a wheezing, fume-belching joke of a car, whose body was built of a mix of fibreglass and an edible resin: left in a busy farmyard, it was said, a Trabant could be consumed by passing cattle in a matter of days. Such were the joys of life in the German Democratic Republic.

When he got to his office Tretow would attempt to hawk as many metres as he could of his company's vile carpets. Their colours seemed calculated to depress or disgust: drab grey, lifeless green, virulent mustard-yellow, a brownish oxblood-red and perhaps the greatest achievement of all, a green-tinged sea shade that managed to make even blue look nauseating. It was Tretow's daily task to offload them to customers throughout the Soviet bloc, who presumably knew no better, and to bottom-of-the-market furniture stores in the West, whose customers were too cash-strapped to afford anything else. Still, it beat being dead, which would have been the alternative had he stayed in Frankfurt.

When he reached his office, Tretow strode jauntily through the entrance hall, giving a characteristically flirtatious greeting to the receptionist, a peculiarly plain and scrawny woman in late middle age. 'Good morning, Fräulein Schinckel, you look particularly lovely today, if I may say so,' he declared.

Fräulein Schinckel did not simper coyly, or feign outrage – her two standard responses to Tretow's phoney advances. Instead she turned her head, avoiding his eye, saying nothing at all. This was not a good sign.

Tretow's stomach was already beginning to tighten as he walked down the corridor – fake wooden panelling on one side, the glazed walls of rabbit-hutch offices on the other – towards his place of work. He paused before he turned the door handle and walked in, only to have his worst fears immediately confirmed.

Two men were waiting for him. They wore normal civilian clothes, rather than uniforms, but they were unmistakably Stasi officers nonetheless: Tretow knew the type well enough by now.

'You will accompany us,' one of the Stasi said. It was neither an order, nor a polite request, but a simple statement of fact. Tretow did not debate it. Over the previous six years he had regularly been summoned to meetings or interviews with Stasi officers as they mined him for information that was useful to them and damaging to their enemies in the West. This, however, felt different. It smacked of discipline and punishment. He was sweating with fear and nausea as he proceeded back down the corridor, sandwiched between the two men.

Bad things were about to happen to Hans-Peter Tretow, he was certain of it. As he got into the Stasi men's car – another Trabant, naturally – he wondered whether his wife would be waiting to meet him when they got to the interview room.

18

FRIDAY

Nick had said that I knew nothing whatever about being a detective and of course he was right. But I did know about project management. I knew about starting with a vacant site and an empty sheet of paper and ending up with a finished house. I knew about planning the work; assembling information and materials; proceeding logically towards an end point; calling in the right professionals to help. So why not apply those problem-solving skills to the questions I faced here?

The task, after all, had already been defined for me by Samira Khan and Tony Wray: save Mariana from jail by uncovering the truth about her past. Of course Yeats, the policeman, had also defined the big problem: no one knew anything about that past. And Mariana was in no state to discuss it, even if she'd been prepared to meet with me in the first place. But architects spend all their lives finding ways round financial, technical and bureaucratic limitations. I'd find a way round this one.

I'd start the same place Yeats had: Andy's computer. Just as soon as I could get hold of it.

The facts of the case had been agreed to everyone's satisfaction, so there was no need for the police to hold Andy's body and possessions any longer. I'd already arranged undertakers to deal with the body. The possessions, however, were my responsibility.

There wasn't much to deal with, just the black nylon case containing Andy's laptop and an overnight bag. A list that was handed to me with the bag informed me of its contents. The bag itself reeked of some disgusting institutional odour that reminded me of that morning-after smell of fag ends floating in stale beer. I didn't bother even opening it, just dumped it in a black plastic bin-liner, tied as tight a knot as I could and slung it in the back of the Range Rover.

It was the computer I was interested in. I took it back to the hotel room where I'd been living for the past couple of nights, plugged in the power cable and asked myself where Andy had put all his research.

Like a lot of people who appear to be chaotic, Andy was very well organized whenever he wanted to be. Dirty plates piled up in his sink for days, carpets disappeared under dust and rubbish, and his desk was invisible beneath the trash scattered all over it. But the things he really cared about – his books, magazines, CDs and DVDs – were always kept perfectly dated and alphabetized, so that he could find anything he wanted in an instant. His laptop, which was essentially his brain in microchip form, was just the same: everything sorted into logical, clearly defined categories. His journalism, for example, was split into folders for each of the publications he worked for. Inside those folders, each finished story had its own file, within which Andy kept all his drafts, copy he'd cut from the finished piece, notes, and so on.

But whatever he was planning to do with Mariana's story, it didn't sound like he was close to a finished product. That meant he'd still be working on it in Scrivener. This was a program that allowed one to collect written documents, notes, pictures, web pages and any other media relating to a given project in one folder called a 'binder'. All the research materials contained in a binder, irrespective of their format, were displayed in the form of cards, pinned to a virtual corkboard. That made it easy for anyone working on a project to see precisely what they'd got … and it also made it simple for me to realize what Andy had been up to.

I looked down the list of Recent Projects in the program's File menu and there it was: a binder he'd called MC, for Mariana Crookham. I opened it, clicked on the Research icon and up popped a corkboard on which there were a dozen cards and one photograph. It was the biggest single item on the board, pinned at the top left – the start of the page – where one's eye naturally rested.

The photo showed the blown-up, slightly blurred, image of a little girl, about six or seven years old. She wore a dress with short, puffed sleeves made of a pale-blue checked fabric, with a little white collar and a blue satin bow. Her golden hair was gathered in two long bunches, held by elastic bands, over which big blue bows, darker than her dress, had been tied. She had clear, tawny eyes, which were looking directly at the camera, and her mouth was caught in a slightly tentative expression, as if deciding whether to smile.

Even as a child Mariana had been ravishingly pretty.

19

Minutes went by as I stared at her face, absorbing every scrap of it, hoping that if I only concentrated hard enough, I would hear what the little girl who'd grown up to be my wife had to say through those half-opened lips. 'Tell me who you are,' I whispered at the screen. 'What happened to you? What did they do to you? Just tell me . . .'

I sent the picture as an email to myself, planning to use the hotel system to print it up. I wanted to be able to carry that image of Mariana with me, like an icon, a totem of faith. In order to send the email I simply opened Andy's Microsoft Entourage application, created a new message, attached the picture and sent it as if from him to me. But once I'd opened Entourage it automatically got to work downloading new incoming messages. I scrolled with guilty fascination through the posthumous mail that had arrived on his electronic doormat. Almost all of it was spam. There was a cheery message from a friend who was on holiday Down Under, with a picture attached of his latest hot blonde conquest. And then came the final unread message.

It had been sent at 09.36 on Thursday morning, just as Mariana's case was being discussed in the magistrates' court. The subject of the message was, 'Good advice for Andrew Crookham', sent by 'warningvoicexxx@yahoo.com'. I opened the message: 'You are investigating matters that are none of your concern. These investigations must cease immediately. Do not return to Berlin. Consider your own personal safety and that of those you love. Remain at home in England. Only bad things can happen if you disregard this advice.'

The message was not signed. I wanted to be able to dismiss it as a sick joke, like one of those round robins that come with instructions to pass them on, or else. But the heavy, nauseous chill that was spreading through my guts said something else. This was a genuine threat. Andy had stumbled onto something in Berlin: something that someone else badly wanted to keep secret. And whatever it was, it surely had to do with Mariana: events in her past, or family connections that could not be exposed to the light. The belief in Mariana that had been snuffed out in court flickered inside me again. This message clearly suggested that there were people out there willing to use violence to stop Andy exposing their activities. Didn't that provide, at the very least, a reasonable doubt that Mariana was the only person who could possibly have killed him? I picked up my phone and called DCI Yeats.

'Very interesting,' he said, when I'd read him the message. 'But it has nothing whatsoever to do with my investigation.'

'What do you mean? It's a threat. Andy's dead. Isn't that what you're supposed to be investigating?'

'Yes, that's right. I'm investigating a murder that took place more than thirty-six hours before this message was sent. Whoever sent the message did not know that your brother was dead. So they can't have killed him, can they?'

'No, I realize that . . . but the point is, this message establishes that Andy had made enemies in Berlin. Whoever sent this message was obviously one of them. But what if he wasn't the only one? What if there were others?'

'But there weren't, and you know it. Still, I will grant you one thing . . .'

For a moment my hopes rose, only to be dashed by Yeats' next words: 'There appears to be someone in Berlin who very badly wants to prevent your wife's past being uncovered. This person has issued an anonymous threat of violence. So my formal advice as a police officer to you is to take this threat seriously. I daresay you are curious to find out what your brother discovered. But limit your enquiries to his computer. Don't do anything else. Don't go anywhere else.'

'What, because it might not be good for my personal safety? You're making exactly the same threat as the person that sent that email.'

'No, I'm not. I have no intention of doing you any harm. But I'm prepared to believe that someone else just might. Your brother got into some very murky water, Mr Crookham. Don't go in after him.'

I put the phone down and stared blankly into space. Another door had seemed to open, only to slam back in my face. Or maybe it hadn't ... Whatever else had just happened, it was now obvious that Andy was on the right track, even if he didn't know it. So there was something real out there that might explain what had happened to make Mariana lash out: something I could still search for. And even Yeats had said I could start my search in Andy's laptop. So that was what I did.

Next to Mariana's little-girl picture on Andy's Scrivener corkboard were a number of cards, several of which contained links to websites. The first took me to a page on a site called StayFriends, whose logo had the slogan '*Schulfreunde wiederfinden*', which I could work out meant, 'Find schoolfriends again'. So it was a German version of Friends Reunited, and it was open on a page dedicated to a Berlin primary school called Grundschule Rudower.

According to the data on the page, this school had 987 pupils listed on StayFriends, from 59 graduating classes, with 740 profile photos of individual pupils and 161 class photos. One of the latter had also been attached to the corkboard. And there, at the right end of the second row of children, was Mariana, standing between a boy with a fierce crewcut and an earnest girl with dark-brown hair whose pinched expression gave an unnerving suggestion of an angry, resentful adulthood to come.

The girl with the dark-brown hair was called Heike Schmidt, and she was a registered member of StayFriends, as was the crewcut boy, whose name was Karl Braun: a German Charlie Brown. It went without saying that the blonde girl in the middle, the girl who became Mariana Slavik, was not listed as a member.

I always carry a Moleskine notebook with me wherever I go, along with a couple of sharp pencils with erasers on the end. I like to take brief notes of what's been said with clients and contractors and make drawings of any changes to the plans. On a building site, a quick sketch is worth a lot more than a thousand misunderstood words. Out of habit I started jotting down a few of the names and places Andy had come up with, taking notes of his notes. Whatever quest he had been on, it had become my quest now. Putting things down in my own writing felt as if I were taking possession of it all, grabbing the relay baton he was holding out for me from beyond the grave.

Going back to the corkboard I followed the trail of Andy's meticulous research. One card was a link to a complete list of Berlin primary schools, divided by districts of the city. The site was open at a page covering the Köpenick district, in which the Grundschule Rudower lay. Another card took me to a website for amateur genealogists, which gave information on all the administrative areas of Berlin, dating back more than a century. Among other things, it specified which districts had ended up in East Berlin and which in West.

Andy had taken the eastern districts and cross-referenced them with the districts on the list of primary schools. Then he'd gone onto StayFriends and searched school after school, looking at the years when Mariana would have been there, scanning every class photo for anyone who resembled her.

I was astonished at the obsessive effort that must have taken. But as Andy used to joke, 'It's not always easy to tell the difference between an investigative reporter and a stalker.' Plenty of girlfriends had left Andy when they realized there was no date so important that he would not cancel it at a moment's notice if he got a promising lead. Nor was it easy for women to accept that he would remember every last detail of the story he was working on but forget anything and everything about them.

The search for that photo had only been one small part of his effort. Another card contained records of all his travel expenses: the easyJet flight from London Gatwick to Berlin-Schönefeld; the two-night stay at a hotel called the Mercure an der Charité, on what was once the eastern side of the Wall; assorted cash payments for meals, cab fares, metro tickets and so on. He'd taken an early-morning flight out and an evening one back, giving him three full days' work. But that, as would soon become clear, had not been nearly enough.

All the notes Andy had jotted down as he was working were filed on another card: notes that included his own commentary on what he was doing or discovering. It felt as though Andy's dry, sarcastic voice, given a low, rasping edge by the cigarettes he was always trying (not very hard) to give up, was whispering in my ear, like a kind of haunting as I read:

Leads 1: School

- Braun: Only two listed in online Berlin phonebook: odd, expected more.
- Braun 1: away in Mali on UN humanitarian work, the do-gooding twat.
- Braun 2: no idea what I was talking about, barely

spoke English but swore never heard of Grundschule
Rudower.

- 8 Heike Schmidts, plus half-dozen Heike Schmidt-
  Somethings ... NB: woman could be married by
  now. Prob'ly not, face like that!
- Schmidt UPDATE: third HS I called v. edgy. Said yes
  had gone to GR school, but denied knowing any girl
  called Mariana. When I described kid in pic, HS
  refused to talk. Quote: 'You must not ask me about
  these things!' Slammed phone down. GOTCHA!!
- Schmidt UPDATE 2: went to home listed for HS in
  phonebook. Apartment building. HS answered
  buzzer. Threatened to call police.
- QUESTION: there's definitely something going on ...
  but what?? And what still so scared of 25 years later??

How I wished I could talk to Andy. I wanted to show
him the email and ask the next obvious question: had
Heike Schmidt been frightened by the same person who'd
threatened him? And was it just coincidence that the
threat against him had followed his contact with
Schmidt?

I jotted those questions down in my notebook, feeling
the thrill of the intellectual chase, understanding for
the first time in my life why Andy had become so
obsessed by the stories he worked on.

The next section of his notes was headed:

Leads 2: Birth Certificate

Unbelievable! No central records office for Germany. So much for Kraut efficiency!! So . . .
- Birth certificates are issued at the place of birth.
- Addresses are registered at office called the Einwohnermeldeamt.
- Can follow people through those offices because have to give previous and next address.
- In East Germany same thing was called ZMK = Zentrale Meldekartei.
- Oh . . . great . . . NOW they tell me . . . There is a central Berlin office for birth certificates.
- QUESTION: who could fake documents in E. Germany?? Was there organized crime (cf. Russian Mafia) and/or resistance movement? Otherwise has to be people in charge of system = Stasi.
- QUESTION: or was name changed in West? When did she go to West? Ask Pete . . . how? What reason for question?
  UPDATE: see chart for certificate trawl . . .

I followed the trail to a separate document and once again was given an insight into the thoroughness with which my brother went about his business.

He'd started out trying to find any record of a Mariana Slavik, born on 14 June 1980. There was no such certificate.

So then he'd asked whether any girl called Mariana Slavik had been born at any time, five years either side of that date. Again, he'd not found any record of any such birth. A note next to that information read: 'NO Mariana Slaviks anywhere. Less than 150 Slaviks in whole German phonebook. Plus, Mariana is weird spelling. Usual way is Mariane, with an "e". Where is this bloody woman???'

In order to find her, Andy had widened his search. He looked at all the girls born on 14 June 1980. There were twenty-eight of them in all, whom he'd arranged alphabetically from Renate Alback through to Heike Zuckerman, with all the data about parents, place of birth and so on that the certificates provided.

None of the girls was called Mariana, or Slavik. Three of them, however, had asterisks by their names: Marinella Knopf, Mariamne Schwartz and Maria-Angelika Wahrmann.

Andy had obviously highlighted them as being the closest to Mariana, but he clearly wasn't convinced that meant very much, because just below the list he'd written:

- Follow these up . . . all of them . . . will have to
make 2nd trip back Berlin . . . BOLLOCKS!!!
- QUESTION: what if birth-date is fake, too? Kid

would still want to keep same birthday, surely –
parties, prezzies, etc. – but easy change one or two
years either way ... check them too, next trip?

- BIG QUESTION: HOW DO I TELL PETE ABOUT ALL
  THIS??
- Talk to Mariana first? Maybe she has reasonable
  explanation ...
- NO ... MUCH BIGGER QUESTION: WTF hasn't P
  noticed any of this himself? She must be the
  greatest shag of all time to pull the wool over his
  eyes so well.

I put my pencil down and closed the laptop. The
bubble of excitement I'd felt just a few minutes earlier
had suddenly deflated, replaced by something much
closer to humiliation. In my head I could hear Chief
Inspector Yeats asking me, 'How well do you know your
wife, Mr Crookham?'

I looked again at Andy's question to himself – 'Talk
to Mariana first?' – and as I did so, my dreams of proving
Yeats wrong seemed like nothing more than pathetic
schoolboy fantasies. There, in writing, were words that
seemed to support the precise scenario that he had
suggested as Andy arrived at our house, bursting with
ideas, and discovered I wasn't there. It was easy to
imagine him unable to stop himself asking Mariana
endless questions about something, driving her to the
point where she suddenly lashed out, and ...

No! That couldn't be it!

Of course, Andy was right, up to a point. I had accepted everything Mariana had said to me without question. And yes, shagging had something to do with it – I felt like I'd won the lottery every time I saw her naked. But that really wasn't the most important thing. It was more that I believed we had something magical, a charmed life, and I hadn't wanted to do anything that would break the spell. So I didn't question her about her family or her past. Instead, I always described my family to her in a way that suggested there wasn't really so much difference from the distance between Mum, Andy and me and the total chasm between Mariana and her background. That way our dysfunctional families bound us together and increased that fantastic sense of being a little team: us against the world with no distractions anywhere.

I loved the woman, all right? Sometimes that means wanting to know every single scrap of information about the person you adore. But in our case it had meant keeping the curtain between us and the outside world tightly shut, for fear that any light should be let in upon the magic. But as any honest magician will tell you, his tricks are not real. They're all just a matter of distraction and illusion. So now I had to ask myself: had our marriage been an illusion, too? And once I saw through the trick, what the hell was I going to find?

20

If I'd understood Dr Wray correctly, Mariana did not consciously know what had traumatized her. But maybe her subconscious had let slip some clues: something in her words or behaviour that had indicated something was wrong, but that I would have missed, or ignored at the time.

That night, over dinner in the hotel restaurant, I found myself going back into the past, taking out all those echoes of happier times and looking at them afresh. I thought about what it must have been like for Mariana to be the product of not one dictatorship but two. She had grown up in a land that had gone straight from Nazism to Stalinism, and though she had only been ten when the Berlin Wall came down, it was always obvious that she had some sort of race memory of oppression and a visceral hatred of anything that resembled it.

She called herself a 'neo-liberal', meaning that she loathed communism, socialism, in fact any form of politics that even hinted at state control or the loss of personal freedom. Stories about the spread of CCTV cameras or the use of spy chips in rubbish bins provoked an anger in her that went far beyond obligatory suburban outrage. She never, ever, talked about the specifics of her East German girlhood, but the Stasi were always bogeymen in her eyes. 'They are still out there, all of them,' she would say. 'The people who led this system are free today . . . they are police officers, lawyers and politicans and they are laughing in our faces. Someone should find them and shoot them in the head.'

Moments like that were very rare, sudden flashes of lightning across a sky that was otherwise calm and sunny. Now, though, the violence of her speech took on a new significance. Just like the email that Andy had been sent it was a reminder of the deeper, darker culture of violence from which it came. And as one thought unfurled into another through a mind relaxed by a bottle of rich red wine, another memory came to me, bearing another clue to her personality.

It was an evening after work, two or three years ago. Mariana and I were having a pint with Nick. He amazed me by saying that he'd decided to go to a therapist. 'I need help,' he said, with a vulnerability that I'd never heard in him before. 'I mean, chasing skirt, never settling down, notches on the bedpost and all that ... it's fair enough when you're twenty, even thirty. But I'm turning forty this year and I'm in serious danger of becoming a sad old lech ... So I think I need some help.'

'Good for you,' I said. 'I'm impressed.'

Nick snorted derisively, thinking I was taking the mick.

'No, I mean it,' I assured him. 'Takes a lot of balls to admit there's something wrong and even more to do something about it.' I raised my glass: 'Here's to you ... you sad old lech!'

Nick laughed and knocked his glass against mine. Then he looked at Mariana, who'd not said a word, and asked, 'How about you, M? You ever had your head examined?'

His tone was perfectly friendly, but he couldn't have provoked a more venomous response if he'd trodden on a rattlesnake. 'Never!' snapped Mariana. 'Psychiatrists are all liars ... all of them! They pretend they can read people's minds when it is all just bullshit. How can they see inside my head?'

'Whoa!' said Nick, rolling his eyes at me. A minute or two later we were very deliberately talking about sport and letting Mariana calm down in her own time. The subject of psychiatry was never mentioned again. But as I sipped my wine, one idea about heads became associated with another glossed-over memory from our earliest days together.

I said we were married a year after we'd first flirted, that day in the car outside the Blacks' house. That's true. But it's not the whole story. It wasn't exactly a smooth, linear process. Nor was this the first time I'd been unable to communicate with Mariana.

After her first few weeks as an intern at our practice, she went away on holiday, then back to college to study for her postgraduate degree. There was just one catch. She didn't give me her address. She changed her phone, too. The only way we could communicate was via email and instant messaging.

It was an incredibly manipulative way of playing hard to get, since she completely controlled the terms of our communication. At first, though, I was too giddy with excitement to care. Our hours of online chat revealed a woman who was clever, funny, well-read, filled with curiosity and original ideas and, above all, totally unabashed about sex. She was blatantly, graphically, hilariously frank about what turned her on and she provoked me into my own outbursts of personal pornography: a filthy honesty that I'd never dared to express to a woman before. As her messages popped up on my screen like darts from a dirty-minded Cupid, I was a junkie, a crack-whore for Mariana's strange, artificial substitute for love.

One night as we were chatting she added a new, visual element to our communications. She'd just told me how she'd gone with some university friends to see a Sheffield United match at Bramall Lane. To prove the point she emailed me one of those pictures of a group of people, laughing hysterically, that make one feel hopelessly cut off from their private joke. Mariana was playing peek-aboo from behind a guy's shoulder, just her red-and-white-striped bobble hat and a huge pair of Jackie O sunglasses visible, like the cutest Where's Wally in the world.

The next picture came later that week as a response to me complaining about a lousy day at work. She wrote back:

− AH, POOR BABY. WAIT A MOMENT I CHEER YOU UP!!

A couple of minutes later a message arrived in my email inbox with a jpeg file attached. I opened it to find a picture of Mariana. She was at the beach, at one of those playgrounds for bodybuilders and fitness freaks, hanging from a pair of gymnast's rings. The picture was taken from the side and showed her spectacular body in profile like a magnificent pendant sculpture. Her left leg was vertical, the toes arched down like a ballerina *en pointe*, while her right was pulled up, the knee bent to form a perfect triangle. Her back and stomach were sleek and lean, the dazzling seaside light glinting off her tanned, sun-creamed skin. Her breasts, in a polka-dot bikini top, swelled beneath the tensed muscles of her arms, behind which I could just catch a glimpse of her forehead beneath a tumble of golden hair. My reply was hardly inspired:

– wow!

And so it went on. Mariana used to complain, only half joking, about what she called her 'gigantic butt'. In reality, it was as perfect a combination of curves as any man ever beheld. One night, she messaged me having just come in from a party, a little drunk I suspected, judging by the way she wrote, complaining that yet another man had been grabbing her:

– HERE, I SHOW YOU WHERE HE PINCHED ME!!

Next thing I knew, she'd sent a low-resolution shot, presumably taken from her computer camera, showing the ass in question only partially covered by a pair of white hotpants Kylie Minogue might have thought twice before attempting. I got the strong impression she had nothing on underneath.

The following night, she gave me a frontal view. She was standing with her hips cocked in front of a full-length mirror in what I presumed was her bedroom, and I hoped to God it wasn't anyone else's, wearing black high heels, hold-up stockings, minuscule knickers and bra. Her left hand – I knew it was hers by the watch on her wrist, which she used to wear to work – was perched saucily on her hip. Her right was holding the camera to her eye. But her face had disappeared behind a blaze of flash, reflected back from the mirror to the lens. She was, effectively, headless.

It suddenly struck me that her face had not been visible in any of the pictures she had sent me. So I wrote back . . .

  – SO HOT!! BUT WHERE IS YOUR LOVELY FACE?
  – NOT TONITE. LOOK REALLY BAD.
  – YOU COULD NEVER LOOK BAD!!
  – HAIR DIRTY, SPOTS. I'M VERY VAIN, I KNOW!
  – FACE! FACE! FACE! _ _
  – NO! I LOOK SCHRECKLICH!!! TOMORROW MORNING, MAYBE

I looked up *schrecklich* on Babelfish. It meant 'terrible'. I told myself that this was just typical female insecurity, that strange combination of vanity and self-loathing that makes even beautiful women see flaws where none exist. Next morning, to my surprise, she really did send me a picture as promised. She was sitting on the floor in her jeans, one leg crossed over the other, her face looking straight at the camera. There was just one catch. She had shot it in such darkness that she was barely visible. Even when I put it through an enhancer program, with the exposure banged way up, all I got was a pixellated image of a flash of blonde hair, the outlines of two huge eyes and a blurred, unreadable expression.

Now, when I thought about the compulsiveness with which Mariana had hidden her face in those photographs, it seemed to connect to her incredible suspicion of any therapist who might want to analyse her. Why does someone hide their face? Because they do not want to be recognized. Why would someone fear analysis? Because a shrink might get them wrong ... or, even worse, the shrink might discover what they were really like. What was it that Mariana didn't want anyone to see? Was there something terrible in there, in her head – something *schrecklich* – that she desperately wanted to be kept hidden? Was that what Andy had somehow stumbled upon – the secret shame that Mariana was willing to do anything to protect ... including kill?

For a few days after she'd sent those pictures, we carried on as before. One night we spent three hours messaging one another back and forth, chatting perfectly happily. Or so I thought, anyway.

I sent her an email the next morning, following up something we'd been talking about. She didn't reply. That night, she wasn't online at all: same again the night after.

I assumed she was busy. Then a week went by without a word and I started to worry. The silence continued and the terrible realization dawned that it was all over: whatever 'it' was. I went through a kind of cold turkey, physically aching for want of her. I lay awake at night wondering what I'd done to put her off. I read and reread every word that had passed between us, trying to work out the point at which she'd decided to bail out. The craving for her became so bad that I seriously contemplated going down to Sheffield and just waiting by the architecture faculty until she showed up.

It drove Nick crazy. 'Can't you see that she's just playing you? She's having a good laugh, jerking your chain and seeing what happens. Open your eyes, mate. This is never going to go anywhere.'

I argued with him: 'Look, I know this is crazy, but she's worth it. And there's a real connection between us, I know there is.'

'You reckon? Well, if your connection is so good, how come you can't even call her? It's not just a little crazy, mate. Talk about a prick-tease . . .'

Two months went by and then, as suddenly as she had gone, Mariana returned. She sent me an email filled with apparent remorse. It read, 'I hope you can forgive me some day. I'm sure you will never answer me but I want that you know this: I bitterly regret what I have done. If you hate me, I have earned it. It wasn't in any way your fault, just mine. I have been thinking of you all the time and I wish you all the best and a lot of love, Mxx.'

I wrote back and told her that I could never hate her. I just wanted to see her again and talk face-to-face like normal human beings. If we could ever be lovers – for though we'd dated, we'd never actually had sex in the time she'd been at the practice – that would be fantastic, I said, but I would settle for being her friend.

'OK, if you want real, natural friendship, you can have it,' she replied. 'But I must warn you I'm a very bad friend, often resentful and touchy. But if you really want that blonde bitch for friendship, she is here for you.'

Before I could reply, she added a postscript: 'Help me move on, change my perception of the world, let me trust someone.'

In retrospect, of course, I came full circle once again to Andy's original question: why had I not seen that there was something seriously wrong with Mariana? Well, I had – in part. Of course I thought it was bizarre, the way she acted. Not to mention frustrating, infuriating, painful and a total waste of time. But as a man you expect a certain amount of crazy, hormonal, emotional manipulation from a woman, just as women, I imagine, expect all the things that most men get hopelessly wrong in their relationships. But we all put up with the drawbacks of the opposite sex when we think the other person is worth it. And Mariana was. Not only that, she proved me right and justified my tolerance of everything she'd put me through by what happened next.

The games stopped. She came back to work with us again. Within a week we were sleeping together and from that moment on she was never, ever, anything but wonderful to me.

'Of course she's changed,' Nick said. 'She wants a job and you're a partner. She'll be wanting a ring next. You're her meal-ticket, mate. Get used to it.'

I didn't think that was a fair explanation back then and I still didn't, even after everything that had happened. If anything, Mariana was our meal-ticket, not the other way round. She had been our way into the footballer market. She'd made us rich. But quite apart from that, the psychology wasn't right. There had always been something true and pure between us, hidden away beneath all the game-playing and manipulation like a diamond in a seam of black, volcanic rock: I was absolutely sure of it, right from that first conversation in my car. And that, it occurred to me now, might have been what bothered Mariana. She felt it just like I did. She wanted it too. But at the same time something about it scared the hell out of her. So she did everything she could to drive me away, until, in the end, she'd run out of tricks and I was still there, waiting for her. And that's when she finally came to me.

At that point I set everything that had happened before to one side. I'd never really known love before: not from my family, nor my first marriage. Mariana gave me the real thing, pain and all. And for that I'd forgiven her everything.

But how could I forgive the killing of my only brother? I had told Vickie Price that I would have nothing if I lost Mariana. But there was no possibility of our marriage surviving unless I could come to terms with what she had done. In that respect, the detective mission on which I had embarked was not just aimed at convincing a judge. First I had to convince myself. And on that thought I finished the last glass of wine, signed my initials to the bill for a meal I'd barely noticed and wandered back up to my hotel room. I wanted a decent night's sleep. I'd be back to work in the morning.

21

SATURDAY

Two days earlier, I'd discovered how much blood a human body can pump out into the open air before the heart gives up and dies. That same day, in the hours between Mariana's court appearance and my visit to the secure psychiatric unit, I'd learned how that blood is cleaned away.

Yeats had called to inform me that the house was no longer a working crime scene. I could therefore take possession of my property again. He gave me the number of a specialist cleaning company that dealt with crime scenes. I called them up, fixed an appointment, told them to collect the house keys from the hotel reception desk and asked what I could expect to see when I went back to the house.

'It'll be totally clean,' the man said. 'You'll never know anything had happened. We start at the centre of the crime scene and work out from there: absolutely every surface, object, bit of furniture, draperies, you name it. The last thing we do is the inside of the front door as we go out. We get rid of any odours, too. All you'll detect is a very slight, fresh, lemony scent. Very pleasant, many of our customers say.'

The lemony freshness of my house awaited me on Saturday morning. But not before I'd checked out of the hotel and gone round to my office. I had expected it to be empty, but Nick was there, wearing a shirt that looked suspiciously as if it had been slept in. He rubbed his hand against eyes as black-rimmed as a panda's.

'I don't suppose you've come to lend me a hand?' he asked as he saw me walk in.

'Afraid not. I just came to get hold of all Mariana's personnel files. I'm going through every scrap of information I can find.' A thought suddenly struck me, 'Oh sod it! Don't tell me the cops took them all ...'

'Copied them,' said Nick. 'Twice. One set for them and one for the defence. Apparently any evidence the police see, the defence has to see too.'

'Well then, I'll take a copy as well.'

Nick looked at me: 'Honestly, Pete, are you sure you want to be doing this? Wouldn't you be better off here?'

'I know you mean well, but I can't come back. Not yet. I'm not trying to be a hero or anything. I just have to find out the truth about Mariana. I'll never have any peace, any closure in my life, until I've done that.'

Nick nodded in grudging acceptance that I was not going to be swayed. Then he looked at Mariana's files. 'Are these going to get you back to work any quicker?'

'I hope so.'

'In that case, bollocks to copying, just take the bloody originals.'

The man from the cleaners was right about the scent: it wasn't entirely unpleasant. He was wrong, however, to say that I would not be able to detect that anything had happened in my living room. The blood on the floors had entirely disappeared. The glazed far wall sparkled. The dining table and kitchen units were spotless. But there were pale, ghostly marks on the wall – a thinning of the creamy white surface – that indicated where the chemicals that had removed the blood had taken away the top layer of paint as well. And on the sofas you could follow the blood spatter by the way the leather was very slightly faded.

Aside from any visible evidence of what had happened here, my mind kept detecting, or perhaps imagining, other, less tangible signs of Andy's continued presence in the building. It wasn't just downstairs that I could still see his body lying on its mattress of blood: it seemed to follow me everywhere. He died in every room in the house.

I wanted to stay, though, because Mariana was present for me in the sight and scent of her clothes hanging in her wardrobe and the framed photographs of us scattered about a random assortment of mantelpieces, bookshelves and walls. All those memories of her stabbed me like acupuncture needles wherever I went, one after the other, all the time. But at least I had that tangible evidence of her. For all my mental images of Andy there was just one picture of him, and then only in a group shot, taken at a party years ago. It was one more indictment on the list of charges against me, one more example of the carelessness with which I'd treated our relationship.

There's no point feeling guilty, though, unless you do something about the source of your guilt. I'd come back home for a purpose. I had to look at my house as a resource. This was where Mariana had lived. This was where her belongings all were. So this was where I would find the most material from which to excavate and reconstruct her past.

There was an outbuilding at the back of the house that I had converted into my personal home office-cum-studio. I took all the files I'd removed from Crookham Church in there, then went back through the house and gathered a pile of Mariana's old diaries, letters, postcards, photographs, address books, her German and UK passports – anything at all that might possibly contain a clue.

I started with the whole question of her birth certificate. According to Andy, none had been issued in the name of Mariana Slavik. Yet I had a nagging memory of seeing just such a certificate, and logic dictated that it must have existed at some point. After all, Mariana Slavik was the name under which she had married me. In order for us to do that, she had to produce her German passport in that name. And to get that original passport she, or her parents, must have had to produce a birth certificate. So I started looking for it.

There was nothing in Mariana's personnel file. The passport had been good enough for us. But looking through a boxfile I'd found at the house, filled with old bits and bobs, I came upon the certificate. True, this was only a photocopy, but it was, or at least purported to be, an official document clearly stating that Mariana had indeed been born on 14 June 1980 in Berlin, the daughter of Fräulein Bettina Slavik. The father was listed as 'unknown'.

If the document was genuine it explained a lot. It was no wonder Mariana never talked about her father: she didn't even know who he was. In a society as ordered as East Germany, with the state snooping into every corner of its citizens' lives, who knew what stigma would be attached to the illegitimate child of a promiscuous young woman?

Of course, the birth certificate could be a fake. That raised the question of how easy it was, or had ever been, to get false papers in East Germany. Andy had concluded that the most likely candidates were the Stasi: the same Stasi that Mariana hated with such a passion. But if there had been criminal gangs in East Germany they could have done it just as easily. Alternatively, suppose the certificate was genuine but someone had managed to remove the original from the archives in Berlin? I wasn't sure who could do such a thing, or why they would want to do it, but it was possible.

So, it suddenly struck me, was something else. Mariana might never have known that her identity was false. If it – whatever 'it' was – had all happened when she was still a small child, she'd have been none the wiser.

That was certainly the impression given by the original CV, still preserved in her personnel file, that she had shown me at her very first interview. It stated that Mariana Slavik had attended a gymnasium (the German equivalent of a British grammar school) in the Bavarian city of Augsburg. She took her Arbitur exams, entitling her to attend university, in 1998. There was a photocopy of her Arbitur certificate attached to prove the fact. Her first degree had been taken at the Technical University of Munich, and she had a certificate of graduation dated June 2002. That was genuine, I was sure. Mariana's ability as an architect was beyond dispute. I'd followed her every step of the way through the later years of her qualification process, and through all that time she'd proved it to me time and time again: she was the real thing.

That's not what Andy had thought, though, and I was rapidly developing a serious posthumous respect for his investigative abilities. I owed it to him to honour the work he had done. So I planned to go through everything of Mariana's that I'd collected and see whether there was a name, an address, anything at all, that correlated to something Andy had uncovered. Maybe then I could work out what had made her kill.

22

A bundle of unopened letters, addressed to Mariana, had been sitting under a paperweight on one of the kitchen work surfaces. It was the usual stuff that gets sent to a prosperous, middle-class woman. A subscription copy of *Vogue*; some bills; catalogues flogging Toast and Boden clothes, White Company linens, Designers' Guild furnishings and Sarah Raven seeds. Mariana had recently decided to create a vegetable garden. She'd said she was looking forward to getting her hands dirty. She wanted to grow the food that we ate. She liked the thought of bringing a garden to life.

I remembered, exactly, where Mariana had been standing in our garden when she told me about her plans, and the light that had shone in her eyes. She had hugged me tight, just from the pleasure of thinking about it all, and the smell of her hair had filled my senses just as the memory of her was doing now.

When I'd brought the letters into my studio, I'd put them on the table quite close to my chair. So when I'd finished with Mariana's office files they happened to catch my eye. Once I'd discarded all the commercial stuff there was only one actual piece of genuine correspondence: an envelope with the logo of a private hospital in Leeds printed on the front, postmarked the day before the killing.

It had been sent by a Mr Timothy Reede. His notepaper proclaimed him to be a Consultant Gynaecologist and Fellow of the Royal College of Obstetricians and Gynaecologists.

'Dear Mrs Crookham,' he began, 'I am writing to let you know that I have received the results of the tests taken during your consultation last week and I am pleased to report that they confirm my initial impression that the Essure procedure which you underwent two years ago continues to be completely effective, without any significant side effects to your health. Occasional heavy periods, spotting and discharges are to be expected with any form of tubal ligation, of which Essure is one. But they are nothing to be alarmed about. I hope this news will reassure you that all is well, Yours . . . etc.' A bill for the consultation and tests was attached. It came to £287.50.

My first reaction was puzzlement. I knew Mariana saw a gynae from time to time like any other woman.

She'd once described what it was like to have a cervical smear. After that I had no interest at all in knowing what went on once she stuck her legs in the stirrups. But I was pretty certain that if she'd undergone some kind of hospital procedure I'd have heard about it. Wouldn't I?

I opened my own computer and searched for 'Essure tubal ligation'. Up popped the first ten of 640,000 possible results. And then the phrases hit me: 'permanent birth control' ... 'sterilization procedure' ... 'hysteroscopy sterilization'.

Children had never been a huge priority in our lives. Mariana was still young, her body clock had barely started to tick, let alone set off any alarms. I certainly wasn't in any hurry. Whenever I bothered to think about it, which wasn't often, I assumed that when Mariana was ready, she'd come off the pill, we'd keep on doing whatever we were doing already, and babies would follow as a matter of course.

Now I discovered how wrong I had been.

Mariana had gone to hospital and had two little nickel-coated springs placed in the ostia, the openings to her Fallopian tubes. These springs caused inflammation in the tubes. That in turn blocked the way between my sperm and her eggs, making it impossible for us to conceive children. Ever. Without telling me, my wife had sneaked off to have the quickest, most discreet, least invasive form of permanent sterilization currently available. Essure, I discovered, is the only form of tubal ligation – that's tying your tubes in plain English – that can be carried out as an outpatient procedure under light anaesthetic, without any incisions anywhere. She really didn't want me to know what she'd done.

What happened next began as a sickly, gut-wrenching feeling in the pit of my stomach, moved up my body to grab my throat then exploded in a wordless bellow of frustration, humiliation and wrath. I hurled my coffee cup across the room and it shattered on the far wall, splashing the remaining dregs of the cappuccino across the wall in a pathetically diminished facsimile of the spatter-pattern of Andrew's blood.

I'd been had. I'd tried to pretend that Mariana could not have killed my brother, despite all the evidence to the contrary, until she herself had shouted out her own guilt. I'd tried to find excuses for her behaviour on the assumption that there must be a reason for it all, one that would somehow exonerate her. Now I realized that the destruction she had wrought was not just a matter of one mindless, psychotic, uncontrollable act of violence. She hadn't just robbed me of my brother. She had cold-bloodedly, calculatedly, robbed me of my children as well.

I had to face the facts. I'd been married for six years to a woman who could decide to have herself sterilized and snuff out the life inside herself without saying a single word to me before, during or after the procedure. The woman I had adored had been a figment of my imagination. The woman I had actually married now looked suspiciously like a monster.

MINISTRY OF STATE SECURITY HEADQUARTERS, NORMANNENSTRASSE, BERLIN: 1984

The Stasi liked to take their time when interviewing suspects. Yet Hans-Peter Tretow's interrogation was remarkably swift.

Whether by coincidence or deliberate planning, it was conducted by the very officer who had first questioned Tretow on the day he defected from the West. He had been promoted to the rank of major. His hair was thinner, though somewhat better cut, and his skin more lined, but the watery pale-blue eyes hadn't changed: this was the same man all right. It seemed that the major had photographs that he wished to discuss: surveillance shots, acquired by the Stasi using hidden cameras. He placed them one by one, directly in front of Tretow, on the table that sat between the two men.

'We have film footage, too,' said the major. 'Both pictures and sound. It's quite a movie. You are filth, Tretow. I hope you know that.'

'I know that this is illegal, yes.'

The major frowned in incredulity at what he had just heard. 'Illegal? You make it sound like a traffic offence. This is not some minor technicality. This is a crime that disgraces the good name of the German Democratic Republic. Our society has no room for this kind of decadence. You should have left it behind when you left the West. Indeed, you promised to do so.'

Tretow looked puzzled: 'Sorry?'

Several cardboard document-holders were piled by the major's right hand. He reached for one of the files, flicked through its content and then removed a number of typed sheets. 'Let me see . . .' he murmured, running a finger down one of the pages of text. 'Yes, here we are . . . From an interview between yourself and Herr Direktor Wolf, dated the 19 April 1978. Wolf: "Should you produce information that assists the defence of democratic socialism against its capitalist enemies, then you will be suitably rewarded. But if you fail me in any way, I will make it my personal business to see that you receive the maximum punishment that your crimes merit. Are we clear?" . . . And your response . . . Tretow: "Completely."'

The major lifted his eyes from the file and looked directly at Tretow. 'So, do you feel that you provided the information that you promised us?'

'Er . . . yes, I believe I have done that. I hope so, anyway.'

'I agree,' said the major affably. 'You gave us the means to exert considerable influence upon certain key individuals in Western nations, notably the Federal Republic. This information continues to be of use and you are still available to assist with the operation when required. Is that not so?'

'Absolutely.'

'So, let us agree that you kept your side of the bargain, in that respect at least. But what about Herr Direktor Wolf, would you say that he did as he promised?'

'Of course!' Tretow hoped that his response, however brief, conveyed bottomless quantities of enthusiastic gratitude.

The major smiled. 'Again, I agree. You have a respectable job, a magnificent apartment, a delightful family. You and your wife have been allowed on numerous occasions to buy goods, including fresh fruit, prime meat and the latest Western clothes and electrical equipment from the supermarket reserved for senior officers at our minis- terial headquarters. Your life is good, is it not?'

'Oh yes, very good, very good indeed!'

'So one of the most important, well-respected men in our entire nation has been extraordinarily generous towards you. He has granted you privileges that many decent, hard-working citizens can only dream of, and this,' the major slammed his hand down onto the photos, hitting the tabletop with a crack that sounded as threatening as a gunshot to Tretow's terrified ears, 'this is how you repay him. Are . . . you . . . MAD?'

The major leaned forward across the table, putting all his weight on his left hand. He peered at Tretow like a scientist examining a particularly repellent virus. Then, without the slightest warning, he slapped him very hard on the side of the face. Tretow's head jerked to the side with the force of the blow, and the stinging pain brought tears to his eyes.

The major hit him again. 'I asked you a question. Answer it!'

Tretow was dazed. 'What question?'

The major hit him a third time and then, barely a second later, a fourth, backhanded to the other side of his face.

'Answer the question!' he shouted. 'Are you mad?'

'No!' cried Tretow, and then shrieked in alarm as the major raised his hand. Unable to shield himself with his manacled hands, he cowered helplessly, his head down, shoulders hunched, quivering. A stain spread across the front of his trousers. Returned to the status of a powerless child, recoiling from a violent father-figure, he had acted like a child. He had wet himself.

The major gave a contemptuous sniff at the urine's acidic odour. Then he continued his questioning: 'So when you parade your criminality in front of Herr Direktor Wolf, this is the action of a man who is fully in control

of his mind, who knows what the penalties for misbe-
haviour are, yet still deliberately flaunts his contempt
and ingratitude . . . is that what you are saying?'

'No, no – I mean, yes. I . . . I don't know.'

'Pathetic,' the major sighed. Almost as an afterthought
he added, 'We know you beat your wife, by the way. An
innocent, defenceless woman, who has given you beautiful children . . . what kind of a man do you think you
are, to abuse your own wife so?'

Tretow stammered wordlessly, but the major interrupted his attempts to formulate a response. 'There is
no need to answer. We have just established that you are
a snivelling coward, a pants-wetter, an antisocial deviant.
What do you think we should do with a man like that?'

'I don't know . . .'

'How about this?' The major removed his pistol from
its leather holster, walked round the table and held the
muzzle to Tretow's head. 'Shall I tell you how we rid
the world of vermin? With a single shot, without
warning, to the back of the head. Are you vermin, Hans-
Peter Tretow?'

Unable to speak, Tretow gave a single miserable nod
of the head. He had abandoned all hope.

'Yes, that would be a perfectly reasonable course of
action,' said the major. 'It would be quite consistent
with the terms of your agreement with Herr Direktor
Wolf. He certainly thought so. His first instinct on seeing

these pictures was to order your immediate trial and execution. That would still be his preferred choice. Yet even a man as mighty as the director of our nation's entire foreign intelligence operations cannot afford to let self-indulgence cloud his judgement. There are times when he must force himself to hold his nose and, however distasteful it may be, continue to take advantage of filth and scum. Do you follow me?'

'I think so,' said Tretow, his voice betraying the first faint scintilla of hope.

'You are still of use to the ministry, so you will not be getting the bullet you so richly deserve. Not today, anyway. You will lose your job, of course, and your nice apartment. You will have to tell your poor wife that she will not be able to shop at our special store again. I feel for her, I must say, being reduced to life in the two rooms allocated to the caretaker at a state institution, a mere dogsbody and handyman, which is how you will serve our nation in future. I would not blame her in the very slightest if she left you and took your children with her. She will be rehoused much more comfortably by an understanding state as and when she chooses that option – a fact of which she will be informed in due course. You, however, will remain exactly where we have put you and you will be grateful, pathetically grateful, for that. We have allowed you to live, Tretow. And, when you get to your new place of employment, you will see that we have even provided you with activities to amuse you. But one word of warning – you may do what you wish within certain very strictly controlled limits. But if you step outside those limits by even a single millimetre, you will die. And be sure of this, your death will not be as merciful as a bullet to the head.'

The major reached down and cradled Tretow's battered face in his hand. He examined Tretow's bloodied nose, half-closed right eye and a bruise on his cheek that was already acquiring an aubergine depth of purple and black. He lowered his own face so that it was level with Tretow's.

'Do we understand each other?'

Tretow nodded, feeling his chin rub up and down against the palm of the major's hand.

'Excellent.'

The major returned to his side of the table and pressed a button on his office intercom. 'Remove the prisoner and take him to his new place of employment. No, I will not be here. I feel a pressing need to take a shower.'

And so, as he not only relived the violence he had suffered at his father's hands but understood, for the first time, the toxic effects of total defeat that the old man had lived with since his own surrender in 1945, another chapter in Hans-Peter Tretow's life came to an end and a new, very different one began . . .

23

SUNDAY

That night I lay in bed, once again wracking my mind for memories. But this time I was not searching for clues to Mariana's psychosis. Instead I tried to find something, anything, that I could trust to give me some kind of reassurance. I'd brought Andy's laptop upstairs and opened up the school picture of Mariana full-screen, as though the sight of her at a time of innocence might somehow restore the innocence, or more likely naïvety, with which I had once looked on her. But now even my happiest memories were compromised. I wondered whether her fingers had been crossed when she made those vows at the altar, pledging herself to me. I thought of her one night on our honeymoon, lying stark naked on the rim of the deserted hotel swimming pool, daring me to strip off and join her. I could still recall every sweeping line of her body, every play of light upon her limbs. But now it seemed to me that some poisonous evil had been festering beneath her lovely skin.

Yet the bitterness and resentment I now felt were no less toxic. And still a hope remained in me that, even now, some explanation could be given that would explain it all and give me reassurance that my love had not been in vain.

I must have dropped off to sleep some time around two in the morning.

I came to with a start. The numbers on my digital alarm clock read 3.27. I propped myself up on one elbow, blinking as I tried to get my bearings. What had woken me? I listened hard but could not detect any sound of movement within the house. My immediate instinct was to lie down again and try to go back to sleep, but I was awake now, my nerves on red alert and demanding answers. Muttering swear words to myself, I got out of bed and went to the window.

I looked out across a back garden lit by a full moon strong enough to cast shadows across the frostbitten lawn. There was no one there. To my left were the outbuildings in which I had my studio. My eye was caught by the brief glimmer of a moving, flickering light against the studio window. Was it coming from inside? Or was it just the twinkle of reflected moon-light? The light vanished. I watched the window for a couple more minutes. The light did not reappear. I told myself it must have been the moonlight playing tricks on my senses and went back to bed, rolled onto my right side, drew the blankets up over my shoulder and waited for unconsciousness to rescue me again.

No such luck. My mind resolutely refused to switch off. The words of the anonymous email went round and round in my brain: 'Consider your personal safety ... bad things can happen ...' My skin continued to crawl with the prickle of undischarged adrenalin. Then I heard a very faint, muffled 'chunk' from downstairs: just once, then silence again. It sounded very much as though the front door had been unlocked and opened. I lay there, trying to find reasons not to gather up the courage to investigate, my previous nervous tension now transformed into full-blown fear. Someone was in my house. I was sure of it. What was I going to do?

I got out of bed a second time. If I was going to confront an intruder, I wanted to be partially dressed, at the very least, and as well armed as possible. But with what? I wasn't an American. There was no loaded pistol in my bedside drawer. I'd have to make do with something all too English.

I pulled on the jeans I'd discarded on the bedroom floor and padded across to the wardrobe, my ears straining for any sound suggesting that someone was coming upstairs. On the top shelf of the wardrobe, right at the back, was an old leather cricket bag filled with gear I'd barely touched since I left school. I reached up, stretching towards it, leaving my back totally exposed to any attack.

My fingers groped in the near total darkness, feeling their way past Mariana's old hatboxes and a pair of my cowboy boots until, at the absolute furthest extent of my reach, they touched the soft, cracked leather of the cricket bag. I stopped and cast my eyes back into the room, searching through the gloom for any sign of the intruder. I could see nothing, but that did not mean he was not there, lurking, waiting for his moment to strike.

I told myself not to be so melodramatic. All I was doing was making myself even more scared than before. I stretched up again, grabbed the cricket bag and very carefully pulled it out, making sure that I did not bring an avalanche of boxes and boots down with it. The bat was in there. It seemed absurd to be setting out to confront a burglar who might have a knife or even a gun gripping an ancient Gray-Nicolls, but it was a great deal better than nothing, and a full-force blow could do some serious damage. I knew the layout of the house better than any intruder and there was a very strong likelihood that I'd be bigger than him. 'Come on,' I told myself. 'You can do this.'

I pulled back my arms so that the bat was over my right shoulder, ready to strike, and made my way out of the bedroom. I stopped as I reached the landing, which ran across the house with rooms on one side and a gallery, looking down onto the living room, on the other. The visibility was a little better now, the interior of the house cast in a palette of greys, blues and black by the moonlight coming in through the glass wall. I could see at once that I was alone on the landing and all the doors to the other rooms were closed. Very slowly, cautiously, I edged out onto the landing, forcing myself to step into the open. I had to get close enough to the gallery edge to see down into the living room itself.

There was still no sound of anyone else in the house; no footsteps on the stairs; no onrushing attacker; nothing to stop me getting to the handrail and looking over it.

That's when I discovered that I was wrong. There was not just one intruder in the house. There were two shadowy figures, dressed from head to toe in black, their trousers tucked into boots, their faces masked and their forms rendered oddly robotic by lights that shone at the very centre of their foreheads.

One of them was sitting on the leather sofa, just as Andrew must have been on the night he died.

The other was standing over him, holding something in his right hand, some kind of tube, maybe thirty centimetres long: not far off the total length of a kitchen knife. With calm, deliberate movements, the second figure was raising his hand and bringing the tube down onto the upper legs and torso of the other man.

They were recreating the killing.

I opened my mouth to shout at them but I could not make a noise emerge from my throat, still less form any coherent words. My legs were shaking so much I had to take one hand off the bat-handle and grip the handrail to keep myself upright.

It was the calmness of the exercise that was so eerie and yet so mesmerizing. After a number of blows had been struck, the one on the sofa held up a hand to pause the exercise and fractionally altered his position. Then the second one repeated the slow-motion stabs, but this time the one on the sofa got up and staggered towards his mock assailant.

This cool, calculating re-enactment of my brother's death sparked the anger I needed to overcome my fear and inhibition. My shout when it came was little more than a strangled, 'Hey!' but it was enough to get their attention. The two little lights turned as one towards me. They remained still for a couple of seconds as I advanced towards the stairs. Their stillness conveyed an impression of absolute confidence. I might panic, but they would not. They knew that they were in full command of the situation.

Then the one who'd been playing Mariana's role, the

smaller of the pair, turned to the other as if to give or receive instructions. The light on his forehead briefly illuminated the shoulder of his companion's black, military-style combat jacket, a black balaclava and a small, burka-like glimpse of the face beneath. He turned back and raised his right hand, holding the tube out towards me, apparently about to shoot.

I scrabbled backwards, trying to escape, but it was not a bullet that hit me but a dazzling beam of light, strong enough to force me to screw up my eyes. I tried to feel my way along the handrail towards the stairs, but the beam followed me, still focused on my eyes so that I could not open them fully or see what was happening below me. Then, as suddenly as it had struck me, the torch was switched off. I opened my eyes but could see nothing: the dazzle had destroyed my night vision. If the two men attacked me now I would be completely helpless. But there was no rushing patter of rubber-soled boots on the stairs. In fact, the only noise I heard was that of the front door being opened and then closed.

I could see a bit better now and was able to negotiate the stairs. Somewhere in the distance a car engine started. I turned on the lights. The house was empty. There was no sign whatever that anyone had been there. The invasion was over.

For the second time in less than a week I dialled 999,

this time asking for the police. No, I said, the intruders were not still on my premises. No, I had not been harmed. No, they had not appeared to be carrying any weapons. Nothing seemed to be damaged or stolen.

'Well, then, there's nothing we can do,' said the operator. 'If you do discover that there has been any damage or loss to your property, call the station on Monday morning, make a formal report and you will be issued with a case number for insurance puposes.'

'But I think this may be linked to a murder enquiry. It's being conducted by Chief Inspector Yeats.'

'In that case, sir, I suggest you call him. Goodnight.'

24

'Thanks,' said Yeats when I called his mobile number a few hours later. 'You just made me a hundred and forty quid.'

'Sorry?'

'Taking a call out of hours gives me an automatic four hours' overtime. Great stuff. So, how can I help? Have you had another email?'

'No, it's not that. It's something else, something real this time.'

I ran through the events of the night before, adding a discovery I had made when I'd finally risen from another, equally restless couple of hours' sleep: 'Someone had a look at my laptop. It was in the studio where I worked. I'm sure they were in there before they came in the house. I left it closed, I'm certain. But it was open when I went in there just now.'

'Maybe, but looking at someone else's computer isn't

exactly a capital offence. These intruders don't seem to have committed any crime that's worth investigating, not the way our budget and manpower are at the moment.'

'But it has to be linked to Andy's death. I mean, they were acting it out in front of my eyes. And this happens a couple of days after someone sends him a threatening email. There has to be a connection.'

'Possibly, but it could just be a coincidence. I mean, I can see how this must all be very disturbing to you, so soon after you've suffered a very traumatic loss, but I still don't think it has any relevance to my investigation. Nothing you have told me has any bearing on your wife's case. There's no new relevant evidence. And those intruders could just have been a couple of crime freaks out on a jolly.'

'Breaking into someone's house and acting out a murder – what kind of jolly is that?'

'Not one you or I would consider, maybe. But you've got to understand, Mr Crookham, a lot of people have very strange ideas about crimes and criminals. Women write fan mail to rapists. Sadistic killers on the run get help to hide them from the police. So would it surprise me if a couple of idiots decided to sneak into the house and re-enact a murder they'd read about in the papers? No, not at all. And if they gave you a nasty surprise, it was probably no worse than the one they got seeing you appear at the top of the stairs. Chances are they thought the house was still empty.'

'What about my computer, then?'

'I don't know . . . maybe they hoped they'd find some snaps of your wife they could flog to the paper. If you can show me that a crime has been committed, of course I will take appropriate action. Until then I'm sorry, but there's nothing I can do.'

I drove down to Kent that afternoon, stopping for coffee every fifty miles or so, desperately trying to stay awake as the endless motorway rolled out in front of me. All the way down I tried to think of a better explanation for the identity of the intruders than Yeats had come up with, but without any joy. Why on earth would someone who had made threats to Andy, thinking that he was alive, then try to act out his murder? It was madness, but then so was everything else. So far as the police and the lawyers were concerned, my wife had killed my brother out of the blue, for no reason that anyone could explain. All the evidence appeared to agree with them. The sheer insanity of that was still more than I could handle. I could barely drive straight, let alone think straight.

I was due to meet Vickie at the gastropub where I'd booked a room for the night, just to give her Andy's belongings and talk through arrangements for Andy's funeral the following morning.

Vickie was everything Mariana was not, in ways that had once seemed to put her at a disadvantage, but now looked more like qualities to be admired. She was a redhead, and shorter and plumper than Mariana, with bright-blue eyes hidden behind glasses because, as she had told me on one of the few occasions we'd met, 'Contact lenses are much too fiddly for my sausage fingers and I'm bloody well not having laser-guns fired at my eyes.'

That was Vickie all over: practical, energetic, down-to-earth and, under any remotely normal circumstances, full of warmth and good humour. She'd never dieted in her life, could not give a damn about the latest fashions, and was totally unimpressed by wealth or celebrity. For a man like Andy – completely focused when he worked, but completely hopeless in everyday, practical living – she must have been the perfect partner.

There wasn't much sign of good humour about her now, though. Her hair was tied back in a straggly, unwashed ponytail and the eyes with which she looked at me with such bitter suspicion were red-rimmed with too much crying and too little sleep.

'I'm sorry,' I said, struggling to find the words to make things better. 'You know, for . . .'

For what, exactly? I'd committed so many offences so far as Vickie was concerned, I didn't know where to begin. 'For everything . . .'

Vickie said nothing, but just by the look on her face the message was unmistakable: you can do better than that. I took a deep breath: 'I know I screwed up. Not just in the past few days – though that was bad enough – I mean for years.'

'Yes, you did,' she replied. Then something seemed to distract her. I followed her line of sight and saw that there was a mirror on the wall behind me. Vickie had seen her own reflection.

'I look such a mess,' she said.

'I'm not exactly at my best right now, either,' I replied. 'Here, let me get you a drink.'

'No thanks,' she said, rubbing a hand across her eyes. 'I'm not really in the mood for it.'

'Sure? Well, we'd better get this over and done with, then. Andy's stuff is all in the back of my car.'

I led her back outside. As I opened up the back of the Range Rover I reached in to get the two bags and then stopped. There were a few unanswered questions left over from Andy's Berlin notes: things I'd never got round to following up. I handed Vickie the bin-liner containing his overnight bag then said, 'I've got his computer with me too, but is it OK if I hold on to it, just till tomorrow? There are a couple of things from his trip to Berlin that I just want to check. I'll give it back to you right after the funeral, I promise.'

She shrugged disconsolately: 'Yes, I suppose so. I mean, of course – whatever you want.'

'I'm afraid that doesn't smell too good,' I said, nodding towards the bin-liner that was now sitting between us on the tarmac. 'Do you want to open it up?'

'Might as well,' Vickie said. 'God knows what he's got in there.'

She bent down, gingerly undid the knot and then recoiled as the full, pungent blast hit her. 'Oh my God, what is that?' she almost shrieked. 'It smells disgusting, like ... urgh! ... antiseptic, really cheap scent and one of those pine fresheners people hang up inside a car.'

I laughed rather nervously at her description, not sure whether she would appreciate any sign of humour on my part. 'I was thinking fag ends and beer myself, but you've obviously got a better nose than me.'

Now Vickie gave a hesitant smile, a tiny echo of her usual vivacity. She raised her nose, gave the purse-lipped sniff of a snobbish wine connoisseur and said, 'I detect a hint of ... mmm ... gentleman's urinal, too.'

This time we both laughed, cutting through the tension that had stood like a wall between us. As the sound died away, Vickie grimaced. 'Oh, that's terrible. I shouldn't be joking at a time like this.'

'Of course you should,' I reassured her. 'Andy would hate it if you didn't. You know how he always liked a really good laugh.'

The back of the car was still open, so I lifted the overnight bag out of the bin-liner and perched it at the edge of the boot. 'So, are we brave enough to go in?' I asked. 'All right then, here goes ... Whoa! That is pungent!'

The smell rasped my nose and throat. Vickie wrinkled up her face: 'My eyes are watering!'

'I know,' I agreed. 'What's he got in there, mustard gas?'

I turned to one side, took a deep breath of clean air, then plunged my hand into the bag. It came back up carrying a small, slightly damp cardboard box, decorated with a picture of Chinese ivory chess pieces set against a brown background. On the front of the box were the words 'PRIVILEG After Shave Lotion'. On the side there was more writing in both German and a script that looked like Russian and then, in English, the words, 'Made in German Democratic Republic'.

Inside stood a spectacularly ugly brown bottle with a pseudo-ivory top that had been screwed on loosely enough that some of the contents had leaked.

'That,' I declared, holding the bottle up for Vickie to inspect, 'is genuine communist aftershave.'

'Yuck! I pity the women who had to snog men smelling of that.'

'I doubt the girls smelled much better.'

Vickie smiled to herself. 'Andy told me he'd got something in Berlin he wanted to surprise you with, but he never said what it was. He probably knew I'd only tell him to throw it away, horrible muck like that.'

'That's Andy, though, isn't it? Going all the way to Berlin and that's what he comes back with. Bet he didn't remember to get a present for you.'

She shook her head, beginning to laugh again. 'No.'

'Not even something from the Duty Free?'

'Not a thing!'

'But he does track down the nastiest aftershave in the entire history of mankind.'

'Good thing he never went to North Korea,' she said. 'God knows what he'd have found there.'

It wasn't the funniest line anyone had ever come up with, but to the two of us in that cold, damp, gloomy car park it didn't matter. We staggered about like drunks, helpless with the giggles, letting go of all the accumulated tension and pain and letting a small scintilla of joy back into our shattered lives.

'Come on,' I said, getting my breath back and wiping my eyes. 'Let's go and have that drink.'

We ended up having supper together, swapping stories about Andy over a couple of bottles of wine. Right at the end of the meal, after I'd asked for the bill and made sure that Vickie had a cab home, she seemed finally to run out of energy, falling quiet and looking more sombre, more thoughtful.

'Are you all right?' I asked. 'Anything I can do?'

'I wasn't sure whether to tell you this,' she said. But . . . it was just, well, Andy wanted you to be his best man.'

'His best man – me?' The possibility had never occurred to me. Had I thought about it at all, I'd have assumed Andy would have chosen a fellow-journalist or one of his pals down in Kent.

'Yes. Andy was really proud of you, his big brother. He didn't say this, but I think he was hoping, if you could get to know him a bit better, you'd be proud of him, too.'

'I had no idea,' I said, wishing so much that I could have heard and accepted the offer. 'He never said . . . I mean, I just didn't know that at all.'

25

MONDAY

A solitary magpie rose from the graveside at the sound of the funeral party's approach, leaving its burden of sorrow behind. The bird was as monochrome as its surroundings: grey sky, black trees, white snow and black-clad mourners. The ground was hard with frost and the only sounds of life came from the cawing of crows. 'A murder of crows': that, it occurred to me, was the correct collective noun.

After Andy's body, death-cold, had been laid into the ground people milled around the graveyard for a while, stamping their feet, making jokes about the freezing temperature and waiting impatiently for instructions on how to get to the reception Vickie had organized in the pavilion of a cricket club, not far away, where Andy used to play. It was barely half past nine. A lot of the mourners had missed breakfast to get here and were in serious need of coffee. Amidst the surprisingly large turnout I recognized Andy's agent, Maurice Denholm. He'd got Andy a couple of book deals: nothing block-busting, but proper hardbacks all the same, published by a respectable company and reviewed, albeit briefly, in the Sunday broadsheets. We'd met at one of the launch parties, seven or eight years ago.

'Peter,' Denholm said, putting on a suitably sombre expression and grasping my hand with one of his while the other squeezed my upper arm. 'I'm so, so sorry ... Must be terrible for you. If there's anything I can do ...'

'Actually there is.'

A momentary look of alarm flashed across Denholm's face as he realized his bluff had been called, instantly replaced by his usual air of professional affability. 'Splendid! Just name it, dear boy, and it shall be yours.'

'Did Andrew mention anything to you about any work he was doing on my wife, Mariana?'

'I'm not sure I follow you.'

'He was doing quite a bit of research about her back-ground. He'd flown to Berlin, started digging around there. I just thought that if he'd been planning a book or something, he might have told you.'

As I'd been speaking Denholm took on a look of dawning comprehension, followed by genuine surprise and even excitement as he suddenly joined the dots of what I'd been saying. 'So that's what he meant!' he said. 'My word – he had been stirring, hadn't he?'

'What do you mean?'

'Well, he told me he was working on a story about false identity, someone living their life on the basis of a lie. He said he didn't know what to do with it, whether to tell it straight, as non-fiction, or use it as the basis of a novel. I tried to get him to tell me the details, but he became very coy about it. Now I see why. He was investigating his own sister-in-law.'

Denholm narrowed his eyes at me: 'So, did he have a hot story?'

As I considered how to answer him I looked away for a moment, letting my eye wander over the churchyard. I'd arrived early and my Range Rover was parked quite close to the church gate. A man was standing beside it, dressed in a charcoal-grey coat. I frowned and screwed up my eyes, trying to make out his face in the gloom.

'Andy's story,' Denholm repeated. 'Was it any good?'

'I'm not sure,' I said, dragging my attention back to our conversation. 'I'm still trying to work it all out myself.'

Before we could continue the conversation, Vickie bustled up. 'Ah, there you are!' she said. 'The two most important men in Andy's life! We're all leaving for the drinks now, so just join the convoy and it'll take you straight to the cricket club.'

Denholm ushered her to one side. I gathered he was making his apologies: he had to get back to London. I glanced back at my car. The man was still there, looking straight at me.

I walked towards him down the churchyard path. As I got closer I could see that he was slim, with high cheekbones and bleached blond hair swept back off his forehead: a few years older than me, perhaps, but in rather better condition. His coat was perfectly cut and beneath it his tie was black, out of respect for the occasion.

'Mr Crookham?' he said. His voice sounded German.

'Yes.'

I wanted to get straight into the driver's seat and clear off as quickly as possible. But without making any fuss about the matter, the German was blocking my way.

'I have been asked to pass on some advice,' he said.

That word again: advice. That was what the email had offered Andy. Now I was getting it too and it scared the hell out of me. 'Was it you?' I asked, struggling to get the words out as my heart thumped out of control and my knees seemed to buckle beneath me. This was the second time in a couple of days that I'd experienced serious fear and it wasn't getting any easier. 'Was it you that sent the email?'

However the German had expected me to respond, it can't have been like that. I saw a flicker of genuine surprise, even puzzlement, cross his eyes before he managed to restore his equanimity and say, very calmly, 'I am sure that you are curious about the death of your brother. Such a tragedy and so hard to understand. It is only natural that you would wish to find out more about why your wife ... your lovely wife ... would do such a thing. But my friendly advice to you is: contain your curiosity. Do not investigate. It can only lead you into harm.'

The message was horribly familiar: the words so close to those of the email, with the same warning to stay away from Mariana's past. So too was the potential for darkness and violence that seemed to lurk behind the messenger's impeccable appearance and the icy politeness of his speech. This man, whoever he was, came from a world I neither knew nor understood. But with every day that went by, I was more certain that it was the world in which Mariana had been raised.

I managed to ask him, 'Are you threatening me?'

'Absolutely not. I am trying to warn you only. Stay away from all of this. From your wife, from your brother and his questions—'

'How do you know about my brother's questions?'

He continued without acknowledging what I had said: 'from all of it.'

'Who are you? What's your name?'

The man thought for a moment. 'You can call me Mr Weiss,' he said, making it sound like 'Vice'.

'So who do you work for, then?'

'That is not important,' Weiss replied. 'All that matters is that I deliver my message, which I have done, and that you understand it and act upon it. I urge you, Mr Crookham, pay attention to what I have said. And now I must leave. I offer my sincere condolences to you upon the death of your brother. Good day.'

He left without waiting for my reply. I watched him walk down the road and as he got further away he became little more than a black silhouette outlined against the backdrop of a country lane. I suddenly had a flashback to another black figure: the man sitting on the sofa, playing the role of Andy. Were they one and the same? I felt caught in the coils of a conspiracy I could not begin to understand, as trapped as a diver in the grip of a giant, writhing octopus, pushing one arm away only to be seized by another. And what made it worse was that I was the only one who could see or feel this creature. Everyone else just wanted to tell me that it didn't exist, that I was just imagining it. Maybe I was. Maybe the whole thing was just some kind of paranoid delusion. And maybe that thought was even more frightening.

As I got into the car my pulse was racing. When I held my hand out in front of me it was shaking. I tried a breathing exercise to calm myself down: taking long, slow breaths and pushing out my stomach as though it, too, were filling with air. Gradually my nerves settled. And then another thought struck me.

I leapt out of the car, raced round to the back, lifted the tailgate, pulled back the boot cover and looked inside. My case was still there. My wellies were still there. All the junk that accumulates in any car boot was still there.

But Andy's laptop was gone.

26

I wasted ten seconds staring at the space where the laptop should have been, feeling sorry for myself before my brain finally kicked into gear. That was no delusion. Someone really had taken it. And anyone who wanted the laptop that badly almost certainly wanted more besides. If they could get into my car that easily, they could get into Andy's flat as well. That was enough to make me dash back to the driver's seat, start up the engine and set off after Vickie and the rest of the mourners.

She was standing just inside the door of the pavilion, greeting everyone as they arrived for the reception, just as her parents should have been standing at her wedding. I barged to the front of the line, apologizing frantically and making daft expressions and hand signals indicating that I had to get through to take my place alongside Vickie. Which, come to think of it, was where I should have been in the first place. I was the dead man's brother. I ought to have been greeting and thanking all the friends who'd come to see him off. At that precise moment, though, that was the last thing on my mind.

'Do you have the keys to Andy's place?' I said, when I finally got to where Vickie was standing.

She looked alarmed.

'Well, it's . . . it's our place actually,' she said. 'What do you want from it? I mean, does it have to be now?' Vickie frowned. 'You all right, Peter?'

I nodded a little too forcefully. 'Sure. But I really do need those keys . . . I'll bring them back . . .'

'And then you'll tell me what's going on?'

'Promise.'

She reached into her handbag, took out a bunch of keys and detached two of them from the ring. 'That's the Yale, and that's for the other lock, just below it. Do the other one first.'

'Thanks,' I said. And then, as an afterthought, 'What was Andy's postcode?'

'Don't you know?'

'Well, I need it for the satnav.'

She shook her head sadly. 'You two . . . You were supposed to be brothers . . . You never even came to our house.'

'I'm sorry, I should have made the effort, I know. But please, the code?'

Grudgingly, Vickie recited it.

'Look, I've got to go,' I said. Catch up with you later . . .'

I pushed my way back out again and made it to the Range Rover in one piece before I stumbled up into the seat, closed the door and slumped my head against the steering wheel.

'Get a grip,' I chided myself, leaning back into my seat and blinking hard. I cleared my throat, rubbed a furtive hand across my face and punched Andy's code into the satnav.

'At the first opportunity, turn around,' said the prim female voice from the machine.

'It's a bit bloody late for that,' I muttered, and headed off.

Only now did it occur to me to be scared. What if Weiss was there when I arrived? What if he had someone else with him? He must have had at least one accomplice, otherwise he'd have been holding the laptop when I saw him. And of course, there'd been two men at my house the night before last. So now I had a choice: I could either follow the satnav's suggestion and turn around, go back to Yorkshire and forget the whole thing, or I could act like a grown man and deal with my own problems for myself.

'You have reached your destination,' said the voice a few minutes later.

'You sure?' I argued.

I'd had a picture in my mind of a scruffy flat on the first or second floor of a terraced house. But the satnav woman was telling me to stop outside a whitewashed period cottage on the main street through a village on the outskirts of Ashford. It wasn't a big place, but it had a real four-square solidity to it: very simple and unapologetic in its plainness.

As I got out of the car, the nerves kicked in. I had to make myself walk up to the front door, wondering all the time whether someone was watching me as I came. An image planted by countless films and TV shows came to me – the man walking into a trap, a gun aimed at his head. I could almost feel the sights lined up on my skull and the impact of bullet on bone. I had to make a conscious effort to keep walking.

The house stood in a small patch of land, with space on all four sides, so I could walk round it easily enough, my heart pounding against my ribcage as though I were halfway through a marathon. I couldn't see any broken windows or smashed-open doors. When I came full circle and tried the front door it was shut: both locks. My pulse began to slow down a little. Unless they'd tele-ported in, I couldn't see how there could be anyone inside.

I unlocked the door, went in and turned on the lights. Now I could relax enough to take stock of my surroundings. The cottage had been given a thorough modernizing, with nice new oak floors and halogen downlighters recessed in the hall ceiling, but Andy and Vickie had kept plenty of old rustic touches: the wooden beams, the bare brick fireplace. They had a good eye for furniture, too. The stuff in the downstairs living room wasn't fancy, but it was well chosen. There were lots of books on the shelves, as you'd expect from a writer, and some great framed photographs on the wall: an assortment of people and landscapes that were all very different, yet somehow seemed connected both to each other and the room where they were hung. Perhaps they'd been taken on Andy's assignments, with a story behind each of those images: a story that I'd never heard.

It didn't look as if anyone had been here. Everything was very neat and tidy, with none of the devastation I had expected to find. The kitchen and dining room were equally undisturbed. A pile of correspondence sat on the dining room table next to a box of headed notepaper with matching envelopes. Beside the paper stood an empty screw-top bottle of Aussie Chardonnay and a glass with a few dregs left in the bottom. I thought of Vickie dutifully answering the letters of condolence, keeping herself going with another sip of wine. I owed it to her, if no one else, to find out why her man had died.

Upstairs, the master bedroom and bathroom were equally untouched. There was just the second bedroom to go. I assumed that Andy used it as a study and I was right. This was where he'd worked, all right. And it looked as if a twister had torn through the window.

Whoever had been here had ripped the room apart. Every book, every box-folder, every one of the old interview tapes that Andy kept in carefully labelled boxes had been taken from the shelves that ran down the full length of one wall, examined, then thrown down on the floor. Every drawer of his filing cabinet had been emptied. The top of his desk was bare except for a large monitor screen – I remembered Andy telling me that he simply plugged in his laptop when he was working at home – and all the clutter that had been on it was now strewn beneath it along with all the other devastation.

The savage thoroughness with which the room had been taken apart contrasted sharply with the restraint that had been shown elsewhere and the extreme care that had been taken to go in and out of the property without leaving any trace. It was all of a piece with the man who'd been waiting for me by the Range Rover: that same sense of self-control and violence cohabiting seamlessly. A calculation had been made. The best use of limited time had been determined and all the intruders' energy had been concentrated on the one room most likely to produce something of value.

And yet, whatever they were looking for, I had a strong feeling that they had gone away empty-handed. The screen of the computer was smashed, leaving it staring blackly like an empty eye-socket. It was the one example of pointless destruction anywhere in the house, and it suggested frustration: a parting shot, perhaps, as whoever had been here had left the room.

Was that really what had happened? I imagined Weiss and his accomplice, or accomplices, leaving the house, knowing they still had one more shot. The funeral was public knowledge. I was bound to be there . . . Then the triumphant smiles as they opened up the car and found the laptop.

I am not a violent man. The constant tension and temper I'd been feeling since Andy's death were not natural to me. I'm no hero, either. I did a few terms in my school cadets, just because my mates were in it, but I'd never in my adult life had a fight, or fired a gun. As I stood in the middle of Andy's office though, surrounded by the contemptuous desecration of his entire life's work, I realized that I wanted very badly to take my revenge for what these bastards, whoever they were, had done. I wanted to hit back.

27

Back at the cricket pavilion, things were beginning to wind down. Just half a dozen guests were left and Vickie was already starting to clear up, scurrying about the place, picking up cups and plates and wiping down tabletops. At first glance, her energy seemed undiminished, but there was a palpable sense of strain about her. She was running on her last reserves of energy, barely able to maintain the brittle façade that had got her through the day. As I gave her back her keys I had the uncomfortable feeling that I was about to smash it down and leave her utterly exposed.

'I'm afraid I've got some bad news,' I said.

There was a brief flash of panic in Vickie's eyes as she answered, 'What kind of bad news?'

'It's your house – someone got into it.'

Her eyes widened and she put a hand to her mouth.

I reached out to touch her shoulder. 'It's OK,' I said. 'I don't think they took anything. I'm afraid they made a bit of a mess of Andy's study. But it looks like every other room in the house was untouched.'

'But why?' she asked and I could see that she was fighting for every last shred of self-control. 'What did they want?'

'I think it's to do with the research Andy was doing, looking into Mariana's past. He may have stumbled on something someone wants to keep quiet. Or maybe they're just afraid he did – I don't know ...'

'Oh God ...' she began to take short, quick breaths. 'What if they come back?'

'Come over here,' I said, guiding her to a chair. 'Sit down.'

She bent over with her head in her hands and I got down on my haunches so that our heads were roughly on the same level.

'They're not coming back, I promise. They got into my car and stole Andy's laptop. Everything he had was on there. I'll bet you anything you like they've gone back to wherever it was they came from. You'll be safe, I'm sure.'

'I don't care,' she said, her voice catching as the tears began to flow. 'It's too late. They've wrecked it, haven't they? That house was the one thing ... the one thing I had left ... the one place I could still feel Andy ...

And those . . . those bastards have taken that from me. I can't go back now . . . I just can't . . . Not now they've been in there. Oh God . . .'

She let out a wail of pure, primal pain and broke down in heaving, racking sobs. I stayed with her, offering words of comfort, fresh tissues and a glass of water until she had recovered some kind of composure.

'Is there anything I can do?' I asked, 'Anything at all?'

Vickie looked me straight in the eye, took a deep breath and said, 'Yes, you can go . . . I'm sorry, Peter, I've done my best to understand what you're going through. I've tried to be reasonable. But when I look at you, all I see is the unhappiness you've brought into my life. Your wife killed the man I loved. I don't know why. I don't really care. What difference does it make? Andy's never coming back. Now I've lost my house as well. Just go . . . right away . . . please.'

There was nothing to be said, nothing that could ease her suffering or my crushing sense of shame. I went back to my car feeling as low as at any point since Andy's death and further away than ever from any kind of resolution.

And yet something was going on here that just didn't fit with the cosy consensus opinion that the police and the lawyers seemed to have about the case. I called up Iqbal and told him I had new information on the case.

'Really?' he said, conveying a massive weight of scepticism with that one short word. 'Perhaps you should tell me about it.'

I ran through the events of the past few days: the email; the break-in at my house; my meeting with Weiss; the raid on Andy's place and the theft of his computer. 'So what are we going to do now?' I asked at the end.

'I am not sure that there is anything we can do,' Iqbal replied.

'What do you mean? Surely the police will pay attention now that there's been another two incidents.'

Iqbal gave the sigh of a long-suffering man whose patience has been tested to the limit. 'Mr Crookham, please, consider what you have just told me. Or, more importantly, what you have not just told me. You talk about a threatening email, sent after the man who was threatened had tragically met his end. You say you met this German gentleman who called himself Mr Weiss, but you have no proof of his identity, no number plate of his car and thus no means at all by which he might be traced. Nor do you have any actual evidence that he stole your brother's computer, let alone that he broke into your brother's house, and certainly not that he was one of the individals who broke into your house and did nothing but enact a distasteful, but hardly illegal, re-enactment of a tragic crime.'

'Look, I know I don't have any proof,' I said. 'But I'm absolutely certain Weiss has had a hand in all this. It was obvious by the way he acted. You'd have thought so too if you had been there.'

'But I was not there. Nor were any police officers. So they would have nothing to go on. As for the break-in at your brother's house, I am afraid to say that this is an all-too-common occurrence. There are unscrupulous criminals, Mr Crookham, who take the trouble to read their local papers. They see the funeral notices and they know for sure that the home of the deceased will be empty at that time. So they take advantage of this opportunity and commit crimes very like the one you described.'

'Oh yeah? And these criminals, do they get in and out undetectably? Do they ignore every room in the house – all the TVs, cash, jewellery, everything, but target a journalist's study? Does that sound like the work of a typical provincial low-life to you, Mr Iqbal?'

'There is no need to use that tone with me, Mr Crookham. I have given you my professional opinion, based on many years of experience in criminal law. I can say with absolute certainty that the police would take a very similar view to their colleagues in Yorskhire. Now, if you do not mind, I have work to be doing. As and when there are any developments in your wife's court proceedings, I will, of course, keep you informed. Good day to you, Mr Crookham.'

The phone went dead and so did any hope I had of persuading anyone to take my concerns seriously. Iqbal was right. The police would only be as irritated as he had been by my unfounded allegations against an unknown man. So now what?

I couldn't face just driving back to York and giving up. I'd had it with being told to be sensible, do nothing, let the system do its job; of taking the advice of people who seemed more interested in an easy life than the truth. But there would be no easy life for me until I finally found out for sure who Mariana really was and what had made her capable of such terrible destruction. And there was only one place I could do that.

I called Janice, my secretary. 'Could you do me a favour? Can you get me on a plane to Berlin?'

'Of course,' she answered. 'When do you want to go?'

'Right now.'

28

Ninety minutes later I was in the departure lounge at Gatwick, eating lunch, when my phone rang. It was Janice. I assumed she was calling with some additional information about the hotel booking I'd also asked her to arrange, but I was wrong.

'I just had the oddest call from a German lady,' Janice said. 'Well, she said she was German, anyway. She was definitely foreign, she couldn't speak English very well. She said her name was Bettina König, and that she was Mariana's mother. She'd heard about what had happened. Apparently some magazine over there just ran a story about ... you know ...'

'Yes, I know,' I said, thinking: Bettina was the name on the birth certificate.

'Anyway, said Janice, 'this Mrs König had seen the story and wanted to find out what had happened to Mariana. I asked her why she didn't just call you directly and she said she didn't have the number, which sounded a bit fishy . . .'

'No, that's possible. Mariana hadn't spoken to her mother for years. They'd had a big falling-out. I've never even met her myself.'

'Oh,' said Janice, and I could almost hear her filing the information away for further use. 'Well, she left a number. Would you like me to give it to you?'

'Might as well,' I said, trying not to betray my excitement. No point in giving Janice even more good gossip material.

I took the number, called it and heard a brisk, female, '*Hallo?*' on the other end of the line.

'*Frau König, er . . . ich bin Peter Crookham, der . . .*' Shit! What was the word for husband? Got it . . . '*der Ehemann von Mariana.*'

There was an excited, 'Ah!' down the line, followed by a quickfire blast of German that made me realize just how limited my grasp of the language really was. '*Sprechen Sie Englisch?*' I asked.

'Little bit, *ja . . .*'

As slowly and clearly as I could, I tried to explain Mariana's situation, that she was awaiting trial in a secure hospital, not wanting any communication with me or anyone else.

'But maybe I can write, yes?'

'Yes, of course.' I gave her the address and then added,

'But do not expect her to reply . . . Now, Frau König, may I ask you something?'

'Sorry, I am not understanding.'

'May I ask you some questions?'

'Why questions?' Her voice suddenly sounded suspicious, or was that just anxiety I could detect? Perhaps it was just a conditioned reflex. For anyone who had lived in East Germany, with secret police and informers everywhere, the idea of being questioned must have been pretty scary.

'It's nothing, really . . . I was just curious about Mariana . . .'

'What is, "curious"?'

'Er . . .' I wracked my brain for the right word: 'Ah – *neugerig*?'

'*Ach so, ja.* OK . . .'

'Right, well I wondered if you could tell me when and where Mariana was born and . . . I know this sounds crazy . . . er, *verrückt* . . . but when she was born, what was her name? Because there is no Mariana Slavik listed anywhere.'

Now the anxiety in her voice changed to a fearful anger: 'Why you ask this questions? What you want for know?'

'I'm just trying to find out about Mariana's life and her family – your family. Her father, for example . . .'

'No! Not to be talking about the father of Mariana! I must say nothing. You must say nothing . . . nothing!'

'But Frau König, if I could just find out ...'

But it was no good. Bettina König had hung up on me. I tried to call back twice more but there was no reply. I gave it an hour, waiting until I was by the departure gate, then tried again. The number was now unobtainable.

Mariana refused to speak to me. Her mother would not answer any questions. But the intensity of Bettina König's reaction told me plenty. She was hiding something about the father and the more I thought about it, the more it seemed to me that he was the key to the whole thing. I imagined a man who could give his wife and daughter new identities, while making himself disappear. Was this also the man who had sent Weiss to England to steal Andy's computer? I wondered whether he had been responsible for the trauma that had been buried like an unexploded bomb, deep in Mariana's subconscious.

Something had happened in her childhood days in East Berlin, that was for sure: something that was still important more than twenty years later. There were no answers to any of those questions: not yet. But just being able to ask them gave me something to work with: something to take to Berlin.

29

As I walked down the long corridors at Berlin-Schönefeld Airport that led to the arrivals area the notion came into my head that Mariana might be waiting there to greet me. It was crazy, of course. I knew perfectly well that she was locked up in a secure unit several hundred miles to the west. But still the image of her persisted and I actually felt a pang of disappointment when I came through the swing doors and did not see her standing amidst the small knot of people waiting to greet the Gatwick plane.

Not far away, though, there was a small cafe, and my eye suddenly caught a flash of blonde hair. It belonged to a young woman who was bent over a laptop so that her face was almost entirely hidden. Once again, my rational mind was aware that she could not possibly be Mariana, and yet I had to walk a little closer and get a proper look to make sure. And once again the disappointment, when it came, caused a sharp burst of physical pain. It struck me that this was liable to happen constantly in Berlin, a city filled with Aryan blondes, but in a way this unwanted shock therapy was a help. It focused my attention and gave me one more element of motivation. The whole purpose of being here, after all, was to make that pain go away for good.

A man was sitting at the table behind the blonde, directly in my line of sight as I was looking at her. He was quite small, slightly built and, judging by his silver hair and well-worn face, in his late fifties at least, possibly older. He was wearing a brown pinstriped suit in an old-fashioned double-breasted cut, with a beige shirt and nondescript tie. The formality of his clothing made him stand out from the casually dressed air passengers and their families all around him. Perhaps that was why I noticed him so clearly. I made my way out of the terminal, along the covered path that led to the train station, glad to be out of the snow that was falling on this corner of Germany just as it had on North Yorkshire.

I was halfway to the station when I thought I saw the man from the airport behind me. I turned my head to check and, sure enough, there he was, now wearing a grey loden coat over his suit and making his way at a gentle pace, pulling a small wheeled suitcase behind him. The thought entered my head that I was being followed. It was absurd. There were plenty of other people making precisely the same walk: why should this one, grey-haired man be any different? Still, I started walking a little faster and it was with some relief that when I got to the ticket machine and cast furtive glances around me I could see no sign of him.

Ten minutes later, I was sitting on a double-decker commuter train to central Berlin. About a minute after it pulled out of Schönefeld, I saw the man a third time as he came towards me, dragging his case with some difficulty down the aisle of the carriage. As he walked by, as wrinkled and scrawny as a Rolling Stone, I found myself tensing up, my armpits prickling, but he didn't even glance in my direction before heading upstairs. I muttered under my breath, 'Calm down, for Christ's sake.' If I was going to get jumpy every time anyone happened to get on the same train as me, I'd be a wreck by the time I left Berlin.

I checked into my bland, soulless, but perfectly functional hotel room around five in the afternoon. My mood had improved as I had started to rough out a plan of action. And item number one was: get a little help.

Thank God for iPhones and Google. It only took one search to bring up a mass of responses to 'detective agency berlin'. The first few numbers I called didn't do the kind of work I needed, were fully booked or simply charged too much for their services. The next place had a website with a glossy corporate façade, but it was obvious within a few minutes of stilted conversation that the man who had answered the phone constituted the entire corporation. That wasn't too encouraging, and nor was his response to something I said as I was trying to explain my quest.

'I think my wife's father may possibly have been involved in some kind of criminal activity in East Berlin,' I said. There was a disapproving grunt in my ear. Ignoring it, I continued, 'Something that caused him to fake her identity papers. Maybe he faked his papers too, in order to escape justice.'

'Not possible!' said the man. His voice was heavily accented, his English about as good as my German. 'In the DDR was very little crime. All major crime – all of it! – was solved.'

He couldn't keep the pride out of his voice. Dear God, I thought, he sounds like one of the Stasi himself.

'Er, right . . . I must have got that wrong, then. Sorry to have bothered you,' I said and hung up.

My hopes of finding anyone to help me were beginning to fade when I dialled the next number: a place called Xenon Detektivbüro.

'You must speak to our director, Mr Haller,' said the girl who took my call. 'He speaks excellent English.'

'Even better than yours?' Good grief, that was the first even vaguely flirtatious remark I'd made to anyone in ages. Signs of life, perhaps?

She gave the sort of giggle that brightens any middle-aged man's day. 'Oh yes, much better! I put you through now.'

I'd only just begun to explain my reasons for coming to Berlin when Haller interrupted me: 'Of course! Mr Crookham, of course! My apologies, I should have recognized your name. I have heard a little about the tragic circumstances of your brother's death. It has received some attention in the media here. So . . . you were saying about your wife . . .'

I ran through a brief account of what had happened and my reasons for coming to Berlin.

'You say you think she had a false birth certificate?' Haller asked.

'Yes. I have a copy of it with me, but my brother did not find a matching certificate in the records here in Berlin.'

'And you are sure she was born and spent her early life in East Berlin, or in any case East Germany, not West?'

'Yes . . . why?'

'Well, there is only one way that anyone from East Germany could have obtained false documents, and that is through the Stasi.'

So Andy had been right.

'You mean her father was in the Stasi?'

'Sure, it is possible. Many, many people were in the Stasi.'

'I think I just spoke to one of them,' I said and described my conversation with the previous detective.

Haller laughed, 'Yes, that sounds like Stasi. You know,

many detectives here in Berlin, in fact I would say the majority, are ex-Stasi. This kind of work is all they know and they are very, very good at it. However, luckily for me, since they are my competitors, most of them are also very, very bad at business. It goes against their nature. Many of them still believe, even now, that communism was the true way. I have one working in my team. I will ask him what he thinks about your father-in-law.'

'So you will take the case?'

'Of course!' said Haller. 'I would be delighted. So, you are in Berlin now?'

'Yes.'

'Excellent. May I suggest we meet for a drink when I have finished my duties here? Shall we say 18.30?'

'That sounds fine. Where shall we meet?'

'The Hotel Adlon. Our most famous hotel, right by the Brandenburg Gate, just a few hundred metres from the Reichstag: what could be a better place for your first rendezvous in Berlin? I will meet you in the lobby bar.'

Only after I had ended the call did it strike me that Haller had described Mariana's father as my father-in-law. As strange as it may seem – perhaps because I'd never met or had any sort of contact with him – that had never struck me before. The man whose story I was trying to uncover, whose actions might explain what had turned his daughter into a killer, was one of my relatives. We were family.

30

The Adlon was a grand hotel in the classic style, just as Haller had promised, right in the heart of the city. Haller himself was sitting on one of the high chairs by the bar, upholstered in café-au-lait leather. He got to his feet to shake my hand. He was at least as tall as me, but more solidly built, though there was no hint of a gut beneath his pale-blue shirt, tucked into belted black trousers. He had sandy hair, just starting to thin at the temples, blue eyes, a strong chin and a hearty laugh. He couldn't have been more stereotypically German if he'd tried.

'Would you like a cup of tea? They have proper English Earl Grey here. Or perhaps a glass of beer?' he asked.

'A beer sounds good.'

Haller called the barman over and gave a series of fast, incisive orders, specifying precisely which beer he wanted and how it should be served. Then he turned his attention back in my direction and said, 'Come with me a moment. There is something I would like to show you.'

He led me through the hotel and out onto Parisier Platz towards a simple, almost block-like façade of sand-coloured limestone, punctuated by vertical strips of plain, unadorned windows, like frames on an old-fashioned roll of film. Something about it rang a bell: I'd seen it before but couldn't recall when or where. Still, my memory lapse was surely forgivable. It certainly didn't look like anything much.

Haller must have read the scepticism on my face because he laughed and said, 'Not so impressed, huh? OK, let's go in. Maybe you will change your mind.'

We went through an equally nondescript entrance into an anonymous office-block reception area, and then my jaw fell open in wonder as I gasped, 'Bloody hell,' at the sight in front of me. For beyond the reception the building opened up into a rectangular, glass-roofed central atrium, much deeper than it was wide. Above it stretched a glass roof, supported by a dizzying whirl of metal struts. It became lower and narrower as it reached the far end of the building, creating a kind of tunnel effect. To the left and right the long side-walls were clad in what looked like very flat, toffee-coloured wood, almost like a veneer. A geometric grid of interior windows looking out onto the atrium echoed the stark simplicity of the façade. But that was where any vague link with architectural normality stopped.

Directly opposite where we stood, the entire far end of the atrium was filled with an extraordinary, brooding structure, like a great open cavern made from twisting, swirling metal. From its mouth emerged a glittering glass canopy which covered the entire lower third of the atrium. It was as though something utterly alien had taken up residence inside an apparently normal, human environment and it was, at one and the same time, spectacularly beautiful and distinctly menacing.

'The DZ Bank building, by Frank Gehry!' I said, with the delight of a quiz contestant getting the right answer.

'I thought you would like to see it, being an architect,' said Haller. 'However, there was another reason that I brought you here. This is a good image for you, a sort of metaphor, perhaps, for Berlin itself. On the outside, the city is like this building. It is very orderly – very German. The tourists are all quite safe as they visit all our sights, or take a walk in the Tiergarten. The government sits in all its fine new buildings, all of them very light, very airy, to symbolize the new, safe, peaceful Germany. However, there is always, at the heart of this place, something else that is dark, strange and powerful. This is a city that has seen too much, suffered too much. Did you know that in the last two weeks of Hitler's life, when the city was under attack from the Russians, at least 300,000 people died, soldiers and civilians? That is like one hundred 9/11 disasters. After that, when the Red Army came, countless thousands of women were raped. Mothers and daughters alike were violated: two generations emotionally scarred for life. Thousands of them gave birth to their Russian rapists' children. And then the pain of the communist years, the Wall cutting one part of the city off from the rest . . . I guess what I am saying is that this city is like a person who has been attacked and abused and now has to live with too much pain inside them. On the outside, they may seem normal. On the inside . . .' Haller shrugged. Then he smiled, 'OK, now you must have your beer. You have had to listen to me make crazy speeches . . . I think you need it!'

We walked back to the bar. The beer was cold and delicious, the central heating warm, and the other customers at the bar or settling down at tables looked sleek and prosperous. It seemed crazy to be talking about murder and suffering in such surroundings, but that, I supposed, had been Haller's point.

'Those things you said about Berlin . . .'

Haller grimaced, self-mockingly. 'Ach, pay no attention. It is what you might call, I think, a pet theory.'

'Well, it made sense to me. In fact, it really made me think about Mariana. Everything you said about the normal exterior, and the hidden pain inside, is true about her, too. I never knew before, but it's becoming more obvious every day. And I think she suffered too, just like the city. I suppose you could say she's a true daughter of Berlin.'

'Whereas I am an adopted son ...'

He started telling me about his life, how he'd worked as a cop in Hamburg before quitting the force and coming to Berlin, Germany's frontier town, the place where new money could be made.

'Hold on,' I interrupted. I leaned across the table and spoke in a low voice: 'There's a man over there, three tables away. He keeps looking at me ...'

It wasn't the man in the brown suit this time, but a completely different individual. He was much younger, wearing designer shades and a white shirt. He lit a cigarette, displaying an expensive-looking watch and a heavy gold bracelet on strong, tanned wrists.

Haller checked him out and laughed. 'Maybe you have made a friend for the night! This is Berlin. Anything can happen!'

I fell back in my chair, laughing along with him to cover my embarrassment. 'That's not what I meant. It's just ... I keep thinking someone's following me. There was a man at the airport and on my train. Now this ... I feel like the Stasi's after me, or something.'

'Twenty-five years ago, maybe,' said Haller. 'Not now. And in any case, if you were being followed by anyone who had ever been a Stasi officer, you would not know it. They were the world champions of surveillance. They had a system that made it possible to follow people even when they changed everything about their appearance: clothes, hair, beard, glasses, skin . . . no matter how good a disguise might be, the Stasi could see through it.'

'How?'

'They assembled scientists, doctors, anthropologists, zoologists, experts of every kind, to study the specific markers that make us individuals. The way we walk, the posture of the body, the shapes of eyes, ears, noses, lips . . . everything that is unique to an individual. Stasi officers were trained to apply three of these markers to anyone they had to follow. This enabled them to pick the target up no matter how they were dressed, or how many people were surrounding them.'

'Like biometric ID systems . . .'

'Yes, but planted in a human memory instead of a computer.'

'That's scarily impressive . . .'

'Sure,' Haller agreed. 'The Stasi were very good at their jobs. You know, they held police in the West in total contempt. They thought we were soft, decadent, no good at our jobs. Maybe they were right . . .' He smiled to himself: 'In Germany we call our foreign intelligence agency the Bundesnachrichtendienst, BND for short. It is like your MI6. They used to have an office in Munich above a flower shop. The final training exercise for Stasi officers was to look at a picture of a BND agent, get into West Germany, travel to Munich and then pick up their selected agent as he or she left the flower shop and follow them without being spotted. The proof of how good they were is that no one in the West had any idea of this until the Wall came down and ex-Stasi officers told them what they had been doing.'

'So they wouldn't have any trouble following an English architect . . .'

'Exactly.'

'Well then, let's get a couple more beers and I'll try to relax and tell you why I am here . . .'

31

For the next half hour or so we went through the case in much greater detail than the sketchy outline I'd given over the phone: my experiences in the week since the murder and my brother's research into Mariana's background. I gave Haller my documents and he took notes of his own, interrupting me from time to time to ask sharp, pertinent questions. He had a tough, forensic intelligence that reminded me of DCI Yeats back in York. The first time he ventured an opinion of his own was when I told him about my encounter with Mr Weiss outside the churchyard.

'You say his manner was polite?'

'Yes. I felt as though he was threatening me, but the way he did it was very civil, if that makes any sense.'

'Well, that does not sound to me like a former Stasi officer. Secret police, like criminals, see no reason to be polite. Quite the opposite, I should say. For them the pleasure is in making the threat as openly and violently as possible. They enjoy the fear and humiliation they see in your eyes. Perhaps he has changed to fit in with the new realities. The intelligent ones can do that.'

'So . . . do you think I'm crazy?' I asked.

Haller gave me an amused, quizzical look: 'I'm sorry. Why would I think that you are crazy?'

'Well, everyone else I've talked to about this has acted like I'm making it all up; connecting things that are just coincidences; adding two and two to make five . . . or actually, more like fifty.'

Now his expression turned more serious. 'No, I do not think you are crazy. I am not sure that you are drawing the correct conclusions from your experiences. However, I do not doubt that something serious is happening here.'

'So what are we going to do now?'

'We? I do not think that there is a "we". You agree my terms, which start with a basic charge of 1,500 euros per day. And then my team and I start researching through archives, interviewing witnesses and preparing our report. In the meantime, you might as well return home.'

'No. I'd rather come with you. I think I can help.'

'With due respect, Mr Crookham, you are an architect. I would not tell you how to construct a building.'

'Maybe, but if you were my client, paying my bills,

then you would certainly be welcome to visit the building site and I would anticipate regular meetings to discuss the progress of the build and go over any minor problems, alterations and so forth. Of course, I would insist that you wore a hard hat when you came on site. But that is because building sites are dangerous places and kill many more people, I would guess, than private detective work ever does.'

Haller looked at me with a fixed, impenetrable expression on his face. For a moment I thought I might have pushed him too far. I braced myself for a curt, German farewell and an end to our business relationship. Instead, he nodded: 'All right, then, I concede that you may have specialist knowledge, so to speak, about your wife that may be useful. And, yes, you are paying the bill. But I must make one thing clear ... You may be the client, but when we are working, I am in charge and unless there is a very good reason for you to say anything, I do the talking. Agreed?'

'Yes.'

Haller looked at me, weighing me up. 'I have to say this once again, Mr Crookham. I would far prefer it if you went home and left me to get on with my job. I say this for your own good.'

'Thank you, but I'm staying in Berlin.'

'And that is the principal reason why I am prepared to let you come with me. If you insist on remaining in this city, then I want to know exactly where you are.' Haller sighed and shook his head as if to let me know that he was acting against his own better judgement, then said: 'Ah well . . . I suppose we have a deal.'

We shook hands and agreed to meet at his office the following morning. I made my way back to my hotel, walking through the streets, enjoying the bright lights, the frosty air and the crunch of snow beneath my feet, feeling a nice, mellow beer-buzz. I stopped off for a bowl of pasta and a glass of wine at a little place by the hotel, so by the time I got back to my room I was hardly drunk, but I wasn't stone-cold sober, either.

So maybe that explained why I stared so determinedly at the paperback beside my bed, squinting a little at the way it was lying on the table. It didn't look odd in any way to the normal eye: just a book, on a table, at a very slight diagonal angle to the line of the table and the bed.

Except I'd left it straight, parallel with that line, because that's what I do. It's the architect in me, lining everything up. But maybe it was just the booze playing tricks with my memory. Or maybe I'd knocked it out of line at some point.

It had to be that. The alternative was that someone had been in my room. And this wasn't the kind of hotel where they turn down your bed in the evening and leave a chocolate on the pillow.

I'd spent all day jumping at shadows, imagining people were following me. I wasn't going to lie awake at night fretting about intruders. I brushed my teeth, collapsed into bed, turned out the light and was asleep by ten.

That night I dreamed I was in a florist's shop. I was trying to buy a bouquet for Mariana, but whenever I tried to pick out some flowers I couldn't see them properly any more, or tell the assistant what I wanted. And when I reached for my money, it had gone. I started panicking. I wanted to get out of the shop. But when I got to the door I was hit by a terrible sensation of terror. There was something outside the shop, something dangerous. It wanted to kill me. There was nothing I could do to stop it. And what was even worse, I had no idea at all what it was.

BERLIN: 1988

Hans-Peter Tretow couldn't allow them to talk. That was the one rule that could never be broken. No comparing notes, no complaints, and above all not one single world to anyone outside the group.

'Have I not made this plain?' Tretow said, as though he were personally disappointed, even hurt by their failure to obey him. He looked at the two underlings standing opposite him in the small basement room.

'Yes, sir,' the pair replied in unison.

'Did I not warn you, again and again, that I would take action if you disobeyed me?'

'Yes, sir.'

'And yet you ignored everything I had told you. You defied me. You talked . . .'

'It wasn't his fault, he didn't do anything wrong,' said the taller, tougher, more wiry one of the pair. His name was Friedrichs, and though he lacked all education, his eyes possessed a shrewd, calculating intelligence that Tretow felt obliged to respect.

'Is that true?' Tretow said, turning to Friedrichs' companion, Müller.

'No, sir . . . I mean yes . . . I don't know.'

Müller was both a physical and emotional weakling, Tretow concluded: no threat. Friedrichs was the one he had to deal with first, get him out of the way. Tretow knew how he planned to do it, but finding the precise moment would not be easy. He played for time.

'Make up your mind!' he shouted at Müller, intending to intimidate. 'Tell me what happened.'

Friedrichs stepped in, speaking when his friend could not. 'He was upset by what happened at the weekend . . . you know, in Potsdam. I could see it, so I went to have a word with him, tell him everything was all right. That's all.'

'Impossible! I was told about this conversation. That means words must have been overheard. Either that, or one of you spoke to someone else and they in turn passed the message on. Well, is that it? Is that what happened?'

Müller looked at him with pleading eyes. 'No . . . I swear . . . I, I—'

Friedrichs went to reassure Müller, briefly turning his back. That was the opportunity Tretow had been waiting for. He picked up a length of old-fashioned lead water-pipe, taken from a junk-filled storage cupboard, and swung it with all his strength at Friedrichs' head.

Friedrichs shouted out in pain and surprise, but even though his head began to bleed profusely, he did not go down. It took several more blows, delivered with all Tretow's strength, to render him unconscious. The cramped underground chamber echoed to the pounding of the metal pipe against Friedrichs' skull and the arms he threw up in a desperate attempt to ward off the blows, Tretow's own rasping breaths and the panicked shouts of alarm from Müller cowering in the far corner. Tretow had never previously considered what hard, physical labour the act of taking a human life might involve. By the time he turned to Müller, his chest was heaving, his arm and wrist ached and he had broken into a muck sweat that made the pipe feel as slippery and evasive as an eel in his hand. Yet Müller seemed to accept his fate quite passively and there was a grim, labouring relentlessness to the beating Tretow gave him.

Finally, the job was done. Both bodies lay immobile on the floor. Tretow did not, however, intend to take any chances. He placed a cushion over both faces for long enough to ensure that even if the pipe had not killed them, asphyxiation certainly would. Then he collapsed, exhausted, onto the basement floor, sitting on the bare concrete with his back up against a wall. As he contemplated his new-found status as a murderer, he felt neither triumph nor guilt. It was more that he had been faced with a grim but necessary task that he had completed without unnecessary fuss or emotion.

Now further tasks presented themselves. The two bodies would have to be disposed of. First, however, he needed to extract the maximum possible benefit from what he had just done. It was important that no one else should stray as Friedrichs and Müller had done.

32

TUESDAY

I woke early to find a text on my mobile. 'My office 08.30 Haller'. A hot shower finished with a blast of cold water and followed by a couple of strong cups of coffee at breakfast dealt with the residual effects of last night's drinks. When I stepped outside and scanned the pavements on either side of the road I could see no trace of anyone following me amidst the scurrying crowds of winter-coated Berliners, some keeping their hands warm round their own cardboard cups of takeaway cappuccino.

So much for my paranoid delusions.

I got a cab out to Haller's office, which was above a coffee shop, deep in the heart of what had been East Berlin. To the right, the neighbouring building was covered in scaffolding and plastic sheets, and the full width of the pavement was filled with stacked, snow-topped rolls of loft insulation. To the left stood an apartment block, its façade pockmarked with gaps in the rendering through which bare brick could be seen like knees behind the holes in a pair of jeans. I walked past a rich warm waft of coffee-scented air to the front entrance, pressed the buzzer marked 'Xenon Detektivbüro' and heard the same cheerful voice that had greeted me on the phone less than twenty-four hours earlier. 'Come on up, Mr Crookham. There is a lift. We are on the third floor.'

Less than a minute later, I was looking at the voice's owner, a smiling young woman with lively brown eyes set in a Middle Eastern-looking face. I was just introducing myself when Haller appeared.

'Aha!' he exclaimed, giving me a vigorous handshake. 'So you have met our beautiful Kamile. I must warn you, Mr Crookham, you should be very careful. Kamile comes from a very traditional Turkish family. If you dishonour her in any way, they will take a terrible revenge. Or, even worse, make you marry her.'

Kamile gave the polite laugh of a dutiful employee who has heard the same line a thousand times before. Then Haller got down to business: 'OK, so we must go to our first appointment. Mariana's schoolfriend, Heike Schmidt, is expecting us at her apartment.'

'You set that up very quickly.'

'I charge a lot of money. However, I try always to earn it.'

For all his command of English, Haller had an odd

habit of always saying 'however', each syllable clearly separated, when a simple 'but' would have done. We left the office. Outside, Haller cast a disparaging eye to either side. 'This is not the most salubrious location, however it is very cheap. And one thing I learned very early in this business was that it does not always pay to have fancy offices. Clients think it means you are spending all your money on rent, when you should be spending it solving cases.'

He walked me over to a new 5 Series BMW: fast cars, presumably, counted as a legitimate crime-fighting expense.

'I was talking to a colleague last night, the one who was in the Stasi, about your situation,' he said, getting in.

'And you trust him?'

'Sure.' There was a surge of power as the car purred into the road. 'We've worked together for five years now and he has never let me down. He pointed out to me that it was perfectly possible for Stasi-trained operatives to allow themselves to be spotted, in a deliberate way, to make the person they were tailing feel uneasy and paranoid.'

I shivered uneasily. 'Well, if that's what they wanted, they succeeded.'

'Yes, I am afraid that this is something at which the Stasi were specialists. There is a word in German,

Zersetzung. I do not know how you would say it in English exactly; however, it means the total, ah . . . obliteration of a person's inner being.'

'You mean like, "soul-destroying"?'

'Yes. However, to the Stasi this was not just a phrase. It was also one of the principal aims of their work: the literal destruction of a human soul. The aim was to do this so as to be able to take complete control of the subject.'

'Is that what they're trying to do with me?'

I looked out of the window, trying to imagine the bland streets outside as they must have been a quarter of a century earlier, when the Stasi watched everything, monitored everyone and hung over every aspect of East German life like a poisoned fog.

'We do not know for sure that anyone is trying to do anything,' said Haller. 'However, if they are, I would guess that what they want to do is scare you and make you decide you would be better off going back home. And I have to say, maybe they are right . . .'

I turned my face away from the passing street scene, back towards Haller. 'No, I'm not backing down. I can't.'

He sighed. 'Your presence is complicating matters, you know that?'

'Maybe. But I've had enough people telling me not to get involved. I don't have the choice. I'm in it now and I'm not stopping till I find out the truth.'

'Then you may have a long wait. Who can say what the truth ever is?'

We sat in silence for a minute or two and I looked back out of the window until I felt able to start the conversation again. 'There's something I don't quite get. We keep talking about the Stasi like they're still around. But the Wall came down more than twenty years ago. Who are these people?'

Haller sighed as he collected his thoughts. 'They are . . . OK, you have heard, I am sure of Odessa, the organization for former SS officers? Like in the movie, *The Odessa Files* . . .'

'Yes.'

'Well there are similar organizations for ex-Stasi personnel. They have names like the Insider Committee, or – and this is a kind of sick joke – the Society for the Protection of Civil Rights and the Dignity of Man. In part they are social groups. Men get together and talk about the old days. They tell each other how Germany is going to the dogs, things like that. In part, also, they are political campaigns. These guys want the world to see how great the old communist state was. Many of them still dream that they can make it come back.'

'Like Nazis trying to bring back the Reich . . .'

'Exactly. And also, to be frank, some of these organizations are criminal gangs. They carry out extortion, robbery, acts of violence, just like any other gang.'

So there were East German gangs. Well, that made sense. Weiss had a tough, criminal air about him. 'And you think one of these gangs is after me?'

'No, I think that *if* anyone is after you, it *may* be one of them. We cannot be sure.'

'But these guys must all be getting on a bit. I mean, even someone who'd been in their early twenties when the Wall came down would be mid-forties now, and most of them would be older than that.'

Haller crossed an intersection, turning his head from side to side and checking his rear-view mirror as he answered, 'Sure. However, there are always new recruits – young men who can't get regular jobs, who want to be part of something, to throw their weight around. There is something we call *Ostalgie*, which means nostalgia for the East. People forget the bad things: the oppression, the informants, the secret police, the short-ages of everything. All they remember is that they had jobs and homes, and everything like schools and health-care provided for them without having to pay. It's not hard to persuade such people that you are trying to bring these good things back, even if all you want to bring back is your power.'

Haller was leaning forward now, looking over the steering wheel at the buildings on either side of the street. 'Excellent!' he said, with a snappy nod of the head, pulling the car over to the side of the road. 'So now we arrive. Please remember, I will talk for us both. You stay out of my way.'

'If you say so . . .'

'*Ja*, I do.' Haller unclipped his safety belt. 'Let's go,' he said. Then he paused with his hand hovering just above the door handle. He looked at me: 'Oh, and one other thing . . . Those Stasi men you think were following you yesterday . . .'

'Yes?'

'They're not following us today. I was checking all the way.' Haller grinned. 'Or they don't want to be seen, at any rate . . .'

33

The city was filled with buildings painted in a palette of pale earth tones: sand, ochre, pale dove grey, sage green and dusty brown, with just the occasional flash of a pale dusty pink or blue. Heike Schmidt lived in an old, buttery-yellow apartment house, four storeys tall. The front door was painted a deep claret and opened, unlocked, onto a hall floored in drab grey-green linoleum. Two rows of metal post boxes were set into the wall to the left of the entrance. Haller scanned the nametags beneath each box and said, 'Top floor. Up we go ...'

There was no lift. We made our way up a wooden staircase to the third floor. Haller led the way along the landing till he came to a door. He gave it two sharp raps. The door opened a fraction and I could see a sliver of a thin, brown-eyed female face.

'Fräulein Schmidt?'

'Yes?'

Haller held up an ID card in a leather holder. He switched to German: 'May we come in, please?'

A few seconds went by and then I heard the rattle of a chain and the door opened.

'Come in,' said Heike Schmidt.

She can't have been more than a few months older than Mariana, but her face had an exhausted, grey-skinned pallor and the eyes which observed us with nervy defensiveness were lined and sunken. It wasn't so different from the way Mariana had looked that day at York Magistrate's Court, and it made me question for the first time whether that air of devastation and defeat, which had seemed so unlike her, had in fact been the true representation of Mariana's inner self. Perhaps the only difference was that Heike Schmidt had never been able to construct a lovely shell around her with which to fool the world. The two women certainly looked like casualties of the same psychological assault.

Lost in thought, I was only half-aware of a voice saying, 'My name is Haller, this is my colleague from England, Mr Crookham.'

'Crookham . . . ?'

I realized Heike Schmidt was looking at me, expecting an answer. 'Er, yes . . .' I replied. I assumed I was allowed to speak when directly spoken to. Haller did not attempt to stop me, so I continued, hoping that my fumbling

German made some kind of sense: 'You spoke to my brother a few weeks ago, Andrew Crookham.'

Big mistake. Heike Schmidt stiffened. 'Oh . . . I . . .' she stammered. We'd only got a few feet inside her door. Any second now she was going to shove us back out again.

'Fräulein Schmidt, we need your help in connection with a serious crime,' said Haller.

'I do not understand. Are you police?'

'No, we are not.'

She frowned: 'But the woman I spoke to, from your office, she . . .'

'She did not say we were the police, I can assure you of that,' Haller interrupted. 'I am a private investigator. I am fully licensed and above board.'

Heike Schmidt pursed her lips. She pulled back her bony shoulders and as she stood as tall as she could I realized how intimidating Haller and I must have seemed as we towered over her. 'I don't care,' she said. 'I can't talk to you.'

Haller attempted to adopt a more ingratiating tone. 'Please do not be alarmed Miss Schmidt, we just want to ask you a few questions. You are not in any trouble.'

'I will be, if I answer your questions. Please go . . . Now!'

Haller turned back to the door, but I stayed where I was. 'Come on,' he said to me. 'You heard Fräulein Schmidt. We must go.'

I took a deep breath, slowly exhaled and as Haller insisted, 'Come on!' I reached into my jacket pocket and pulled out a piece of paper. I held it out to Schmidt and looked her in the eye, desperately trying to make some kind of connection.

'Miss Schmidt . . . Do you recognize the girl in this picture?'

She said nothing. But she kept looking at Mariana and I saw her blink a couple of times, as though she were fighting back tears.

'She is now my wife,' I said. Haller had stopped quite still and was saying nothing now. 'I don't know what her name was when you knew her,' I went on, 'but she's called Mariana Crookham now. And she is in very serious trouble.'

'In England?' Schmidt asked.

'Yes.'

She chewed her lip, curiosity fighting against fear. Curiosity won: 'What kind of trouble?'

'She's accused of murder. And I'm trying to prove her innocence. Was she your friend . . . when you were little girls?'

Heike Schmidt gave a fractional, barely perceptible nod of her head.

'Please . . .' I implored. 'I'm sure that I can help her, if only I can find out what happened to her when she was young.'

Schmidt's eyes widened as the fear took charge. 'No . . . no . . . not that . . .'

'Please.'

'I can't. They will . . . It's impossible.'

'Is there anything, anything at all you can tell us. About her father, perhaps?'

'Her father?' The words were cackled, almost drowned, in nervous, panicky laughter. 'There was no father. The place where we met, it wasn't that school. It was an orphanage.'

34

We spent an hour or so in a nearby cafe while Haller's staff tracked down the address of an old state-run children's home near the Grundschule Rudower. Then we set off to find it. I'd always imagined Berlin as a dark, claustrophobic, crowded city, crushed beneath the weight of its history. But as we drove back the way we had come and then headed out into the south-eastern suburbs, much of it was remarkably open. The long, straight roads lined with low-density office and retail developments reminded me of the casual, land-grabbing sprawl of so many American cities.

'Didn't I tell you that Berlin was decimated?' said Haller. 'In 1939 there were almost four and a half million people in Berlin; by 1945, less than three million. All through the fifties people were walking across from East Berlin to West, then flying out of the city to the Federal Republic. That's why the commies had to build their Wall. They were running out of people. Even now, it still feels a little empty. Do you know in Paris there are twenty thousand people per square kilometre? In Berlin, just four thousand.'

I grinned. 'You seem to have all the facts at your fingertips!'

'Well, facts are my business. Also, I never had a proper education, so now I always want to learn more and more. I love information – like your brother, the journalist, maybe. Was he the same?'

'Yeah, I'm just discovering the lengths he would go to to get to the bottom of a story. Maybe that's what killed him . . .'

'Hmm . . .' murmured Haller as he switched lanes, deftly slipping from one line of traffic to another.

'What is it?'

'I think you should learn from his mistakes.'

'How do you mean?'

'Well, you are like your brother in this way, you are always chasing after a story that is in your head. First you try to find this other person who might have killed your brother, a person that no one believes in but you. Then you decide, no, I accept it was my wife who did this, but she must have a reason. Then you decide what that reason is: her father was in the Stasi and he did terrible things to her, so you try to prove that. But because you start with this story, like a theory you want to prove, you look at the world through a pair of blinkers. You see a man on the train – he must be Stasi also. Another man catches your eye at the Adlon ... *ach so*, more Stasi, sent by your wife's father, surveilling you. However, what is the first thing that we discover for sure? That your Mariana lived in an orphanage. There was no father in her life. So now, what do we do with your theory?'

'I see what you mean.'

'My advice is, don't think about stories, or theories. Concentrate on facts. OK, so now we are getting close.'

We had driven south through the city. By a mixture of dead reckoning and surreptitious glances at Haller's satnav I reckoned we were back within a couple of kilometres of his office. The area was dotted with low-rise housing blocks, strung out through the kind of open space that looks far better on planner's sketches than it ever does in reality. The blocks that faced onto the main roads had shops, bars and cafes on their ground floors. The buildings were interspersed by fields given over to allotments, stripped bare of their plants by the winter, and building sites guarded by chain-link fencing. At one vacant, apparently neglected lot a large poster mounted on a billboard showed a model of the development that might one day be standing there. A florid, prosperous-looking man in late middle age was standing behind the model, looking down on it approvingly. At the bottom of the poster was a company name: Tretow Immobilien GmbH.

The voice from the satnav said, '*Sie haben Ihr Ziel erreicht.*'

We'd arrived. Haller brought the car to a halt and looked at the sign.

'Thanks a lot, guys,' he muttered. 'I guess they don't need orphanages any more.'

I got out and looked through the fence at the expanse of frosty, barren ground where Mariana had spent her childhood. After the speed with which we'd got to Heike Schmidt and found the name of the orphanage, I'd been lulled into assuming that we'd turn up, find a gloomy, doom-ridden old building and somehow all the questions about Mariana's past would magically be answered. But all we had now was an emptiness, an absence. It was almost as though the old forces that had once ruled here were covering their tracks, removing the evidence of what they had done. I remembered seeing news reports, soon after the Wall came down, about how Stasi officers had desperately shredded all the documents that could reveal the full extent of their crimes. The orphanage, it seemed, had been shredded as well.

'Cheer up,' said Haller. 'Investigations are not supposed to be easy. Otherwise anyone could do them. However, we can still find out what happened here. All we need are witnesses. Come.'

He drove a little further down the road until we came to a line of shops. There he made his way from one store to another, talking to any customers or staff who looked old enough to have remembered the orphanage. Finally, he struck lucky. We'd gone into a butcher's, past a placard on the pavement that consisted of a cheery pig holding a blackboard on which were written the bargains of the day. Inside, a small elderly woman was inspecting the sausages arrayed in a chiller cabinet with sharp, magpie eyes. 'Ha!' she snorted, after Haller had enquired about the orphanage and its inhabitants. 'You want Old Fredi. He was the ABV round here.'

'So where will I find this Fredi?'

'Is it past midday?'

Haller consulted his watch. 'Yes, just.'

'Then he will be at the *Kneipe* with all his cronies, like he always is, getting drunk and talking about the good old days.'

'How will I recognize him?'

'Just ask the barman. He will show you. Everyone knows Old Fredi. They may not like him. But they know him ...'

Haller thanked the old woman. As we left the store I asked, 'What's an ABV?'

'*Abschnittsbevollmächtigter*,' Haller replied, laughing at the look of bafflement that crossed my face at the tongue-twisting word. 'It means, literally, someone who has power of attorney over a district. In practice, that ABV was a man officially appointed by the state to observe the people in an area and report antisocial behaviour.'

'Like an official snoop?'

'Exactly.'

'But I thought the Stasi had hundreds of thousands of people snooping for them unofficially.'

'Yes, they did. But for the Stasi, there was never too much information.'

'OK . . . and a *Kneipe*?'

'It's the Berlin term for a bar . . .' Haller nodded his head at the door into which he was heading. 'Like this one.'

35

The French modernist architect Le Corbusier described a house as a machine for living. Well, this *Kneipe* was a machine for drinking. It had almost no decoration, no homely touches, no attempt whatever to create a welcoming, comfortable atmosphere. It was simply a space with a bar down one side of the room covered in fake wood laminate and provided with a series of pumps for draught beer. A couple of high round tables stood in the middle of the room, ringed by wooden stools. Lower, rectangular tables were placed round the remaining walls. The barman gestured at one of the tables, where three men were sitting. 'Over there. The one in the brown sweater.'

I had expected a decrepit old geezer. In fact, Old Fredi turned out to be a tough, gnarled, shaven-headed man, who exuded an air of resentful tension like emotional BO.

Haller pulled up a chair, sat down at the table and motioned to me to do the same. Then he put a 100-euro note on the table, slid it towards Old Fredi and said, 'Can I buy you fellows another drink?'

Fredi looked at him with glowering suspicion: 'Who's buying?'

'Does it matter?' Haller asked. 'I'm not a cop, this is nothing official, I was just told you could help me with a business enquiry.'

'Who's the boyfriend?'

'A business associate.'

I said nothing. From the moment we had stepped into the bar every word had been spoken in German. It was taking my full concentration just to follow what Haller was saying and make sense of the Berliners' strong accents.

Fredi reached out and slid the note towards himself before shoving it in a trouser pocket. 'Three more litres of beer, and six double schnapps,' he said. 'And some pretzels.'

'And potato chips,' said one of the other men at the table.

I saw Haller glance in my direction. 'I'll get it,' I said.

'Beer for me too,' Haller said.

I got the round in while Haller began making desultory conversation with Fredi and his drinking pals. It took a few seconds to distribute all the glasses and snacks. Fredi took a good long drink from his beer stein and wiped the foam off his lips. Then he picked up his first glass of schnapps and downed it in one.

When the empty glass had been slammed back down on the table Haller spoke: 'Tell me about the orphanage.'

'What orphanage?' Fredi replied, smirking as though he'd just said something spectacularly clever.

'The one round the corner,' said Haller.

'Oh, that orphanage. It was a building, filled with children ... who didn't have their mummies and daddies, boo-hoo!'

Fredi basked in the supportive laughter of his pals, drank some more, then looked up at Haller and asked, 'What else do you want to know?'

'I want to know what happened there that was so bad a woman would not want to talk about it more than twenty years later.'

The men stopped laughing. Fredi narrowed his eyes and said, 'No, you do not want to know.'

Haller looked right back at him. 'I'll be the judge of that.' He placed two more notes on the table. I tried to banish the thought that they'd soon be appearing on my bill.

Again Fredi pocketed the money. He seemed to need Dutch courage pretty badly because he ignored the beer and sank his second schnapps. When he looked around at the other men, as if seeking their advice or encour-

agement, their eyes were blank, giving nothing whatever away. Whatever Fredi was going to say, they didn't
want to be part of it.

Finally he muttered to himself, 'I must be mad,'
then said, 'There was a man at the orphanage, a caretaker. There were rumours that he was hurting the
children . . . hurting them very badly, if you know
what I mean.'

Haller had jotted a couple of notes on a small pad.
'Did you pass these rumours on to the authorities?'

'You mean, did I report them to the Stasi . . . like I
was supposed to?' There was a bitterness in Fredi's voice,
a simmering self-hatred. 'Yes, of course I did. That was
my job. But I only did it once. Then it was made very
clear to me that they were not interested in hearing
anything about the orphanage. They were very specific.
They wanted to know about everything that happened
in the rest of my area. But at the orphanage . . . nothing!'

Haller looked up from his pad: 'So what was the
name of this caretaker?'

'I've forgotten.'

Haller reached for his wallet again: 'Maybe I can help
you recover your memory.'

Fredi shook his head. 'No, it would make no difference.
I do not want to remember. That would not be a good
idea. In fact, it would be a seriously bad one. Understand?'

'So this man is still around?'

A shrug: 'Possibly.'

'Where?' Haller asked.

Fredi laughed derisively and waved an arm in the air as if tracing it across the sky. 'Here, right here. He watches over us all . . . like God!'

His pals snickered and shot nervous looks at one another. I wasn't really concentrating on them, I was trying to make the connection and then it came and without thinking at all I blurted out, 'Of course! The name at the orphanage . . . Tretow! Tretow Immobilien!'

Haller gazed up at the ceiling, shaking his head at my stupidity and his for allowing me to come with him. A look of genuine fear crossed Fredi's face and he snapped at me, 'Shut up! Are you trying to get us all killed? Get out of here. Now. Both of you! I'm not saying another thing.'

Haller got up, grabbing my arm and almost dragging me out of the bar and onto the street.

'That!' he almost shouted when we were standing on the pavement. 'That, right there, is the reason I didn't want you coming with me. Shit! Serves me right for letting an amateur come along on a job . . .'

He stalked off down the street then stopped, pulled himself together, took a deep breath and turned back to me.

'I'm sorry,' I said, meaning it. 'I didn't mean to screw it up like that.'

'It's OK ... We weren't going to get much more anyway. However, next time you have a bright idea, just wait till we are in the car.'

'So now what? Do we track down this Tretow?'

'And say what? We don't know what he did, or when. We have no evidence ...'

'Well we have to do something. Mariana was in that orphanage. He was obviously harming the kids there ... and for some reason the Stasi were turning a blind eye to it. He could be the key to everything.'

'Exactly. Which is why we have to get our facts straight before we approach him. We will only have one chance. We must not waste it.'

An uneasy silence fell between us as the door of the *Kneipe* swung open and one of Old Fredi's drinking pals, the one who'd asked for potato chips, came outside. He looked at us, then concentrated on the tricky task of pulling a packet of cigarettes from an inside pocket, extracting one and lighting up, his shoulders hunched against the wind. He dragged the first long breath deep into his lungs and then walked over in our direction.

'You still want to know about the orphanage?' he asked.

'Maybe,' Haller replied.

'I can help you. But I need some of that money you were handing out to that tight-fisted bastard Fredi, because he won't be sharing any of his. And this one ...'

he jerked his chin at me, 'better keep his mouth shut this time.'

Haller peeled off another hundred and handed it over. 'So . . . ?'

'There's a woman round here, Magda Färber. She worked at the orphanage, looking after the children. She'll know what went on there.'

'And are you going to help me find her?'

'Another hundred . . .'

'Fifty. I can find her myself. You can save me some time, but that's all.'

'She works at the school now, part-time, serving lunch to the kids. She'll be out in an hour or so, once they've cleaned up.'

'How will I recognize her?'

The man gave a hacking laugh. 'Magda? Can't miss her. Look for the orange hair. Same colour as an orang-utan . . . and about as filthy too.'

Haller handed over a fifty. 'Then she's perfect for an ape like you.'

36

'She does not resemble an orang-utan to me,' said Haller, and I agreed. The Magda Färber who came walking out of the kitchen entrance of the Grundschule Rudower might have given her hair a startling, vivid ginger dye job, but the rest of her was hardly ape-like. She was small, trim and made up like a glamour girl, albeit one from the mid-1980s. Her stonewashed jeans weren't exactly Paris fashions, her short, quilted ski-jacket was a cheap, garish pink, and her face had been given a battering by time and poverty. But compared to the soaks on Old Fredi's table she was a vision of beauty.

'Bet she said no and he never forgave her,' I speculated.

'Very likely. Let us see if she says yes to us.'

Färber did indeed agree to talk, and for the price of a cup of hot chocolate at a nearby cake shop, not a stash of high-denomination notes. But the tale she told was not what we had expected.

'Of course I remember, Herr Tretow,' she said. 'He was a lovely man. And so friendly. He always used to ask how I was and compliment me on my appearance. He used to say I looked so young and pretty it was hard to tell me apart from the children sometimes. Of course that was a very long time ago. I was barely twenty...'

Haller gave her an impish smile. 'But you are still a very attractive woman today. If I wasn't married ...'

Färber looked at me with raised eyebrows and gave an exaggeratedly limp, drag-queen flick of the wrist: 'Ooh, listen to your boss, the charmer! Is he like this with all the girls? Hansi was just the same, bless him ... Herr Tretow, that is. He had a golden tongue, that man. Mind you, his wife was a total bitch. She walked out within weeks of them getting there, taking the children with her. She was spoiled, that was her problem. She'd been used to the good things in life and when her husband had a bit of misfortune, she didn't stick by him like a good wife should. Oh no! She went off to find some other man to leech off. Let me tell you, that was not the way I'd been taught a proper socialist woman should behave. Poor Hansi was devastated. His children were his pride and joy, his life. And then she made it so hard for him to see them, it was awful watching him suffer so.'

If Haller was surprised that Färber's opinion of Tretow was the exact opposite of what we'd expected, he didn't show it. 'Can I get you some cake?' he asked. 'Or some strudel, maybe?'

A large helping of spicy apple pastry, topped, like the hot chocolate, by a generous dollop of whipped cream, duly appeared, and Färber tucked in with an appetite that belied her slender figure.

Haller made inconsequential chit-chat while she ate, and then, almost as an afterthought, added, 'Of course, there are stories, idle gossip I'm sure, about things that happened at the orphanage . . . to the children. People have even suggested that Herr Tretow might have had something to do with it all.'

A heavily laden forkful of strudel came to an abrupt halt in mid-air, halfway between the plate and Färber's already opened mouth. She put it back down, rattling against the plate, and fixed us both in turn with a fierce stare.

'That is nothing but a pack of lies and slander,' she snapped crossly. 'I know people said things, cruel things. But they never had a shred of proof. Hansi was devastated. I remember him pouring his heart out to me, begging me not to pay any attention to it all. And I believed him. You know why . . . ?'

Färber glared at us again, daring us to reply, before providing the answer herself: 'Because he never got into any trouble. Not once. No one came to investigate. Hansi was never taken away for questioning. He certainly wasn't arrested. And you gentlemen must know what this country was like in the old days – the good old days, if you ask me. The authorities knew what was going on. It wasn't like now when there are gypsies and Turks stealing things without anyone trying to stop them; drug addicts everywhere; the streets filled with muggers, rapists ... even murderers. We had none of that because any criminal was caught and dealt with at once. And if Hansi had been doing anything wrong that would have happened to him too, and I would have said, "Good riddance. You deserve it." Because that was how it was. The guilty were punished and the innocent had nothing to fear. But Hansi was not punished. So he must have been innocent.'

She picked up her fork again and shovelled down the final mouthfuls of strudel before anyone could challenge her logic.

'Another slice?' Haller asked when she'd finished.

'Oh, I couldn't eat another crumb.'

'Some coffee perhaps ... for your digestion.'

'Oh yes, that would be nice.'

Haller ordered and then took out a copy of the picture of Mariana as a little girl. 'Do you recognize her?' he asked.

Färber looked at the blurred image for a moment, frowning before her face cleared and the frown gave way to an affectionate, even indulgent smile. 'Ah, my little Mariana! Our princess. Of course I recognize her ...'

'What can you tell us about her?'

'Well, I don't know what happened to her, if that's what you're asking.'

'No, it's not that. We're more interested in how she was back then. What can you remember about her ... and about her family?'

Färber shook her head disapprovingly. 'Oh the parents, they were bad people. Traitors, that was what I heard. The father was executed, most likely, and quite right too. The mother was in prison. That's why Mariana came to us.'

'That was standard practice, wasn't it?' Haller asked.

'Absolutely! When a woman committed a crime against the state, her children were taken into care. Well, they had to be, you see. You couldn't have them staying with the family. That would be a bad influence. They'd never grow up right.'

I'd kept my mouth firmly shut until now, but I could stay silent no longer. 'But Mariana, she wasn't like them, is that what you're saying? She wasn't bad ...'

'Oh no,' Färber cooed indulgently. 'She was adorable. So pretty, with that lovely smile ... Hansi used to say it broke his heart to look at her because she reminded him so much of his own daughter. I think she was his favourite of all the children, whatever he said. Do you know what happened to her? I've often wondered. It was all so crazy at the end. The Wall came down. The country fell apart. The children just seemed to drift away, like ghosts. No one knew what was happening.'

I saw Haller give me a silent, barely perceptible 'no' signal and feigned ignorance. 'No, I'm afraid not. But how about Mr Tretow. Have you kept in touch with him?'

'Oh, he's far too important these days for the likes of me! No . . . he was another one who just seemed to disappear. One day he was wiping the floors and keeping the old hot-water boiler going, same as usual. The next he was gone. But as I say, that's how it was . . . I think of him too, now you come to mention it. It was such a happy time we all had back then . . .'

The interview petered out with a few more reminiscences of Färber's youth. As we made our way from the coffee shop Haller asked me, 'So what did you make of her?'

'She was obviously in love with Tretow, though I'm not sure if he was with her.'

'Agreed. And what she said about the rumours, how they weren't true: what was your opinion of that?'

'Well, if we hadn't just met Old Fredi, I'd have been tempted to agree with her. If anything had been going on, the way East Germany was, someone would have reported it. But we know that Fredi did report the rumours and was told to mind his own business.'

'So?'

'So the Stasi, or whoever, knew exactly what was happening – whatever it was – and chose to ignore it.'

'Why?' Haller asked, his question followed by a high-pitched beep as he unlocked the BMW's doors.

'Two reasons I can think of. One, that they didn't give a damn what happened to those kids because half of them were the children of criminals . . .'

'If the victims are not important, that is a reason not to make a serious investigation, maybe. That is true everywhere in the world. However, is it a reason to order someone to ignore reports of a crime completely? No. So what is your second answer?'

'Because the person committing the crimes was protected. For some reason, Tretow had friends in high places.'

'I agree, that is the obvious conclusion,' said Haller, looking in his rear-view mirror as he prepared to pull away. 'However, how can it be true? This man was a caretaker, a janitor. You heard what Färber said. He was walking up and down the corridors with a bucket and a mop. Why would anyone protect him?'

'I haven't the first idea.'

'Me neither!' he admitted, with a chuckle. 'Or, to be exact, I have no idea that is supported by evidence, by facts. I can guess, of course, however that is not enough. So we need to find someone who might be able to tie these loose ends. Someone who also knows what happened to Mariana, and who can explain why her parents were in prison in the first instance.'

'Well, I wish I knew who that person was,' I said.

'You do. It is the mother, Bettina König.'

'But she refuses to talk.'

'To you, maybe. However, it is possible that she will feel more comfortable with me. I come from the same country. I am not the man who took her daughter from her.'

'But I didn't do that!'

'Of course not. Still, she may have told herself that is what happened and she may blame you in some way, even if it has no good reason, for the trouble her daughter is in now.'

'Oh come on, that's crazy . . .'

'No, it is the natural reaction of a mother who is sick with worry for a daughter she has not seen or talked to in many years. In any case, there is another reason why I do not think you should come with me on this interview. One day, God willing, you will be reunited with your wife . . .'

'I hope so.'

'And when that day comes, I think you will both want to reconnect with her past, her family here. So it is better that her mother can think of you as her son-in-law, not as some kind of interrogator. Let me ask the questions.'

'So what can I do while you're interviewing the mother? I know you don't want me getting into trouble, but there's got to be something. I can't just sit in my hotel room all day.'

'Oh yes, there is something all right,' said Haller. 'Something you will remember for the rest of your life . . .'

MINISTRY OF STATE SECURITY HEADQUARTERS, NORMANNENSTRASSE, BERLIN: DECEMBER 1989

Barely a month had passed since cheering crowds had smashed the first chunks of concrete from the Berlin Wall, but already the headquarters of the Ministry of State Security had been reduced from arrogant, oppressive efficiency to total, panicking chaos. Order and discipline had collapsed, replaced by fear, self-pity and a desperate frenzy of self-preservation. Groups of sullen but still passive East Berliners had started gathering round the perimeter of the sprawling complex, as yet unable to break the habits of a lifetime and take decisive action against those inside it. For the Stasi within, all normal duties had been suspended as every available man and woman set to work to destroy the evidence of the previous forty years of brutality and oppression. In the canteen all the talk was of what would happen if the growing mobs ever discovered that there was nothing whatever to stop them rising up, walking into the complex and tearing everyone in it limb from limb.

Hans-Peter Tretow thought it was pathetic. The very people who were still intent on covering their tracks, who lived in such fear of their people's revenge, were in the same breath bemoaning the tragedy of the Wall's collapse and reassuring one another that their life-times of service to the communist state had not been in vain. Could they not see the glaring contradiction staring them all in the face? Tretow was at least honest with himself. He knew what he'd done and what the consequences would be should any proof of it enter the outside world. He also knew that the same information that had gained him a degree of power when the Wall was up would protect him when it came down. And so he was on a mission both to secure what he required, and to deny it to anyone else.

As Tretow walked down the corridor to the office where his control agent worked, he passed a sweaty, red-faced man in jeans and a cheap, garishly patterned ski jacket struggling under the bulk of a large cardboard box. From the picture on the side, Tretow saw that it contained a shredder. The man caught him looking and rolled his eyes. 'Can you believe it? All our shredders are burning out. I had to go to the West to get another one.'

Tretow could not stop himself from laughing. Without their ability to bully the rest of the population, these people were revealed as clowns. And what was even more delicious was that they had no idea how funny they were.

The Stasi man stopped and glared at him. It occurred to Tretow that this particular man might, even now, be able to make his life uncomfortable, so he held up his hands in a gesture of appeasement and said, 'Sorry, mate. It just seemed crazy, the idea of the Wessis, of all people, selling us shredding equipment. Here, let me give you a hand.'

For a few more seconds the sullen stare was unbroken, but then the man relented and said, 'Yeah, all right . . . thanks.'

They carried the box up two flights of stairs and along a series of corridors before arriving at a large, open-plan office. The first thing that struck Tretow was the noise of a dozen or more shredders working non-stop. Files were being passed, like buckets of water at a fire, along human chains from the metal cabinets lining the walls to the shredders mounted on tables in the middle of the room. Tretow's eye was caught by the sight of a man suddenly exploding in rage, screaming at the shredder in front of him.

The man on the other end of the box shrugged his shoulders. 'What did I tell you? That's another one gone. Might as well let him have this one . . .'

Surveying the chaos of the scene, Tretow realized that there was no way of telling which files would be destroyed and which would remain intact long enough for someone outside the Ministry of State Security to discover them and start investigating their contents. It merely confirmed his initial instinct that if he wanted to survive, let alone prosper, he would have to take care of himself.

Once the box was delivered and the shredder unpacked, he made his excuses and found his way back to the office from which his own personal contribution to the Stasi's attempted destabilization of the West had been managed. It was empty: his control was presumably fully occupied helping his colleagues eradicate every trace of the past. Three large green filing cabinets were lined up against one wall. One of them had already been ransacked. The drawers were open and, as Tretow could see at a single glance, quite empty. For a moment he feared that he might have arrived too late. Then he pulled on the top drawer of the second cabinet and discovered a new problem. This one was still full, he could tell by the weight of it, but it was also locked. That, however, he was prepared for. He'd taken a crowbar from his toolkit at work and slipped it inside his winter jacket. It didn't take long to jemmy open the lock or to work out that the files in this cabinet all pertained to technical and administrative matters: endless forms requisitioning equipment, memos responding to orders or plans for proposed missions. Some of them might prove interesting, but Tretow didn't have time to work out which they were. Whoever had emptied the first cabinet might soon be coming back for the contents of the second, and every time Tretow heard footsteps in the corridor outside he was gripped by a spasm of fearful anxiety, waiting for the moment when the office door would open and he would be discovered.

He told himself not to be so feeble. Today of all days he would be able to bluff his way out of any situation, no matter how compromising. He turned back to the third cabinet and forced it open. This time he struck gold. It contained the neatly alphabetized personal files of all the agents his control was running and the targets of their various blackmail, entrapment and subversion schemes. Three drawers down he found the letter 'T' and a decade's worth of his data, filling four file-holders. That impressed him, he had to admit. Even better, one of the files was filled with strips of photo negatives, slipped into clear plastic holders, along with two flat boxes containing small reels of Super-8 film. A smile of profound satisfaction wreathed Tretow's face, which was only temporarily dimmed by the realization that he had nothing in which to conceal the files from prying Stasi eyes. No sooner had the problem occurred to him than it was followed by the obvious solution: hide in plain sight. Who, after all, would question one more harassed individual scurrying through the building with another bunch of files?

And so it was that Hans-Peter Tretow seized control of the physical evidence of his life as a Stasi asset. There were, of course, still a few witnesses to deal with. But that was surely just a matter of time and careful planning.

37

WEDNESDAY

'The guards were waiting for me,' said Karin Martz, a plump, homely, unexceptional-looking woman in late middle age. 'As soon as my feet touched the ground, they started shouting at me, giving me orders. They never used my name. Here a prisoner had no name, only a number. We were treated at all times as something less than human. We had to keep our eyes permanently lowered, so that we did not make contact with any other prisoner. We were not allowed to speak to anyone except for our interrogators. No one ever spoke to us. We did not exist. We were non-people.'

Frau Martz was guiding a party of a dozen or so people, of whom I seemed to be the only foreigner, through the Hohenschönhausen custody and interrogation centre on the north-east fringe of Berlin. For more than forty years it had been a blank, grey space on official East German maps, a dead zone whose purpose was never revealed to the mass of the population. The Stasi brought political prisoners and suspected enemies of the state to Hohenschönhausen and then questioned and tortured them until they confessed to their crimes. To many Berliners and most Germans, it was as much of a blank now as it had ever been. But Haller had wanted me to come here, and now I was beginning to understand why.

He'd called me first thing in the morning: 'I am on the way to visit Frau König. She lives in Nuremberg now. So I am confident that I will be able to clear up much of the mystery today. I will be back this afternoon. Shall we meet at my office at seventeen hundred hours?'

'Good idea. I can't wait to hear what you've discovered.'

'And what about you . . . are you following my suggestion?'

'Yes, boss. I'm booked in for the early afternoon tour.'

'Excellent! It will tell you a great deal about this city, this country . . . and, I think, about your wife.'

Hohenschönhausen's grey prison walls and octagonal guard towers now stood amidst a sea of capitalist normality, flanked by a tree-lined street of semi-detached suburban houses on one side, and an automotive breakdown and tow-truck service on the other. Within the walls, the blandly unattractive brick buildings had the unmistakable stamp of state-funded mediocrity, little different from the worst kind of municipal architecture back home. We were standing now in a large unloading bay. Again, it could have been anywhere. But the apparent normality was as deceptive as that of the cattle trucks that took Jews to Auschwitz. This unloading bay was not intended to receive commercial goods, but people transported against their will and deprived of all their rights: people just like the guides at Hohenschönhausen, all of whom were former prisoners.

Martz led us indoors, along a corridor. A cord was strung along the wall at waist height. 'That was for the guards,' she explained. 'As we walked along, they would pull the cable. This would turn on red lights, further along the way, so that people would know they were coming. Any other prisoners who were not in their cells would immediately be locked away and the other guards would remain out of sight. We were denied any human contact beyond the absolute minimum required to control and interrogate us.'

She paused and cast an eye at the group, four of whom were women. 'When I first arrived here I was made to stand naked in front of a female guard. I was having my period, but she forced me to remove my tampon in front of her. Then she searched me, inside and out. It was a total physical violation. But she did not care in the slightest. Once you accept that a prisoner is a non-person, then it is irrelevant how you treat them.'

I thought about Mariana's mother. Was she strip-searched as Martz had been? If so, as I was about to discover, that was the very least of her problems.

We came now to a corridor that was no different from any other bland, linoleum-floored workplace purgatory. Identical doors covered in cheap veneer opened onto indistinguishable offices with drab green metal cupboards and matching green curtains, their fabric too thin to keep out the daylight. Each office had a desk, with a fake leather office chair behind it and, somewhat incongruously, a stool on the side nearest the door.

'I was interrogated in a room like this,' Martz said. 'The interrogations took place over a space of several months, always at night, although they sometimes continued into the following day. Twenty-two hours was the longest. I had to sit on a stool, like that one, always keeping upright, no matter how tired I became.'

'Excuse me, but what had you done to be arrested?' I asked, regretting it almost immediately as several pairs of eyes swivelled round to look at me.

'Nothing,' Martz replied. 'I simply had a discussion one day with a friend about the idea of defecting to the West. I was not considering doing it, just talking about it. But that was enough.'

'And was she the one who betrayed you?'

'So many questions! Maybe you should have been in the Stasi!'

There was a ripple of nervous laughter from the other members of the tour party. While they went off to look at the interrogator's office, Martz looked at me quizzically: 'You are English?'

I'd been speaking in German, but my foreign accent and beginner's grammar must have been obvious give-aways. 'Yes.'

Now she was almost staring at me. 'Your face looks familiar to me, as though I have seen it somewhere before. Have we ever met?'

'I don't think so. This is the first time I've been to Berlin. Maybe you're thinking of someone else ...'

She gave a sharp, decisive nod. 'Yes, I have it now ... A few weeks ago: a month, maybe two, there was another Englishman, very much like you. But now I look at you, I think he was younger, maybe, and not so tall.'

I realized she must be talking about Andy. Had he come here, following the same trail that I was on?

'It might have been my brother. His name was Andrew Crookham ... Andy for short.'

'Ah yes, Andi ... Like you, always asking questions ... in German that was, I may say, even worse than yours.' She gave a little laugh, then caught herself and asked: 'You said "was". Has anything happened to your brother?'

'He died. Suddenly.'

'Oh, I am so sorry. Please forgive me.'

'It's all right,' I reassured her. 'It's actually nice to think of him being here. I'll be able to imagine him as we go around.'

'So now you follow in his footsteps ... I hope it is a good journey. OK, let us continue ...'

We went down some steps to a basement corridor. The floor was bare. Cables and pipes ran along the ceiling, from which single, bare lights were hung at roughly ten-metre intervals. Thick doors, painted in a pale duck-egg blue, each with a small spyhole cut at head height, lined the corridor on either side.

'Welcome to the U-boat,' said Martz. 'It is called that because it feels like the inside of a submarine, no? So ... let us start with a standard one-person cell ...'

She opened the door onto a totally stark chamber, with bare concrete on the walls, floor and ceiling. It must have been a little over a metre wide and maybe two metres fifty long. High up on the far wall was a small window, made of glass blocks that let in light but were impossible to see through. Its sole contents were a bare wooden bed-frame and a galvanized steel bucket, with a lid. The doorway was too narrow to allow more than two people to peer in, so we stood in line and took it in turns.

When we had all finished, Martz said, 'This is, in fact, the exact cell in which I spent six months in solitary confinement. During the day, I was obliged to sit on the edge of the bed, with my back straight, eyes wide open, not relaxing in any way, or lying down, or even leaning against the wall. Many days, I was completely exhausted, having spent all night being inter-rogated. Even so, I was not allowed any rest at all. Every five minutes, the peephole would slide open and a guard would check to make sure I was not disobeying these orders. The guards who watched me would never say anything, not a single word. The only people who ever spoke to me were my interrogators. Sometimes there were breaks in my questioning when days, even weeks, went by in total silence. It got to the point where I was desperate to be interrogated again, just for the human contact ... Now, would anyone care to step inside the cell for a minute or two?'

We stood there sheepishly. As I tried to summon up the strength to accept Martz's invitation I caught the eye of another one of the party, a younger guy. He grinned and gestured, 'After you.' So I took him up on the offer. 'I'll try it,' I said. It didn't seem like a big deal. After all, I'd spent a whole night locked up in York nick. I was used to the spyhole treatment. How hard could this be?

'All right, then,' said Martz. 'Go in. Sit on the bed. Look directly at the door. Do not move. Understand?'

Her tone was harsh, uncompromising, frighteningly convincing. 'Er, yes . . .' I stammered.

I walked into the cell. Martz waited while I positioned myself on the bed. Then, without another word, or any acknowledgement at all, she slammed the door shut with a harsh, metallic clang.

It was nothing whatever like York. Somehow the unrelenting years of hostility, terror and pain had permeated the atmosphere and stained the concrete itself. The whole space seemed to be closing in on me, the walls squeezing me from the side, the ceiling lowering till it would crush me, the air emptying from the cell. I gripped the edge of the bed till my knuckles showed white beneath the skin, feeling sweaty, struggling for breath, light-headed. It took every ounce of self-control for me to keep from shouting out to be freed. Gradually the panic attack subsided. My pulse slowed. I sat there for what seemed like an age, time crawling by, and then the peephole slid open. I mustered as cheery a grin as I could manage and said, 'Can I come out now . . .'

The peephole slid shut.

'. . . please?'

Total silence descended upon the cell. More time went past, as slowly as before. I was starting to get angry now. This was getting beyond a joke. And yet I did not move from the bed. My rational mind told me that there was nothing anyone could do to force me to stay in this cell, let alone obey the prison rules, and yet some deeper, more fearful instinct kept me still until at last the door opened and Martz said, 'Prisoner, leave the cell.'

When I came out I saw several faces among the group looking at me with expressions of surprise and concern: I must have looked even worse than I felt.

'How long do you think you were in there?' Martz said, less sternly now.

It had felt like an age, but there was surely a limit to the time anyone could keep a tour group waiting. 'I don't know,' I finally said, desperately trying to sound relaxed about the whole thing: 'Fifteen minutes?'

'Five,' said Martz.

'Five?'

'Ask your fellow visitors . . .'

I looked around to see nodding faces, some earnest, others smiling encouragingly.

'God, I never would have believed it . . .'

'And I was in there for six months. It was two months before I was allowed to wash, or brush my hair. I stopped menstruating completely. At the time I thought it was shock. Later I discovered that the Stasi put the contraceptive pill into our food, every day, with no breaks. The isolation was the same for everyone. I remember once, when I was being led to interrogation, I passed a male prisoner. This was very unusual. Someone must have made a mistake. Of course I was ordered not to raise my eyes to look at him but I managed to catch a glimpse. He had a ragged beard and matted hair like Robinson Crusoe on his island. I wished I could have talked with him, just for a moment. At that point, I had not exchanged a single word with any other human being for twenty-seven days. I feared that I had lost the power of speech. But my cell was like a queen's boudoir compared to some of the others. Come . . .'

As we followed Martz down the corridor she hung back for a moment until I was level with her. 'You are very like your brother,' she said to me in a voice too low for anyone else to hear.

'How do you mean?'

She smiled: 'He too was the only one who went into the cell . . . You look surprised: why?'

'I don't know, really. . . I mean, I'm not surprised that Andy went in the cell. That was the kind of person he was. It's more that you think we were alike . . .'

'Oh yes,' she said. 'It is obvious that you were brothers. Perhaps you had more in common than you thought?'

38

Martz excused herself and went back to the head of the line. 'And now,' she said, 'the rubber cell.'

In German the word she used was '*Gummizelle*', which sounds childishly silly to an English-speaker, like a Gummy Bear. The cell, however, was stark, brutal and utterly horrifying.

'As you can see, this cell is entirely lined in padded black rubber, making it pitch-black and soundproof. Prisoners would be given heavy doses of drugs to make them feel disorientated. For days, they would stumble to and fro, not knowing where they were, falling against the walls, losing track of day and night, up and down, any kind of reality at all until they cracked and began talking to themselves, screaming for mercy, losing control of their minds and bodies. Every single word they said was recorded, just in case there were useful pieces of information there, in amongst all the crazy rubbish. When prisoners were let out, the cells were washed down, to get rid of all the blood, the vomit and the shit. A crew of female prisoners did that, working in the early hours of the morning, like chambermaids getting a hotel room ready before the next guest arrives. And there was always, always another guest.'

By now a heavy fog of depression had settled upon our group, an overwhelming sense of sadness, horror and impotent outrage at the evil human beings could do to one another. It defied belief to think that this had all been going on in my lifetime. This was not some black-and-white newsreel from the forties. People had been screaming in the rubber cells while I'd been buying U2 albums, copping off with my teenaged girlfriends in the back row at the Odeon, growing a series of stupid eighties haircuts and agreeing with my sixth-form mates that, yeah, Thatcher was a total fascist bitch.

I thought of Mariana growing up in the midst of all this. Her parents might have been tortured in these very cells while she was packed off to the orphanage to suffer God knows what. For the first time I began to understand why she had never been able to cope with even the thought of her own family. There must have been so much pain there, so much damage that had never been repaired. I desperately wanted to be able to talk to her then, but all the words I longed to say lay stillborn upon my tongue, thought but unspoken for want of the only person on earth I wanted to hear them.

And then Karin Martz showed us what to me was the most appalling torture of all, the purest distillation of East German evil.

It began with another steel door and another cell. Two buckets, one somewhat deeper than the other, were suspended on chains from the ceiling, directly above one another, about a metre apart. Three wooden rails ran horizontally across the cell, one above the other, just behind the buckets. Two more rails were arranged a few centimetres above the ground, one behind the other.

'Can anyone guess the purpose of this unusual arrangement?' asked Martz.

'Did it have something to do with water, perhaps?' asked one of the party.

'Yes,' Martz agreed. 'Something to do with water.'

'Perhaps the prisoners were forced to drink from the buckets . . . like animals,' another suggested.

'They were treated worse than any animal,' said Martz, matter-of-factly. 'So, can anyone tell me?'

We stood there dumbly, unable to come up with any better ideas. Perhaps that was just as well.

'It worked as follows,' Martz said. 'The prisoners were taken behind the rails, then bent double, between the top two rails, and secured so that they could not move.

Their face was directly above the lower bucket, which was filled with water. They therefore had to hold their head out in front of them, or their face would drop into the bucket and they would drown. But this meant that the top of their head was directly underneath a hole in the bottom of the other bucket, which was also filled with water. So the water would drip down onto them – the famous Chinese water torture. At first this would just be a little irritating. But as time went on, hour after hour, each drop became an agony. Their body would be screaming for relief from the strain of being bent over. All they would know was pure, all-consuming pain. And the only movement of any kind available to them would be the blessed relief of lowering their head . . . in which case they would drown.'

One of the women in the group started crying. 'Please,' she begged her husband, 'take me away from here. I can't stand any more of this.'

He put a protective arm round her, 'Of course, my dear,' he murmured. 'Right away. Don't worry, it'll be all right.'

Then he glared at Martz and almost shouted, 'Look what you've done to her! How can you force us to see this brutality . . . this inhumanity? Shame on you!'

The rest of us stood in an embarrassed silence, shocked by the accusation, but unable to do anything to counter it. Finally, when the couple had made their way out of the corridor, towards the steps that would lead back to the normal, safe world of twenty-first-century Berlin, I broke the silence. Being British, of course, the first thing I did was apologize.

'I'm so sorry,' I said to Martz. 'I'm sure we all know that it's not your fault ... I mean, you did not intend to upset that poor woman.'

Martz looked at me with a strange, quizzical half-smile on her face. 'Are you sure? In truth, I am happier when this place does that to people. It shows that they understand what it really means. It is the people who can walk through this hellhole without being touched, and then go away to have beer and pizzas without a second thought ... they are the ones I despise.'

The tour continued for a little while longer: more corridors, more cells, more misery. As we finally left the U-boat and stepped back out into the open air, a voice piped up, 'Please excuse me for asking, Frau Martz, but how do you live with all this? I shall never forget this day. How do you forget five years?'

'I don't,' she said. 'When I go to sleep, I still have nightmares. Sometimes my husband has to wake me, just to silence my screaming. In my apartment there are no curtains on the windows, no doors anywhere except the front door and the lavatory. This is quite common, you know, among former prisoners. We have to have light. We cannot bear to be closed in. We have to live every day with what was done to us, and what makes it worse is that the men who abused us have never been punished in any way. So the only thing we can do is to work here, as guides to our own misery. It is an act of remembering. We want people to understand what was done here. We want them to be vigilant so that it can never be done again.'

And so the tour came to an end. The other members of the group said goodbye to Karin Martz, each trying to find the right words to convey their gratitude for the tour and their sympathy for what she had endured. I hung back till they had all dispersed and said, 'Frau Martz, may I ask you one last question?'

She smiled: 'Of course: what would you like to know?'

'Well, my wife is German, born here in the East. I think her parents may have been here, some time in the eighties. It seems likely they were arrested as political prisoners in Berlin, so I imagine they came here. I know it sounds crazy, but I don't know their names, not what they were called then, anyway. Her mother is now called Bettina König. My wife is called Mariana. She was Mariana Slavik before we were married.'

Martz sighed, 'I am sorry, Herr Crookham, but I cannot help you. There were so many of us, over so many years. And of course you do not know these people's names, for we had no names. We were crossed out, erased. To be honest, even now it is sometimes all I can do to remember who I am, or even to accept that I exist as a human being. So your wife really has no parents. She is a child of the nameless, a child of numbers ...'

As I walked back through the gates of Hohenshön-hausen I hoped to God that Karin Martz was wrong. I flagged down a cab and gave the driver the address of Haller's office. When I got there, I hoped, the ghost of Bettina König would be replaced by the truth about a real, flesh-and-blood woman.

39

Haller was dead.

Just before five o'clock I pressed on the buzzer outside the front door of his office building, expecting to hear Kamile's ever-cheerful greeting, only to be met by total silence. Two more rings later a sobbing, barely comprehensible voice told me the office was closed and only relented after I explained who I was and why I was there.

A Kamile I hardly recognized met me on the second floor. Her eyes were puffy and red, her cheeks streaked with mascara-stained tears, her nose sniffling.

'Are you all right?' I asked, as if the answer wasn't blindingly obvious. And then, without waiting for a reply, 'What's the matter?'

That's when she told me about Haller. As we went into the office, where a couple more of the agency's staff were trying to answer a clamour of phones through their own tears and stunned disbelief, she explained what had happened. 'He was coming back from the meeting on the A9, the autobahn. He'd called me ... It must have been just a few minutes earlier ... He was sounding very cheerful. He wanted me to tell you that he had some fantastic information.'

'Did he say what it was? Anything at all about Frau König?'

'No ... He doesn't like ...' Kamile stopped and with a conscious effort corrected herself ... 'Didn't like discussing anything important on a cellphone. He had intercepted too many calls himself. He knew how easy it was. That is probably why he did not call you.'

'So then what happened?'

'It seems he ... he smashed into the back of a truck. The police say he must have lost control. He was going quite fast, about two hundred kilometres an hour. But that was how Haller always drove. He had been trained as a police driver himself, so he knew what he was doing.'

'Do the police know what happened – why he lost control?'

'I don't think so. From what I could understand, the road conditions were not dangerous, there was not too much traffic on the road ... and where it happened, the road was straight.'

'And he wasn't drunk or anything?'

Kamile looked shocked. 'Mr Haller would never, ever drive when he was drunk. He was a good man ...'

'I'm sorry. I didn't mean to offend you. It's just ... there has to be an explanation.'

'The police will investigate and they will find out,' Kamile said, pulling herself together. 'Excuse me for one moment, please ...'

She went away to help a colleague who'd been waving at her frantically. I was left trying to come to terms with the shock of another sudden, totally unexpected death. In all my life, I'd never known anyone die violently. Now it had happened twice in a week. It made me feel as though I was bringing death with me wherever I went, like the carrier of a fatal virus.

The phone on the reception desk had started ringing again. Kamile looked at it for a moment, then turned back to what she was doing, evidently believing it to be the more important priority. Eventually the voicemail must have cut in because the phone fell silent. Seconds later, it started again and was once more ignored.

I was about to leave, trying to find the right moment to say goodbye to Kamile. The phone started trilling a third time. There was something insistent about it that made me feel as though this was the same person trying again and again to get through, rather than a random series of callers. No one else was going to pick it up, so maybe I should, if only to take a message.

'Hello?' I said, sounding very English, not thinking to use the German, 'Hallo.'

'Mr Crookham? Am I speaking to Peter Crookham?'

It was a woman's voice, German, but clearly very comfortable speaking in English.

'Yes,' I replied, a little hesitantly, wondering how on earth she could possibly have known it was me.

'Good . . . Now, please listen to me very carefully. My name is Gerber. I am an agent of the federal government. You are in great danger. At all costs, do not leave the Xenon Detektivbüro office. One of my colleagues will come and escort you from the building. Go with him. He will make sure you are safe.'

'What the hell is going on?'

'We have reason to believe that Herr Haller's death was not an accident. You too may now be a target. Please, stay precisely where you are.'

The line went dead. I was left standing beside the desk as Kamile came back to the reception area and asked, 'Did you answer the telephone? Who was calling, please?'

'It was for me,' I said. 'A woman . . . she said that Mr Haller's death was not an accident . . .'

Kamile gasped and held her hands to her mouth.

'She also said I was in danger.'

She lowered her hands. 'How is this possible?'

'I don't know.'

'Do you believe her?'

'I think so, yes – I don't know. She said I had to stay here. Someone would be coming here, to escort me to safety.'

'But what does she mean? Who would want to . . . to kill Herr Haller? He was such a kind man . . . And you – I don't understand.'

She looked as though she were about to faint.

'Here, sit down,' I said, guiding her to her chair behind the reception desk. I'll get you a glass of water.'

'No, thank you . . . it's all right. I will be fine. What are you going to do?'

'I want to get a look at the street, see if there's anyone out there waiting for me. Where is the nearest window?'

'There,' Kamile said, pointing at an office door. 'In the meeting room.'

I walked across to the door. It led into a room in which half-a-dozen chairs were arranged round a long table with a grey laminate top. At the right-hand end of the table a projector was suspended from the ceiling, facing a whiteboard on the wall to my left. Beyond the table two windows were covered with slatted fabric blinds. I went round to one of the windows, opened the blinds a fraction and peered out.

The street outside looked completely normal. I tried to remember whether any of the cars parked across the way had not been there when I arrived. There was a pale-blue Ford Mondeo that I couldn't recall seeing before. From where I stood it was impossible to see if there was anyone in it. A few people were walking up and down the road: a mother with her two small children; a couple of teenagers, too busy smooching to pay any attention to the world around them; a stocky, red-faced man in a bulging hoodie. None of them looked as if they were about to kill me. But that probably wasn't the kind of thing you advertised.

Behind me I heard the sound of a door buzzing and the click as it was opened. Two voices spoke, one male, the other female, the words indistinct. Then Kamile appeared at the door to the meeting room.

'There is a man here for you,' she said.

I nodded in acknowledgement. I walked out of the meeting room, into the reception area.

And there, not ten feet away from me, was Mr Weiss.

40

He looked exactly the same as he had done at the funeral. His coat was as immaculate now as it had been then. His blond hair was entirely unruffled. Only his tie had changed: a dark red replacing the black of mourning.

His hand reached inside his jacket. Cursing myself for being such a gullible fool, I waited for the gun that would blow me away.

Instead Weiss got out an identity card and held it up, facing me. In the few seconds I had to examine it, I couldn't make out the name of the agency for which he worked – even by German standards the words were unusually unintelligible – but the eagle logo of the German state and horizontal black, red and yellow stripes of its flag were plain enough.

'I work with Agent Gerber,' he said. 'I have been asked to apologize to you for any alarm she may have caused, but also to assure you that the danger you face is very real. Please come with me. Immediately.'

For a moment more I stood there, dumb and indecisive. Then Kamile sniffed back her tears and said, 'You should go. But wait one second . . .'

Weiss grimaced impatiently, itching to be off, while Kamile darted behind her reception desk, rummaged in a drawer and then handed me a business card. 'If you need to call me about Haller,' she said. 'Or if you need help.'

'Thanks,' I said, taking the card and shoving it in a trouser pocket.

'Now we go,' Weiss snapped, and I followed him out of the office. When we reached the landing he ignored the lift, but opened a side-door onto the emergency staircase.

'Go up!' he hissed in a harsh, urgent whisper. 'Fast! I will follow you.'

I started running up the stairs in front of me. As I rounded a corner between one flight and the next I glanced back over my shoulder and saw Weiss behind me. He was looking back down the stairwell and this time he did have a gun in his hand. For the first time, the seriousness of my situation became real to me. Weiss wasn't fooling. He really thought there would be someone after us. And if he was armed, the chances were that they would be, too. I felt the skin on my back prickle in horrible anticipation of the bullets that might soon be ripping into me.

He glanced back up at me and gestured angrily upwards: 'Don't stop!'

I ran again, sprinting up the stairs with frantic urgency. At the top of the stairwell there was a fire door. I slammed the metal bar down and felt a blast of icy air as it opened onto a walkway that ran along a narrow strip of flat roof, the tiles dropping away sharply on either side. The building was shaped like a hollow square with a courtyard in the middle, as were those on either side. We were on the side of the square nearest to the road.

Down below, three men ran into the courtyard. One of them looked up, caught sight of us and pointed upwards. The middle of the trio barked orders and the first man ran towards the ground-floor entrance of the building we'd been in, while the other two ran back out of the courtyard into the street.

'*Scheisse!*' Weiss swore as he glared down at the courtyard then started speaking rapidly in short, decisive sentences, his German too fast for me to be able to translate. I realized he had to be wearing some kind of earpiece communications device. He ran past me and dashed out across the slippery, ice-encrusted walkway, beckoning me to follow.

We were heading towards the scaffolding-covered

building next door to Haller's office. From the roof I could see that it had been weatherproofed, with plastic sheeting rising up the full height of the front and rear elevations and over the roof between them. There was just enough open space, though, for us to be able to duck under the plastic. Beyond us stretched another walkway and we made our way along it, heads bent and shoulders hunched beneath the plastic covering. The roof was bare of its tiles, leaving an open wooden ribcage of joists with nothing between them but air. Down below, the floors and ceilings had been stripped away, with only a few paths of loose planking left over the beams and floor joists to allow the builders to get around.

I tried not to look down at the dizzying, vertiginous drop, telling myself that I had spent my whole working life walking round half-finished buildings. This wasn't any different.

Weiss seemed indifferent to his surroundings, moving at a brisk, simian trot, his gun held out ahead of him, occasionally glancing round to check on my progress or peering over the edge of the roof to look out for any threat below. Somewhere down below us a light had been rigged, casting a spectral glow around the interior of the building and throwing grotesque, elongated shadows of our bodies across the plastic above our heads.

We reached the door at the far end of the roof that led to this building's emergency stairs. It was unlocked, and opened at Weiss's push. The stairwell itself seemed untouched by the renovations, with walls and steps of chipped and flaking painted concrete and a bare steel handrail. He started running downstairs, two or even three steps at a time, at a worryingly ankle-twisting, neck-breaking pace, then stopped on a small landing opposite a door onto one of the vacant floors and craned his head forward, listening for sounds of pursuit like a hunting dog sniffing the wind. There were none, so down we went again, grabbing the handrail for dear life as we leapt the last half-dozen steps and swung round, barely touching the ground, to race down the one below.

The stairwell was going by me in a blur of concrete and steel and the sliding and slapping of our shoes on the ground. It was all I could do just to keep my feet on the steps without getting them tangled or slipping as the descent raced on. I was barely conscious of the dark forms, barely registered as men, that suddenly appeared round the corner of the flight below, or the fact that Weiss had stopped dead so instantly that I careered into the back of him.

I heard him mutter a curse: '*Fick mich!*' which was followed immediately by a deafeningly sharp crack that reverberated round the stairwell. Weiss staggered back half a pace, uttered a pained, wincing grunt, fired his gun twice, shooting back down the stairs. Then he shouted, 'Up! Go back up! Go! Go!'

I turned round and hurtled back up the stairs, trying to ignore the screaming protests from my hopelessly unfit thigh muscles and the desperate heaving of my chest as my oxygen-deprived lungs gasped for breath. My hammering pulse blurred my vision, and sweat was trickling into my eyes, but somehow I managed to spot the shadow of a man, up ahead of me, cast on the stairwell wall. Just a few more steps and he would see me too.

I'd just reached a landing. There was a door to my left. Without thinking, I lowered my shoulder and barged it open, yelling, 'This way!' at Weiss as I went.

The door opened onto one of the stripped-out floors of the building. There were no walls, no floorboards, no doors, no glass in the windows: just the structural features that were keeping the building upright. A thin line of planks streaked across the bare floor joists to the wall facing the street and then ran along the length of the wall itself. A man was standing there repointing the brickwork. He can't have heard us at first over the music from the radio he'd placed in one of the empty window frames. But then he turned, frowning in puzzlement at the sound of our footsteps. His expression changed in an instant, and a look of shocked surprise flashed across his face as Weiss fired two more shots at our pursuers, keeping their heads down and buying us a few seconds of time. The builder dropped his sharply pointed trowel and the board on which he'd been mixing the mortar. They clattered onto the planking as he scurried away and cowered in the far corner of the building.

I raced onwards, the adrenalin rush of the chase banishing all my fear of falling. Barely stopping for a moment, I bent down, picked up the trowel and dashed through a gaping door frame that led out onto a small balcony.

The wall of plastic sheeting stretched in front of me as far as the eye could see, blocking me off from the outside world.

'What are you doing?' shouted Weiss.

He had taken cover to one side of the open door. As he darted out into the opening and fired another pair of rounds, I slashed at the nearest shiny green sheet with the sharp end of the trowel, desperately trying to pierce the building's plastic skin.

At the second attempt the trowel caught in the plastic and tore a small hole. I reached forward, squeezing the fingers of both hands into the hole and pulling them apart to tear a bigger rent in the fabric. There were more shots and a harsh metallic clang echoed just to one side of me as a bullet ricocheted away. The hole in the sheet was as wide as my shoulders now. I reckoned I could squeeze my body through.

'Follow me!' I shouted to Weiss.

Then I pushed my way into the hole and flung myself out. And suddenly I was tumbling through the air, thirty feet above the paving stones of a Berlin street.

41

I landed on the rolled-up bales of loft insulation with an impact that caught me smack in the solar plexus, leaving me winded and gasping for air as I bounced and tumbled to the ground. Getting to my knees, I saw Weiss make a much smoother, more accomplished, landing. He ran across to me, wincing, and I saw for the first time that the left arm of his suit was torn and soaked in blood.

'Get up! Keep moving!' he said, dashing off towards the end of the street, barking out orders to whoever was on the other end of his communications link. From up above I heard the sound of more firing, but had no idea where the shots had gone. All I knew was that I had not been hit – not yet.

Seconds later, a silver Mercedes appeared round the corner of the street, raced in our direction and then slewed round in a screeching turn so that it stopped broadsides to us, right across the road. Weiss ran up to it, flung open a passenger door and then grabbed me and shoved me onto the back seat. A moment later he too leapt in. The car was already moving, racing back the way it had come, by the time he'd closed the door behind him.

It took me a few seconds to get my breath back. Then I looked across at him. 'Who . . . ?' I couldn't complete the sentence. The adrenalin that had kept me going through the past few crazy seconds was ebbing away, leaving me stranded. My ears were ringing from the gunshots, my body ached from the fall and my brain had just ground to a halt.

'Someone who fears what you know, or might find out. Fears it enough to kill Haller and try to kill you.'

'But . . . but I don't know anything!'

'Not yet, maybe, but . . .'

There was a woman in the front passenger seat. She gave me a flicker of a smile and said: 'Karolin Gerber. We spoke earlier on the telephone.'

'Oh, right . . . hi.'

Weiss leaned forward and spoke to her in German. 'Are we being followed?'

She tilted her head to one side and glanced in the wing-mirror. 'No. You OK?'

Weiss glanced at the gaping hole of torn fabric, blood, skin and bare flesh with apparent disdain and said,

'Just a flesh wound. Give me the first-aid kit. I will deal with it.'

Gerber did as she was asked, then Weiss passed the kit on to me.

'Open it,' he said, reverting to English. 'Inside you will find a bandage. Tie it round my arm, tight. This will stop the bleeding. I will have it seen to properly later.'

As I was tying the knot I said, 'So that day at the funeral, when you warned me to stay away from ... from all of this. That really was a warning.'

'Yes, what did you think?'

'It sounded more like a threat.'

'*Ja*, maybe ... I wanted you to be a little scared. Clearly, you were not scared enough.'

'But why did you steal my computer? Why did you wreck my brother's study?'

Weiss looked at me pensively, weighing up the pros and cons of what he was going to do next. When he'd reached his decision he said, 'At the start of my career I worked for an agency called the Bundesnachrichtendienst ...'

'The intelligence service,' I said, remembering what Haller had told me during our first meeting.

Weiss raised his eyebrows in surprise, 'Ah, so you have heard of it. Well, then you may know that we were involved in espionage and counter-espionage

317

against the East and, in particular, the Stasi. That was where I first encountered a man called Rainer Wahrmann . . .'

That name, Wahrmann: I'd seen it somewhere before. I wracked my brain trying to make the connection as Gerber went on. 'Wahrmann had a daughter, who was registered with the name Maria-Angelika, although you know her better as Mariana, your wife.'

Now I remembered: 'That name . . . Maria-Angelika Wahrmann. It was on a list my brother made . . . girls born the same day as Mariana.'

Weiss nodded. 'Precisely. Several weeks ago, your brother came to Berlin, trying to find the truth about his sister-in-law. He was a good reporter, well trained in gathering information. He made enquiries at the appropriate official agencies. These enquiries came to my attention. I must say I was somewhat concerned because it was possible that your brother was – though I do not think he knew it – on the track to discovering your wife's true identity. But, you see, there are very good reasons why it has been obscured . . .'

'What reasons?'

'I will come to that . . . When I have answered your first question.' Weiss gave me a wry half-smile: 'A little patience, huh? So . . . it bothered me that if I knew your brother was here, other people might also discover what he had been doing. . .'

'You mean Wahrmann?'

'Possibly.'

'Or Tretow?'

Weiss's eyes narrowed: 'You know about Tretow?'

'He's a property developer now. But in the old days he worked at the orphanage where my wife was sent. And someone was looking after him, warning off anyone who took an interest in what he was doing.'

'And Haller, did he know all this, too?'

'Yes.'

'Then you do not need to ask me why he is dead or who was attacking us just now. And you will also understand why I was concerned about your brother. I feared he was walking blindfold into a minefield.'

'And then he died . . .'

'Yes,' Weiss agreed, 'and in very extreme circumstances. And then your wife was arrested. I needed to know what had happened, exactly what your brother had known. So I came to England . . .'

'And you broke into his house.'

'I apologize, believe me, but I felt I had no choice.'

'And you broke into my car and stole his computer.'

'Again, it was unfortunate, but necessary.'

'My house, the other night . . . was that you?' I looked at Gerber: 'Both of you?'

Their silence told me everything.

'But why?' I asked. 'What was the point of it?'

'Tell me, when you first discovered what had happened, could you believe it? For all the evidence against your wife, did it seem likely, or even possible that she was a killer?'

'No.'

'Me neither, but I knew of people who would have killed your brother without a second thought. So I wanted to go to the scene of the crime and see for myself. It was not my intention to disturb or alarm you. I had not realized you would wish to move back to the scene of the crime so soon.'

'And what did you conclude, then, from your re-enactment?'

'That the police account of the killing made sense.'

'To you maybe,' I replied. 'But then, I get the feeling you know a great deal that I don't about my wife. So why don't you tell me the truth . . . all of it? And if you do, I won't go straight to the British Embassy and tell them exactly what an agent of the German government has been getting up to on UK soil. And then you won't have a major diplomatic shitstorm to worry about. Does that sound like a fair deal to you?'

Weiss gave me another one of his appraising looks. 'You know, Mr Crookham, you are an interesting man. After the first times I saw you, I thought to myself, "He is a big man, physically, but he is soft. He is not a fighter." Now I see you throw yourself from a window, ten metres from the ground because you have already calculated that the fall is safe, and plan your escape accordingly. I hear you making threats against me and your voice is different. I believe that you mean it. You would do what you say. I had wondered what the daughter of Rainer Wahrmann, with his blood in her veins, would see in a man such as you. I think now I understand . . .'

'Well, that's very flattering of you, Mr Weiss. But I asked you a question: does it sound like a deal?'

Weiss grimaced again and sat back in his seat, his jaw clenched and his face ashen. With his good hand he gestured to me to hand him the first-aid box. He rested it on his lap, rummaged through it and pulled out a small blister pack that held two large white pills. He popped the blisters and swallowed the pills before sinking back into the seat.

Only then did he look at me again and say, '*Ja*, we have a deal.'

42

'Stop the car,' Weiss said. 'I need to make a call, in private.'

The Mercedes pulled up and Weiss got out, closing the car door behind him. I watched him pacing up and down on the pavement outside. Judging by the looks on his face and the tension in his clenched left fist he seemed to be having a hard time getting his point across, but evidently he got his way in the end, concluding the conversation with a decisive nod of the head.

As Weiss got back in his seat, the driver leaned his head back and spoke over his right shoulder: 'Where to, boss?'

'Potsdam. Templiner See,' Weiss replied.

'Are you sure that's a good idea?' Gerber asked. 'They need to be prepared, both of them. Otherwise it's not fair. . .'

'No, if we are going to do it, better to do it right away.'

'But what about you? You should see a doctor.'

'I'm OK. Let's just get this over and done with. Go to Templiner See. It is time Mr Crookham met Rainer Wahrmann.'

Weiss looked out of the window, but I doubt he was seeing any of the city we were passing through in the gathering dark of a winter late afternoon. His mind was elsewhere. I wanted to ask him about Wahrmann, the father-in-law whom I had never met, whose exis- tence itself had been a mystery to me, but I hardly knew where to begin. Thankfully, Weiss saved me the trouble.

'What did your wife tell you about her father? How they parted, I mean . . .'

'She said he'd left home when she was a kid. He never even bothered to keep in touch with her, all the time she was growing up.'

'It wasn't exactly like that. It was not the father who left. His daughter Mariana and his wife were taken from him – I was the agent who arranged the transfer. They were moved to a place of safety. He was forbidden any contact with them. To this day he knows nothing about his daughter's life. He has no idea, therefore, of her current situation. The separation was total.'

I thought of the things Wahrmann must have done to be denied any contact at all with his family.

'What kind of a sick bastard is he?' I asked

'Not what you think, maybe,' Weiss replied. 'But Rainer Wahrmann is certainly a most unusual man. In his time he has been a spy, a criminal and a traitor in the eyes of his country. At the time of your wife's birth he was in prison, sentenced to three years in jail.'

'For what?'

'A crime, naturally. His particular offence, however, was unusual. He was found guilty of telling a joke.'

'I'm sorry?'

'Back in the late 1970s, Rainer Wahrmann was a student, a very brilliant one of whom great things were expected, working on his doctorate in economics at Humboldt University. For two hundred years this has been the leading university of Berlin, but when the city was divided it was in the East. It became the place where the country's elite students were sent, chosen both for their aptitude and for their allegiance to the SED – the ruling communist party.'

'So Wahrmann was a communist?'

'At that time, yes. Any ambitious young man was obliged to be, and he was very ambitious, a veritable golden boy: handsome, an academic prodigy, just married to a beautiful young wife. But one night he went to a party at another student's apartment. He had too much to drink and he told a joke about Erich Honecker, the leader of the country. That is how it was:

the East Germans had jokes about Honecker, like the Russians had jokes about Khrushchev and Brezhnev . . . I mean, they were actually the same jokes, just with the names changed.'

'What was the joke?'

'You want to hear it?'

'If it put my father-in-law in jail, yes.'

Weiss paused, like any other amateur trying to remember a joke, his ultra-competent mask momentarily disturbed.

'OK,' he began, 'so Honecker is riding in his limousine through the countryside, way out in the sticks. Suddenly a pig wanders out into the road. Bam! The car hits the pig and kills it, instantly. The driver does not know what to do, so he asks Honecker, "Do you want me to drive on, sir?" Honecker says, "No, you'd better go to the nearest farmhouse and offer to pay damages for their pig." So the driver goes off to pay the damages. Fifteeen minutes go by . . . thirty . . . an hour, and still he has not returned. Finally, the driver comes back. He is walking unsteadily, singing a song. He has obviously been drinking. In his arms he carries a huge pile of gifts and packages: loaves of bread, fresh vegetables, jars of pickle, cuts of meat – everything farmers can provide. Honecker cannot believe what he is seeing. He asks the driver, "What happened?" The driver says, "I don't know. All I said to them was: I have Honecker in my car and I have killed the pig."'

I did my best to summon a polite laugh. 'That's it?'

Weiss did not appear to be upset by the absence of hilarity on my part. 'Yes. Wahrmann told the joke, someone reported him to the Stasi and he was jailed for conspiracy to undermine the state.'

'How can telling a joke be a conspiracy?'

'Very simple. For you to tell a joke, someone has to tell it to you first. Then you must pass it on to other people. Therefore it is a conspiracy. Therefore, also, Wahrmann was a conspirator against the state, a subversive. The official term at that time was *Diversant*. In English, that means "saboteur".'

'That's madness!'

'The whole system was madness. Is that not obvious to you yet?'

I thought of the trivial irritations of my own society's mania for health and safety, political correctness and the requirement to spout acceptable platitudes that no one really believed. Then I considered an entire system in which those niggling absurdities were magnified a thousandfold; in which truth and honesty were abolished by law; where the slightest deviation could lead to imprisonment and torture. That had been the world of Rainer Wahrmann.

'Where did they send him?' I asked.

'First to Hohenschönhausen for interrogation, then to a jail called Bautzen, in Lower Saxony, near the Czech border. The inmates called it The Yellow Misery, because it was made from yellow bricks. But you were at Hohenschönhausen this afternoon, yes?'

'Yeah.'

'Bautzen was worse.'

I tried to imagine how a pampered young student, a golden boy accustomed to privilege and entitlement, would cope with the U-boat, and struggled to imagine something even more degrading. Wray had talked about multigenerational trauma being passed on from parent to child. Mariana's father must have been traumatized all right. I could only imagine the hurt that she had inherited from him.

'My God . . . and he was there for three years?'

'No, just a little more than a year,' said Weiss.

'How come they let him out?'

'A senior party official came to Wahrmann's cell. He told him that while he was in prison his wife had given birth to a baby – his baby. Then he offered him a deal. There was a big international youth congress taking place in Leipzig with representatives from the youth movements of all the communist bloc countries, plus sympathizers from the West. The regime wanted to demonstrate the effectiveness and humanity of its justice system . . .'

I gasped: 'That's grotesque.'

Weiss just looked at me. He did not need to repeat himself: the whole system was grotesque.

'So what was the deal?'

'Simple. All Wahrmann had to do was go to the congress and give a speech describing the error of his ways and expressing the thanks he felt to the system for showing him where he had gone wrong. This had ensured that he would never make the same mistake again.'

It was like something out of *Nineteen Eighty-Four*: a real-life Winston Smith proclaiming his love for Big Brother. 'You mean, he was told to thank the people who had arrested him and, I presume, tortured him, and then sent him to prison for a conspiracy that had never even existed?'

'Exactly.'

'So what did he do?'

'He took the deal. He made his speech – very brilliantly, by the way, I have read it – and went back home to his wife and baby.'

'And then what?'

'Then the golden boy became golden again. He was the living proof that the party was capable of redemption and forgiveness. He wrote a thesis on "The Superior Efficiency of Resource Allocation in Socialist Command Economies" that was published on both sides of the

Iron Curtain. It put him on the fast track. He was given a job in the personal office of the finance minister, writing speeches and position papers. Still in his twenties, he was attending international trade negotiations, bilateral meetings with both communist and Western governments, always singing the praises of the communist system.'

'How could he?' I asked, to myself as much as anyone else.

Weiss carried on regardless: 'Rainer Wahrmann was a star. Official newspapers here carried his articles. Socialist parties in Western Europe used his economic reports as proof that the average worker in the East was far better off than those in the West. But what they did not know was that everything he wrote was a lie. It was all just propaganda. In truth the East German economy, along with all the Soviet-style economies, was a wreck. Wahrmann knew it, but he chose to lie anyway.'

My sympathy and pity for Wahrmann's position was rapidly disappearing, replaced by anger at the totality of his betrayal of principle. 'You're telling me that Mariana's dad knew exactly how bad the system was, how it abused the people it controlled. And still he lied for it? What a scumbag!'

Weiss looked at me with something approaching disdain. 'Oh, so you would be different, huh? You would say, "No, I don't want to see my wife and daughter. I don't want to go back home. I don't want to give them a better life, in a nicer apartment. I would rather stay in jail." Is that your position?'

'No, of course not, but . . .'

'But what? That was the deal. Wahrmann took it. Think of your precious Mariana and what was best for her. Now answer me: do you think he did the right thing?'

'I don't know.'

'Yes, you do. He did the only thing he could do. Or at least, the only thing that any ordinary man would do. But now let me ask you another question. Do you think your wife is an ordinary woman?'

That was a much easier question to answer. 'No. Not remotely.'

'Well, neither is her father. He's smarter than any guy I've ever met. He knew exactly what he was doing. But no one else did. Rainer Wahrmann fooled them all.'

Before I could ask what he meant, Weiss turned away and looked out of the window again. We seemed to have left the city and for the past few minutes had been taking a dual carriageway through heavily wooded countryside or parkland.

'Not too much further,' he said. 'Ten minutes, maybe, fifteen at the most. And then, I hope, your search will be at an end.'

43

We arrived at Wahrmann's house – a smart lakeside villa, built in an early modernist style – at around a quarter past six. Wahrmann must have profited from his life of crime and spying because it had all the trademarks of a rich man's residence: the heavy, impenetrable gates; the speakerphone box by the entrance; the crunching gravel of the drive past perfectly trimmed hedges up to the impeccable white façade. I wondered who would greet us at the door: a butler, perhaps, or maybe a pretty young trophy wife?

Instead we were met by a nurse in a uniform as immaculate as the house itself. She looked at us sternly, gave a nod of recognition to Weiss and then let us in.

'Do not be too long,' she said to Weiss, walking with him across the hall. 'I meant what I said. He is tired. He cannot concentrate for very long.'

'Did you tell him?' Weiss asked.

'He knows this is his daughter's husband, yes,' the nurse said. 'But that is all.' Then her voice changed and her cool professionalism gave way to a note of genuine, affectionate concern for her patient. I wasn't sure whether she was addressing Weiss or me when she said, 'Please, be very careful. He has suffered a very great deal in his life. He should not have to suffer now.'

I had no idea what to expect. From the moment I decided to go to Berlin I had been preparing little speeches in my head for the time I'd come face to face with Mariana's father, whoever he might be. I had always known that he had deserted her, but beyond that my picture of him had been in a constant state of flux. Haller had reminded me not to jump to the assumption that her father had been the source of all Mariana's problems, but what was I supposed to think instead? To judge by Weiss's description, Rainer Wahrmann was a brilliant but completely unscrupulous survivor. But the nurse was describing an invalid victim of tragic circumstances.

She led us across a tiled entrance hall to a heavy wooden door. 'Just him,' she said, pointing at me.

'I need to speak to him,' Weiss insisted.

The nurse raised her hand to stop him. 'No, one person only, I insist.'

She opened the door and I went into what must once have been an elegant reception room, furnished in keeping with the Bauhaus style of the villa itself, but was now Rainer Wahrmann's entire universe. A hospital-style bed had been placed at one end, with a side table beside it, but he was sitting in a black leather and chromed-steel Barcelona chair by the windows that took up almost all the far wall and looked out over the black night-time waters of the lake. It was, I suddenly realized, just like being at home. The room a neutral white: the visual drama provided by the landscape beyond. And here, too, I had found a man making his acquaintance with death.

Wahrmann must once have been very handsome. That was clear from the elegant bone-structure of his face – the strong jawline, arrow-straight nose and patrician forehead – and the presidential sweep of his steel-grey hair. But the flesh of his face and the muscles of his body had withered away, leaving a shrunken, desiccated husk, little more than a scarecrow on which his clothes were hung.

A breathing tube was plugged into his nostrils and ran from there to an oxygen tank on a wheeled trolley beside his chair. He gave a feeble wave in the direction of a second chair, also a Barcelona, opposite his.

'Please,' Wahrmann said. 'Sit down.'

He paused while I settled myself, then added, 'I apologize for not being able to greet you properly. Unfortunately, I am somewhat indisposed.'

He smiled, and though he radiated barely a fraction

of the charm that he must once have possessed, I could suddenly see Mariana in the corners of his mouth and the tawny, feline glint of his eyes.

'I am so sorry you are ill.'

'Leukaemia,' he said, in a calm, matter-of-fact way. 'Another little gift from the Stasi. I am not the only one to have received it. They used radioactive spray as a means of keeping track of those they suspected of subversive activity. Then, after the Wall came down, when old scores were being settled, I was poisoned with thallium. I recovered from the radiation sickness at the time, but who knows, maybe it tipped the balance ...'

Wahrmann gave a shrug of his bony shoulders, then fixed me with eyes that still burned with the life and energy that was fast deserting his body.

'Tell me about Mariana, my little girl. Something has happened to her, hasn't it? Magda, my nurse, wouldn't say anything. Bless her, she only wants to protect me. But my brain still functions, even though the rest of me does not. You have made considerable efforts to track me down. So this must be serious. You have come alone, without Mariana. Therefore she is either unable or unwilling to meet me. Yet you are here anyway. Tell me, what is the reason?'

Once again I ran through the events of the past days as clearly and concisely as I could, ending with Haller's death and my escape from his office. Wahrmann listened patiently, occasionally asking sharp, pertinent questions designed to clarify or amplify particular aspects of my story. I could almost feel the power of his intelligence forcing my own thoughts into a sharpness and coherence I would never have managed by myself.

'So you see,' I concluded, 'if I can only find out what happened to her at that orphanage, maybe I can give Wray the clue he needs to unlock Mariana's mind and give her lawyers something they can use in her defence. I know you've not seen Mariana in years. I know you've not played any part in her upbringing. But you must care about her a little bit, surely. So can you tell me what the answer is?'

Warhmann took a small glass jug of water from a table by his chair, poured some of it into a glass and sipped it thoughtfully. Then he looked at me with eyes haunted by overwhelming guilt and loss as he said, 'I don't know. As God is my witness, I do not know.'

'What do you mean, you don't know? You're her father. You must know!'

'No, I swear that I do not. My own daughter's life is a mystery to me, one that I have never been able to solve. And it is my fault, I freely admit it. I was the one who deserted her. In my little girl's hour of need, I left her in the hands of a monster.'

The confession seemed designed to win him a little sympathy. But I wasn't going to let him get away that easily. 'That doesn't surprise me,' I said, 'from everything Weiss has told me about you.'

Wahrmann's eyes narrowed: 'How much, exactly, has he told you?'

'He said you were a criminal, a traitor and a spy.'

I expected Wahrmann to make an indignant denial. Instead he burst out in laughter that soon descended into a breathless confusion of wheezes, gasps and coughs.

'Are you all right?' I asked. 'I'll get the nurse.'

Wahrmann held up a hand to stop me, shaking his head between coughs. 'No, I'll be fine. Excuse me one moment.'

He composed himself with the help of another sip of water. Finally, he could talk again: 'And what did Weiss tell you about himself?'

'He said he used to work for the BND. That's where he got to know you.'

'That's true,' Wahrmann nodded. 'But since unification, he has been an officer in the federal office for the protection of the constitution: domestic intelligence, in other words. In both cases, however, he has been involved in combating the Stasi, or its former members, and their attempts to undermine the Federal Republic.'

'So he knew you when you worked for the Stasi?'

Wahrmann smiled. 'On the contrary, he knew me when I spied for the West.'

44

Trying to grasp the truth about Mariana's father was like trying to grab an eel: every time I thought I'd finally got it, reality seemed to slip away through my fingers. 'Hang on. Weiss said that you had written lies and propaganda for the East German finance ministry. You were on their side.'

'That's right. In public I did everything I could to sing the praises of our glorious socialist state.'

'And in private . . . ?'

Warhmann sighed. 'How do I explain this? Let's see . . . When I was sent to Bautzen . . .'

'After you told the Honecker joke?'

'Exactly . . . And by the way, it has always been my contention that the real reason I was convicted had nothing to do with any conspiracy against the state. I think the problem was that I told the joke very badly. I was letting down the standard of Marxist–Leninist comedy.'

I frowned in complete bafflement. Would they really have imprisoned a man for that? By now, anything seemed possible.

'Please,' said Wahrmann, 'could you not manage a polite smile at least? That was supposed to be another joke.'

I summoned up an embarrassed chuckle. 'Sorry . . . I'm finding it hard to know what to believe . . .'

'That's all right. It takes a while, I find, for people to grasp the reality of life in the old Soviet bloc. Myself included, by the way. I had grown up believing in the state and the need to defend our revolution. Then I experienced the reality of dictatorship and injustice, and I had my conversion. The road to Bautzen was my road to Damascus. I became determined to do whatever I could to undermine the state and the party.'

'But you gave a speech praising the way you had been treated in prison.'

'Yes. How else was I to be released? The more I appeared to be a reformed character, the more I was trusted and thus the greater damage I could do.'

'So what was the damage, then?'

'In 1985 I was sent to a bilateral trade negotiation in Bonn, the capital of West Germany. On the evening before the talks began there was a grand reception for all the people involved. I saw one of the Western guys I knew from other economic summits, a man called

Dienst, go to the men's room. I followed him in. There was nobody else there. So then I handed him an envelope, turned full circle and walked out of the men's room without saying a word.'

'What was in the envelope?'

'Accurate East German industrial production figures for the past four quarters.'

'Nothing else?'

'No.'

'But what if he just ignored them?'

'There was no chance of that. Dienst was a smart guy. One look at the numbers would tell him that our economy was performing far more poorly than anyone in the West had imagined. Since East Germany was by far the most advanced communist economy, the others must be even worse. Dienst took my figures directly to the BND and told them who I was and what I could potentially provide. Naturally, the BND were very suspicious at first. Many of the Easterners who volunteered to spy for the West were Stasi double-agents. So, of course, were many BND officers: my greatest risk was that one of them would expose me. But finally we agreed terms and set up a system of dead-drops, and I started passing information over to the West on a regular basis.'

'Did your wife, Bettina, know about any of this?'

'No. She knew nothing at all. I wanted to keep her safe.'

'But you were taking a hell of a risk. And you had a family to think about. What about Mariana?'

Wahrmann closed his eyes. I knew he was imagining Mariana, conjuring her up in his mind's eye. For both of us, that was as close as we came to her any more.

'She was the most wonderful child,' he said, opening his eyes again and giving a sad, wistful smile. 'So beautiful, just like her mother. People used to say Bettina should have been a movie star, and Mariana had the same quality. She was sweet-natured, happy, always laughing, and so bright: all the time asking questions, noticing things, wanting to know more. Everyone loved her. Bettina used to call her "My little ray of sunshine". To have a wife like that and a child like that, well, I felt like the luckiest guy in the world.'

As I had done to be Mariana's husband.

'And yet . . . ?' I asked.

'And yet I deserted her. I betrayed her. I did not mean to, but I did.'

'Now my brother's dead, Mariana's in a psychiatric unit and I'm here, trying to pick up the pieces. All because you betrayed your country. Is that what we're saying?'

'Do you really think I was betraying my country? You have been to Hohenschönhausen. You know what sort of a country this was. I was not betraying it. I was trying to save it.'

'But you had a duty to your family. Surely that came first?'

Wahrmann grimaced. 'That was my dilemma, the argument in my head that kept me awake at nights. Of course a man has a duty to his family. But does he not have a moral duty to fight tyranny and oppression also? Should he turn his eyes away from what is happening? Yes, that might be the safe, sensible choice. But if everyone makes the sensible choice, tyranny continues without any challenge. And then what happens to all the families? Are they any safer? Someone has to make a stand.'

'But you made it at the expense of the people you loved.'

'And I have paid for that ever since, as have they.'

I realized that I was being unfair. When Weiss had told me about Wahrmann's deal with the Eastern system, I had accused him of betraying his principles. Now that he was demonstrating that he had not sold out to the Stasi, I was accusing him of betraying his family. Which proved his point: either way he could not win. In that system, no decent man ever could.

'I assume you got caught,' I said, getting back to the story.

'Ja . . . it was inevitable. I lasted less than a year. And then . . . well, you heard what they did to me for telling a joke. For treason it was far, far worse. I was sentenced to life imprisonment, without the possibility of parole.'

I tried to imagine what it must have been like to watch that steel door slam shut, believing that the rest of your life would be spent in such crushing confinement.

'How did you handle it?'

'Oh, I knew how bad things were. I told myself the system would collapse eventually: ten years, maybe, twenty at most.'

'And in the end it was all over in three ... But why did Mariana end up in an orphanage?'

'Because they arrested Bettina, too.'

'You said she knew nothing about your spying.'

'She didn't. But that made no difference. The fact she had done nothing to stop me was enough.'

'How could she have stopped something she didn't know was happening?'

'She couldn't, of course, but that made no difference. They gave Bettina a three-year prison sentence. It destroyed her. The woman I loved died in that prison cell. The woman that came out was just an empty shell, into which anger and poison and bitterness had been poured to fill the vacuum where love and happiness had been.'

'What about Mariana?'

'All children of female political prisoners were taken into care, as a matter of course. All contact with their parents was forbidden: no letters, no presents, nothing. Bettina was released from prison in September 1989. By this time, the old order was beginning to fray at the edges. There were demonstrations against the government. Thousands of people were leaving the country, escaping to the West through Hungary. But even so, no one would tell Bettina what had happened to Mariana, or where she was. Then, in November, the Wall came down and the whole system broke down completely.'

Wahrmann looked feverish. There were beads of sweat on his forehead. It was taking everything he had just to tell his story, but he showed no signs of wanting to stop and I wasn't about to suggest it.

'Day after day,' he went on, 'Bettina tried to contact officials or make appointments, but it was impossible to speak to anyone. Finally, in December, she managed to find an official who told her that Mariana was here in Berlin. Bettina went to the orphanage. Mariana was skin and bone, literally starving, right here in the middle of Berlin. The staff at the orphanage had no money to buy food for the children that were left. They were making do with a few scraps given to them by neighbours, and winter vegetables from some allotments that lay nearby.

'I know the ones . . . So how did Bettina get Mariana back?'

'She simply took her. They were glad to have one less mouth to feed. But Mariana . . .' Wahrmann looked away for a moment, struggling to keep himself together. 'She did not recognize Bettina ... her own mother. She was screaming and crying as Bettina took her to the bus stop. By the time they reached the apartment where Bettina was living with her parents, the fire had gone out. Mariana was silent, dead behind the eyes, like a zombie. The ray of sunshine was gone. She would not talk about the orphanage, not a single word. But it was clear she had been profoundly traumatized.'

I hardly dared ask my next question for fear of what the answer would be: 'Had she been abused ... sexually, I mean?'

'I don't think she was,' said Wahrmann, with an emphasis on the word 'she' that suggested others might have been. 'Bettina took Mariana to a doctor to be examined and was told that she was still, ah ... intact. But something happened to her, that is for sure. Something very bad.'

'Did she ever talk about it?'

'No, never, not a word ...'

'What had happened to you, while all this was going on?'

'All the political prisoners were released from jail in January 1990. I made my way back to Berlin. It was not much of a homecoming. Bettina was filled with rage towards me for what I had done to her and Mariana ...'

Wahrmann's voice drifted away.

'Were you able to earn a living at least?'

'Well, my knowledge of the East German economy was of considerable use to the unification process. I was also able to assist the authorities in some of their investigations of former Stasi personnel.'

'So you put some of the bastards away?'

'Some, maybe ... though many fewer than I would have liked. There has never been a great hunger to pursue the wrongs that were done in the East. Many crimes have gone unpunished. Many victims are unavenged.'

'Meanwhile you and Bettina split, and she took Mariana off to the West ...'

Wahrmann needed another drink of water before he answered: 'Yes, it became ... necessary.'

'Why?'

'Some of my former colleagues in the East were not happy with what I was doing for a government they still perceived as the enemy. Like you, they accused me of treachery, of betraying my countrymen. Attempts were made ...'

I'd picked up the barbed aside but tried to ignore it: 'Was that when you were poisoned with thallium?'

'Yes. Also, the brakes on my car were cut ... They failed while I was driving along a normal stretch of road, on a clear, sunny day.'

Like Haller, I thought: was that what had happened to him?

Wahrmann continued: 'After that there were threats against Bettina and Mariana. So they were given a new family name, new birth certificates, new passports . . . It was best for my little Mariana. I had to let her go to make sure that she would be safe.'

As hard as Wahrmann's two imprisonments must have been, let alone the periods of interrogation that had preceded them, it seemed to me that none of it had come close to hurting him as much as the destruction of his family. His voice was hesitant, his shoulders had slumped and the lines on his face seemed to be grooved even deeper than before.

'And the attacks on you stopped?' I asked.

'Yes. You know how it is. Time passes. I think I ceased to be seen as a threat. My enemies had better things to do, bigger games to play. I went back to Humboldt University, as a lecturer and eventually a professor. I have also acted as a consultant for various banks. That is how I could afford,' Wahrmann waved a hand at the room around him, 'all this. In recent years I have been looking in particular at the way in which the global capital markets have spun out of control.' His eyes glinted with ironic amusement: 'As you know, I specialize in failing economic systems.'

'And did you ever try to find out what had happened to Mariana in the orphanage?'

'All the time. But it was very difficult to track down

the children who were at the orphanage at the same time as Mariana. Many records had been lost or destroyed, and when I did find names of children many had just vanished. Others would not talk. Others became vagrants, junkies. Half-a-dozen at least died very young: overdoses, traffic accidents, even exposure to the cold.'

'And no one thought this was suspicious, all these young people dying?'

'Absolutely it was suspicious. But there was very little evidence. And they were just street kids. No one cared about them. Sometimes I even had the feeling that some people – powerful people – wanted to make sure that there were no proper police investigations. Many former Stasi officials still wield a lot of influence, you know.'

'What do you know about Hans-Peter Tretow?'

'Ah!' Wahrmann gave an exasperated sigh. 'I know he worked at the orphanage while Mariana was there. I am certain he had something to do with the way she is now. I suspect he had a hand in the disappearance of some of the other former inmates. So does Weiss. But we have never been able to link him definitively to any particular crime. And now it is too late. We have a statute of limitations. Beyond a certain point it is no longer possible to prosecute someone for a crime they committed in the past.'

'Well, there's something he's still frightened of, something he doesn't want anyone to know. Think about it: Haller's brakes failed. Does that sound familiar?'

Wahrmann's eyes widened as he too made the connection with his past.

'I was also attacked when I went to Haller's office,' I went on. 'Weiss is sure Tretow is connected to both incidents. So there's something he wants to keep quiet.'

Wahrmann thought for a moment before he spoke again: 'Well, there is of course one crime that is not subject to any limitation.'

'What's that?' I asked, though I already knew what the answer had to be.

'Murder,' said Rainer Wahrmann. 'Somewhere inside her, deep inside, Mariana knows about a murder.'

45

The silence that fell between us was broken by a rap on the door. A moment later the nurse came in. She took one look at Wahrmann then glared at me disapprovingly.

'It's all right, my dear,' said Wahrmann, spotting the unspoken criticism. 'Herr Crookham and I have been catching up on some family history.'

'You need your rest,' the nurse said.

'I shall soon have more than enough of that.'

A brief flicker of pain disturbed the nurse's authoritative, professional façade. 'You really must get back into bed,' she said.

'Just give us two more minutes,' said Wahrmann. 'And then, I promise, I will be a good boy.'

The nurse sighed theatrically, shook her head as if to say, 'What's to be done with you?' and then retreated back to the door. 'Two minutes, and not a second more,' she said as she left.

Wahrmann turned his attention back to me. 'I am sorry I could not have helped you more. But at least you now have some information to help the doctors treating Mariana. That will make their job much easier, I am sure. In time they will find the truth from her.'

'You sound like you think I should give up.'

'What else can you do?'

'Ask Tretow? He knows exactly what happened.'

Wahrmann gave a low, bitter laugh. 'And what makes you think he would even talk to you, let alone tell you anything of value?'

'I don't know. But I'll tell you one thing. I bet he's as curious about me and what I know as I am about him.'

'The difference is that he is prepared to kill. You said so yourself.'

'He can hardly have another go at me, not after what's already happened. That would just be asking for trouble. Anyway, Tretow's a bit short-staffed right now. Weiss's people are already after the men who shot at us. They'll be keeping their heads well down.'

Wahrmann gave an irritable, 'Puh!' exactly the same way Mariana did. 'Listen to yourself, talking like a tough guy. Have you not paid any attention to anything I have said? Have you not heard what happens when a man tries to play the hero? You are an architect. So stick to architecture . . . like I should have stuck to economics.

Mariana has already lost a father. Do you really want her to lose her husband as well?'

'I just told you, I don't think she will lose me . . .'

His hand reached out between our chairs and caught my wrist in a surprisingly fierce grip. 'I don't care what you think, Crookham. I am not prepared to take any more risks. Go back to your hotel: I will ask Weiss to make sure you are protected. Get a good night's sleep. Then go to the airport tomorrow morning and get the first flight back to England. Tell the doctors everything you know. Help my daughter. Help her to get well.'

'But I don't know enough yet. She'll end up in jail.'

'Yes, and in time she will be released, just as her mother and I were released. And that is when she will need you to help her rebuild her life. So promise me you won't contact Tretow.'

'Sure . . .'

'Say it.'

'I promise I won't contact Tretow.'

So I went back to my hotel. Weiss went off to hospital to receive some long overdue treatment for his wound, while Gerber took up position in the front lobby. The agent who'd been our driver took the seat from my bedroom table and stationed himself outside my door.

Five minutes later, I was online, trying to find a way to contact Hans-Peter Tretow.

I couldn't come so close and then just walk away. I

wanted to see the man who'd ruined Mariana's life. I wanted to be able to tell Andy that I'd found the man who'd put him in his grave. I wanted retribution for my brother and for Haller too. And if that meant I had to lie to Rainer Wahrmann, well tough. He'd lied often enough and found reasons to justify that, too.

I began by asking myself: how would Andy have done it? Well, he'd start by doing a basic directory trawl. The online Deutsche Telekom phone book listed four Tretows. Two were women, and neither of the others was called Hans-Peter. But any of them might have been his children: Magda Färber had said that Tretow had kids, and one of them had been a daughter who resembled Mariana.

I called all four numbers.

Two of the quartet – a man and a woman – were out. I left messages on their answering machines. The second man hung up on me before I'd even finished asking whether he knew Hans-Peter Tretow. The final woman, however, was very polite, apologizing for not being able to help me. That was nice enough, but it didn't get me any closer to my quarry. I had to find another way to reach him.

Hans-Peter's company, Tretow Immobilien, was listed in the directory's business section, but when I called I just got a recorded message telling me that the office was closed until nine o'clock tomorrow morning. I thought about calling Heike Schmidt. Andy wouldn't have had any qualms about it, but I couldn't face making her even more fearful by bringing Tretow back into her life. I was about to give up when I remembered Kamile, the receptionist at Haller's detective agency. Her card was still in my pocket.

'You said I could call if I needed any help,' I said when she answered her mobile. I could hear the sound of people talking in the background, glasses chinking and music playing. I guessed she and her colleagues were drowning their sorrows.

'Ah, yes . . . yes, of course.'

'I'm sorry . . . I'm the last person you want to be thinking about right now. But this has to do with Haller's death. I think I know who was responsible for killing him, or having him killed, anyway.'

Now I had her full attention: 'Who is it?'

'A man called Hans-Peter Tretow. And if it is him, he tried to have me and Weiss killed too, this afternoon.'

'But why? What have you, or Herr Haller, done to him?'

'Got too close to the truth. He has some kind of secret he wants to keep hidden. It all dates back to the communist days. And whatever the secret is, it has something to do with my wife Mariana . . . The thing is, I'm trying to track Tretow down. That's why I need your help, to give me a hand finding him.'

'Well, I may not be very useful. I am not a detective.'

'No, but you know the people who are. Could you get them onto this? I mean, they have ways of getting hold of numbers, right?'

'Sure, sure, of course,' Kamile said. 'I will speak to one or two of my colleagues. They are here with me now. Maybe one of them can do something for you.'

When I ended the call to Kamile, the clock on my phone read 20.42. I ordered room service for dinner and waited for someone from Xenon Detektivbüro to call me back. At 22.13 the phone rang. A voice said, 'Is that Herr Crookham . . . Herr Peter Crookham?' But the voice did not belong to a private detective.

It belonged to Hans-Peter Tretow.

46

'You were looking for me,' Tretow said.

'How did you find out?'

'Does it matter? You asked a number of people about me. One of them contacted me – more than one, in fact. So . . . how can I help you?'

He was a smooth bastard, I had to give him that. He didn't sound remotely flustered. But neither did he sound like an innocent businessman who'd just been phone-stalked by a total stranger.

'Well . . .' I began, wondering what to say next. The hell with it: I might as well just get straight to the point. The man had sent his people to kill me. It was a bit late to worry about social niceties. 'I want you to tell me why Haller was killed . . . why people were shooting at me earlier today . . . and what happened to my wife Mariana at a state orphanage where you worked as a caretaker in the late 1980s. Just tell me what the hell is going on.'

'Murder? Shooting?' Tretow replied. 'You should be very careful making false accusations, Mr Crookham. They can have serious consequences.'

'I don't want to make accusations, Tretow. I want to make a deal. I just want to know what happened to Mariana. And all I want to do with that information is give it to her psychiatrist so that he can use it to make her better. Tell me what I need to know and I'll be on the first plane home tomorrow morning.'

There was no denial, no more pretence of ignorance, just a straight question: 'And what if I don't tell you?'

'My wife is in a secure psychiatric unit. My brother's dead. My business is falling apart. Take away my hope of fixing Mariana and I've got nothing more to lose. I'll say anything to anyone who's willing to listen. I'll start joining the dots between a killing in Yorkshire, a crash on the A9 autobahn, a demolished orphanage and the rich, respectable businessman who wants to build millions of euros' worth of apartments on the site where he used to abuse little children. And if I can't get anyone to listen, I swear to God I'll just deal with you myself.'

The threat sounded feeble to me even as I made it. Tretow certainly wasn't about to quake in his boots. He simply said, 'There are two operatives from the BfV, the domestic intelligence agency, at your hotel. Can you leave the hotel without them knowing?'

'I think so, yes.'

'Think so isn't good enough. I need you to be alone . . .'

I remembered Wahrmann's warning and my blithe refusal to accept it. Maybe I'd been wrong. 'What, so your men can kill me?'

Tretow sighed. 'Don't be so melodramatic, Mr Crookham.'

'Really? Was I being melodramatic when they were shooting at me this afternoon?'

'You keep accusing me without the slightest evidence, Mr Crookham.'

'How about the threatening email you sent my brother? I'm assuming it was you, or one of your people, that sent it.'

'Presume what you like. The fact is I had nothing to do with your brother's death. That much is certain. Right now, my only desire is to pursue my business interests undisturbed by unnecessary distractions. I would far prefer a peaceful agreement between two reasonable men. So, can you get out of the hotel?'

'Yes, I believe so.'

'Then I need you to do so in precisely fifteen minutes. Leave through the service entrance at the back of the hotel. Turn left on Chausseestrasse and start walking. What will you be wearing?'

'Black overcoat, jeans. I'm tall, a metre ninety-one. You won't miss me.'

'OK,' Tretow said. 'Fifteen minutes.' And then the line went dead.

I spent the next thirteen minutes looking at every Google Earth and Streetview image I could find of the hotel, making sure that I knew exactly where I was relative to the rest of the building and the exit onto Chausseestrasse. Then I put on my coat, came out of my room and told the sentry I was heading down for a nightcap at the hotel bar. He spoke into a wrist-mike, listened to the response then gave me a nod of approval.

I took the lift down to the basement, then made my way at a jog through the corridors linking all the various storerooms, offices and services that a hotel hides in its underbelly. I was expecting to find a staircase at the back of the building that would take me back up to the ground floor, almost certainly somewhere near the kitchens, and sure enough – there it was. Up I went and emerged within sight of the rear exit. That opened onto a tarmac-covered yard where a couple of cars and a large van were parked. The yard was entirely surrounded by buildings, but on one side there was an arch that led to the street. I walked through it and there I was on Chausseestrasse.

I turned left, as instructed, and started walking. Barely ten seconds later a black VW Passat pulled up beside me, coming in the opposite direction. The front passenger window slid down and a man leaned across from the driver's seat. His hair was grey, his face as drawn and wrinkled as a headhunter's trophy. This was the man from the airport.

His smile seemed to say, 'Yes, you're right. You do recognize me.' But the only words he spoke were, 'Get in.'

47

The Passat pulled up in a side street just a few hundred yards from the Reichstag, the German parliament building. Across the road stood a mini-mall of shops and cafes, all closed for the night. But when we got out of the car the driver led me in the opposite direction, across the pavement and along a narrow path, slippery with half-melted snow. It led between two rows of rectangular concrete slabs, the first couple barely higher than my knee, but the rest rising in size until they towered to almost twice my height. Other paths crossed the one we were on at right-angles, the slabs marching away in every direction, rising and falling with the contours of the ground in an apparently limitless grid. The only light anywhere came from the faint ambient glow of the city, and the slabs cast deep, impenetrable shadows across the path. This army of great dark monoliths looming to either side acted like huge concrete blinkers so that all I could see was the path ahead, unrolling without any visible end.

There was hardly anybody else about. Occasionally a figure or two flitted across my line of sight as they passed between stones far in front of me, moving unheard and only half-seen, like ghosts in a giant's graveyard. But for the most part there were just the two of us, walking wordlessly as we made our way through a sinister, foreboding world of darkness and half-light.

Then a flame dazzled briefly from an impenetrable shadow up ahead, followed soon after by the sharp orange glow of a lit cigarette.

The driver stopped and I did the same but he shoved me in the back and grunted, 'Move.'

I walked towards the burning cigarette and then its owner stepped forward a pace, out of the blackness and, though he was still half lost in shadow and smoke, I saw the face of the man on the poster: the face of Hans-Peter Tretow. Tonight it had none of the prosperous, convivial salesmanship of that image. Tretow's eyes were wary and calculating as they observed my approach, and his mouth was set in a grim downward curve between ponderous, fleshy jowls. He was shorter than me, but bulkier, and though he must, I reckoned, have been somewhere in the region of sixty, there was still a sense of physical power, even menace, about him.

He reeked of money, too. His overcoat had a heavy fur collar, and as he came closer to me I caught a whiff of a rich, spicy aftershave.

'So, you are Peter Crookham,' he said.

I gave a nod of acknowledgement.

'And you are married to my sweet little Mariana ... the murderess.'

'She didn't murder anyone.'

'Nevertheless, a man died. You know where we are?'

'Sure, this is the Holocaust Memorial.'

'Quite so. A place where the German people say sorry for the sins we are supposed to have committed. We did that a lot, you know, for many years. But there is only so long that one can say sorry and only for so many things. Now we are sick of apologies. We have had enough of the past. That is why no one gives a shit about what happened here during the years of the DDR. They want to forget all about it. Understand?'

'If you say so ...'

'Good, because then you will also understand that your threats to me are empty. All your talk of exposing these things I am supposed to have done, of making people ashamed to buy my apartments, forget it.' He threw his cigarette stub to the ground and started grinding it into the slushy ground to emphasize his words. 'No one would print your story. No one would put you on TV. So do not expect me to apologize. Why should I? The ones who should say sorry are Wahrmann, and his dumb bitch of a wife, too.'

'Don't be ridiculous. They didn't abuse their daughter . . .'

Tretow opened his eyes in exaggerated surprise: 'That is what you think? I disagree. They were the ones who left their pretty little girl in a state orphanage, deserted and all alone, when she should have been safe at home. I took care of a lonely, unhappy, frightened child. I was her friend. I looked after her when her father did not. I let her know that even though he didn't love her and was happy to desert her, I would always be there for her. So don't you come here telling me that it is my fault she is now crazy. I did not do that to her. And, by the way, I did not "abuse" her, as you say. Ask her father. Ask how she was made to spread her legs for a doctor.'

Tretow's voice had been rising, his tone becoming more aggressive as he pursued his theme of self-justification. His self-proclaimed role as Mariana's protector made me want to wring his neck. But that last line hit home.

A slow, hungry grin crossed his face.

'Yes, you know about that, I can tell just by looking at you . . . so screw you if you think I hurt that child.'

His refusal to accept any responsibility was getting to me, and the provocation was entirely deliberate.

Tretow was waiting for me to lose control, I could feel it. Fighting to keep my voice level, I answered him back: 'You hurt Mariana all right. And not just her, either. I've seen the damage you did. More than twenty years later and those kids are still wrecks . . .'

'Ha! You mean Heike Schmidt?'

'How do you know I met her?'

'The same way I've known everything you did since you arrived here in Berlin. That fool Haller was too trusting. Old loyalties die harder than he supposed . . . But Heike . . . *ach*, I could tell you things about that girl. I could tell you about Mariana, too. But I am a businessman. I must have something in return.'

'Such as . . . ?'

'Well, you are seeking information. So you should give some information to me. It has been a long time since I saw Mariana. I used to care for her very much and it would please me to know about how she is now and about your life together. For example . . . do you have children of your own?'

Of all the questions to ask, how had he known that would be the one that would hurt me most? He could not possibly have known about Mariana's operation . . . could he? It had to be blind luck, or just a psychopath's intuition for the best means to cause pain.

Tretow shrugged: 'Oh well, if you will not answer me, our meeting is at an end. Goodnight, Mr—'

'No,' I said. 'We don't have any children.'

'Hmm, you surprise me. Do you not want any, or is it Mariana?'

'She can't have children.' I was damned if I was telling him why. 'So, I've answered your question. Your turn. Let's start with Heike Schmidt.'

Tretow sighed like a man who has just had a sip of a particularly fine brandy. 'Ah Heike, she always had a plain, sour face, but she was a natural, just a dirty little bitch. It was in her blood, in her bones . . .'

I thought of the shattered woman alone behind her apartment's locked front door: 'How can you say things like that? She was a child, a little child!'

Tretow leered at me: 'And you think children have no interest in sex? You think they don't enjoy it? Well, you didn't see Heike the way I did, entertaining all those Western politicians and industrialists as though she was born to be a whore. I have films, if you'd care to watch.'

'You sick bastard.'

'Heike didn't complain. She had pretty dresses. She had Barbie dolls. All the other girls envied her. That was how Mariana persuaded her to do it in the first place . . . Ha-ha! You should see your face, Mr Crookham. Such a look of surprise. And yet, you must be desperate to know more. Sadly for you, that will require you to answer another question. More than one, actually. So . . . Mariana, is she still beautiful?'

'Not the last time I saw her. Right now she's a wreck. And it's thanks to you, I know it is . . .'

'Calm yourself, Mr Crookham. Just tell me what Mariana looks like. You know, when she is not committing acts of murder. Tell me, or I walk . . .'

'She's very beautiful, just like she always was. In my eyes, she's the most beautiful woman on earth.'

'And charming?'

'Yes, very charming.'

Tretow nodded affably. 'Good, good, I am pleased to hear that she is still the Mariana I remember. After all, that is how she was able to recruit the other girls. They all worshipped her because she was so pretty. She was the princess of the orphanage. Fräulein Färber probably told you that already, no? So when she invited them to come on a little trip, an expedition to Potsdam, or maybe a picnic out in the countryside, of course they were happy to say yes. The girls, and some boys too, would go to play with their nice, kind new uncles and Mariana would stay with me.'

I thought of the ease with which Mariana had recruited the clients that had made our architectural practice so successful and wondered whether she'd had any idea at all of the pattern she had been repeating. The stain of her childhood was seeping into my own memories of her, tainting everything it touched. I was having to breathe deeply now, slowly and deliberately, just to keep my rage in check: 'Did she know? Did she know what was happening to the other kids?'

Tretow looked delighted by the effect he was having on me. 'I don't know . . . what do you think? The children were always under strict orders not to talk about what happened, even to each other . . . but you know how children are. It is hard for them to keep a secret. But I can tell you this for sure: we spent so many hours together, Mariana and I. She helped me when I worked in my vegetable garden, also. And because she was so special and so useful, I never touched her. A little kiss, maybe, sometimes, but that is all. And photographs, of course. She loved to have her picture taken. Such a vain little creature and so proud of her beauty – perhaps you have noticed that? Well . . . have you?'

'Not really, no . . . I don't think she's particularly vain.'

Tretow did not seem pleased by that reply. 'I think you are just trying to defend your wife, Mr Crookham. Very noble, to be sure. In any case, I knew that Mariana was very, very precious. I was saving her for a special moment, a special client. There was a minister in your own government, a very senior minister indeed, whose tastes . . . well, let us just say that he had seen Mariana's photograph. He would have done anything, given anything, to spend even an hour with her. With a girl like Mariana, you understand, it is the first time that really counts. After that . . .'

I took a pace towards him, raising my fist.

Tretow backed away, both hands up in front of him: 'Whoa! Control yourself. My colleague Mr Meyer, the one who brought you here, is still watching us. Do not be deceived by his appearance. He may look a little old but he is still a very dangerous individual. Also he has a strong sense of civic duty. So when he happens to be walking by and sees a respectable man such as myself being attacked, well, of course he will come to my rescue and then who knows what might happen. So, let us not argue . . .'

Tretow's hands dropped and he stepped forward again, forcing me to back away to give space. 'You should be grateful to me,' he continued. He wasn't bothering to ask me questions now. He wanted to tell me everything about Mariana, all the grisly details, knowing that every word he said, every new revelation, was cutting me like the lash of a whip.

'I treated your wife very well, even when she begged me to let her have a nice uncle like Heike and the other girls did . . . She felt left out, you see. She wanted to be like them. She was worried that maybe it was because she was not pretty enough, after all. That is why she was so keen to pose for photographs and films. She wanted to please me, to prove that she could look pretty if she really tried. Here, I have some pictures . . .'

Now my temper snapped. As Tretow reached into his coat and momentarily looked down to see what he was doing I stepped forward, grabbed him by the scruff of the neck and shoved him hard against the monolith behind him. His head snapped back and hit the bare concrete with a clearly audible crack. Tretow staggered forward with a howl of pain, lifting his hands to his skull, and at that moment I heard the sound of running footsteps just behind me.

I turned and there was Meyer, running straight at me, his hands held low, a dull glint of light reflecting off the bare blade of the knife in his right hand. If he got close to me I was a dead man. But I still had one chance. I stepped towards him and before he could get his knife within range leaned forward and swung a wild right-handed punch, a crude, untrained haymaker towards the side of his head. I was at the very far limit of my reach, but Meyer can't have been expecting such an aggressive response to his charge because his left arm was slow in coming up to block me. My arm skimmed over the top of his counter and smacked into his temple with all my fourteen and a half stones behind it.

Meyer went down like a cartoon cat that's just run into a frying pan. At the same time an agonizing pain exploded through my right hand as my knuckles shattered against his skull. For a second the pain simply served to make me even angrier. As Meyer sank to his knees I swung my leg in a smooth, rugby punt arc that connected with the side of his chin, sending him sprawling unconscious across the path.

Tretow, however, was very much still with us. He still looked groggy and a little unsteady on his feet but he was getting better with every second that passed. Meanwhile, he too had taken out a knife – from the same coat pocket, perhaps, in which he'd claimed to be keeping photographs – and was coming towards me in a slow, crouching advance, the knife out in front of him.

He was armed and I was not. I'd had one lucky shot, but now I had to defend myself without the benefit of surprise. And this time I only had one working hand.

Keeping my eyes fixed firmly on Tretow's knife hand, I stepped backwards. Directly behind me there was a gap between two stones: a cross-path intersecting with the one we were on. If I could get onto that there would be nothing to stop me making a run for it. I couldn't hit Tretow any more. But there was no reason why I couldn't outpace him.

I took another step back . . .

And tripped on Meyer's outstretched arm.

I stumbled backwards, my feet scrabbling for purchase on the icy, snow-dusted slush until I finally lost balance and slipped backwards, instinctively putting my hands out to break my fall and screaming out in pain as my broken bones bore the full weight of my tumbling body against the rock-hard tiles from which the path was formed.

As I propped myself up on my elbows, Tretow appeared in the gap between the stones through which I had just fallen. His shoulders and chest were heaving for breath as he took another step towards me. I lashed out at him with my feet, hoping to hit him in the knee, or at least on the exposed shin bone, but he was able to turn so that my shoes simply collided with his calves, the force of their impact softened by the heavy flesh. I tried again, hoping to trip him this time, but he was ready for me, stepping past me to my left, squeezing between my body and the side of the nearest monolith, the knife coming ever closer to me.

In desperation I kicked my right leg up and across, aiming for his knife hand. Tretow swung the blade towards me and it slashed through the fabric of my jeans and cut across my shin.

Tretow took another pace and now he was standing right over me. I raised my left arm in a pitiful attempt to fend him off, but he knew I didn't stand a chance.

His lips twisted into that predatory, blood-hungry smile and I knew in that moment that he was revisiting an old pleasure: he had killed before.

He leaned forward, grabbing my throat with his left hand as his right pulled back and cocked like the hammer of a revolver, ready to deliver the first deadly stab to my guts. I should have been terrified, but in that moment the sensation that filled me was a strange kind of acceptance. My brother had been killed by the cut of a knife and now I was going to die the same way. It felt somehow like an act of atonement, as though I were paying the price for my wife's act of sin.

For a moment Tretow's face was just a few centimetres from my own, the reek of his aftershave was almost overpowering and his voice was as soft and coaxing as a lover's caress as he purred, 'The answer was in the allotment.'

He seemed to gather himself, summoning all his force for the killing blow . . .

And then his face disintegrated, right before my eyes, as a deafening crack echoed between the concrete slabs. An explosion of blood, bone fragments and grey brain matter spattered across my face, the bones stabbing me like acupuncture needles, and there was a clatter behind me: the sound of a bullet ricocheting off the path and embedding itself in concrete.

Tretow's body slumped forward onto mine, forcing me back to the ground in a gruesome embrace. As I lay there, pinned to the cold, wet, iron-hard path, I screamed, 'Get off me!' and swiped my hands across my face, frantically trying to get the contents of Tretow's skull off my skin and hair. Then I saw a pair of women's leather boots below tight-cut blue jeans and heard the sound of Gerber's voice, like an irritable wife upbraiding a wandering husband as she said, 'You should have told me where you were going.'

But I wasn't paying any attention to her. A sense of calm was slowly cutting through the disgust, the nausea and the panic of my death embrace with Hans-Peter Tretow as I realized that my quest had finally reached its holy grail. Now I knew why Mariana had killed my brother. And I knew what had made her do it, too.

48

THURSDAY

They took me to the nearest casualty department and I was shoved full of painkillers while my hand was x-rayed and plastered and my lower leg stitched up. With my one working hand I washed Tretow's bloody remains from my face and then stuck my head under the tap, tunelessly humming, 'I'm going to wash that man right out of my hair.' It was gallows humour, the song of a man who has walked through the valley of the shadow of death and somehow come out the other side.

While I was still in the hospital Gerber and Weiss interviewed me about the sequence of events that had led me to the showdown with Tretow at the Holocaust Memorial. I had a question for Gerber, too: 'How did you find me in there?'

'With difficulty. I had put a tracker into the lining of your coat while you were talking to Wahrmann. It was my opinion, and that of my colleagues, that you might try to do something reckless. But Tretow chose the worst possible place for me to find you. There are almost three thousand of those concrete slabs and each one of them provides excellent cover, as well as interfering with any kind of signal. It was only when you shouted out in pain that I was able to get a bearing on where you were.'

I looked at the massive plaster mitten through which only the tips of my fingers were visible: 'So breaking my knuckles saved my life . . . doesn't seem too much of a price to pay.'

'It saved your life twice over since you also disabled Meyer.'

'Will he live?'

'Oh yes. He has a little concussion, some whiplash on his neck. That is all.'

'And Tretow . . . He said something to me, just before he died. "The answer was in the allotment."'

Weiss frowned. 'Do you know what he meant by that?'

'Yes, I think so. There were allotments near the orphanage. They're still there, even though the orphanage itself has gone. Anyway, Tretow had one of them. He used to take the kids there, his favourites. I think you'll find something there. Something that explains exactly what he did.'

'We'll start a search in the morning, at first light.'

'There's something else,' I said. 'When I was talking

to Tretow he said he still had films of the kids with men. Important men. You should try to get hold of them before someone else does.'

Weiss glanced at Gerber and she rose to her feet, pulling her mobile out of her bag. As she left the room she was already giving instructions to organize a search of Tretow's home. I turned back to Weiss: 'He also said he had pictures . . . of my wife Mariana, when she was little. He said they were—'

'We found them in his coat,' Weiss said, gently interrupting me. 'They are – how should I say this – very explicit, very disturbing. I would not advise you to look at them now. But maybe we could make copies of them for the benefit of your wife's lawyers. They would, perhaps, help in her defence.'

'Thank you.' I closed my eyes for a moment, thinking of the photographs of herself that Mariana had sent me years before. Had she been aware of the echoes from her childhood, or was she unconsciously playing out the same scenarios as she exposed herself to the camera lens: compelled to do it, but not knowing why?

'So what will you do now?' Weiss asked. 'I can have someone take you back to your hotel. Perhaps you can get an hour or two of sleep before you fly home.'

'Not yet. There's somewhere else I have to go first, someone I need to see.'

49

It was half past five in the morning, still pitch-dark outside and hardly a sociable time to pay a visit. Still I pressed my finger to the doorbell and kept it there, even when there was no answer for ten seconds, thirty ... almost a minute before the intercom crackled and a tired, cross voice asked, 'Who is this?'

'It's Crookham, we need to talk.'

'Go away. I have nothing more to say to you.'

'Please, wait ... Tretow is dead. You're safe now.'

'What do you mean?'

'He's dead, I promise. Let me in and I'll explain it all ...'

Heike Schmidt pressed the buzzer, the lock clicked open and I went up to her apartment. She brewed some coffee, we sat down at her kitchen table and I gave her a version of the account I'd provided for Gerber and Weiss, minus Tretow's remarks about Schmidt herself.

Schmidt was sceptical, almost indifferent at first. But as my story went on and she came to believe that it might be true I could see her interest, attention and even excitement rising. From time to time she interrupted, asking me for extra details, or making me repeat a section she particularly liked, so that I felt almost like a father reading his child a bedtime story. And there was something childlike about her relish of the more gruesome aspects of the story.

'Did his head just splatter, like a watermelon?' she asked me after I'd described Tretow's final moment.

'I suppose so. Something like that.'

'And you were covered with his actual brains?'

'Yes,' I almost retched. 'It wasn't very pleasant.'

'Yuck! . . . So he's absolutely certainly dead? He can't ever get better?'

'No. He's gone forever and he's not coming back.'

I felt as though I'd been talking to Schmidt's eight- or nine-year-old self. The abused and exploited girl that had been hidden away inside her for so long was crawling back out into the light.

'Now can I ask you some questions?' I said.

'Sure,' she replied.

'There are really just two things I want to know. The first sounds absurd, I know, but did Tretow ever wear aftershave when you knew him?'

Schmidt did not say a word. Instead, she burst out

laughing, and not just for a second or two, but a full-blown attack of the giggles. A couple of times she tried to compose herself enough to talk, but then she collapsed again, leaving me unnerved, even alarmed by her manic emotion. I felt embarrassed. Finally, Schmidt took a deep breath, wiped the tears from her eyes and said, 'Yes, he certainly did wear aftershave. In fact . . .' she started to giggle again. 'In fact . . . Control yourself, Heike! . . . In fact, we used to call him Mister Stinky because he always smelled so strongly. And the stuff he used was really horrible, too!'

'Privileg?' I asked.

'Yes! That's so funny! How did you know?' she squealed delightedly. 'When he first arrived at the orphanage he used to talk about the good old days when he had the finest French and American cologne. But now he had to make do with . . . what did he call it? Yes, "cheap communist muck". Later, when . . . when we were all working for him, he sometimes got good stuff again. But we still called him Mister Stinky anyway.'

Suddenly the demon that had haunted my imagination from the night of Andy's murder was brought right down to size. He was nothing more than Mr Stinky, a grubby pervert who soaked himself in cheap, malodorous perfume to cover the stench of his corruption.

'Why did you want to know about Privileg?' Schmidt asked.

'My brother had found some while he was here. I think he was wearing it on the night he died. I think the smell of it and the memories it brought back was what made Mariana . . . you know, go crazy.'

'My God, that's terrible. Do you think he knew about Tretow, that he used to wear it?'

'No, I'm certain he didn't. Knowing Andy, he'd have done it as a joke.'

'But not a funny joke, I am afraid . . .'

'No, and my next question isn't much fun, either . . . I have to know: what happened at Tretow's allotment?'

Heike Schmidt said nothing. She sat quite still for several seconds then got up and went to her kettle, the old-fashioned metal kind, sitting on a gas hob. She fussed with it distractedly as she made herself another cup of coffee.

'Want one?' she said, not even bothering to turn in my direction.

'No thanks, I'm fine.'

She opened a drawer in the unit next to the oven and pulled out a packet of cigarettes. 'Supposed to have given up,' she said. Any hint of childish innocence had disappeared now. This was an adult woman: one who had seen and suffered too much.

She held her hair back with one hand as she bent down to get a light from the hob. Finally, she brought her coffee cup and a saucer over to the table with her as she sat back down. She flicked some ash into the saucer: 'Do you mind?' she asked.

'Of course not. Go ahead.'

Schmidt smoked her cigarette right down to the filter, not saying a word before she finally stubbed it out in the saucer. Then she grimaced. 'Stale . . . tasted horrible.' She swallowed some coffee to take away the taste of the tobacco. Only when all that was done did she start to answer my question.

'Tretow always made it very clear to the children that, you know, worked for him, that we must never tell anyone what went on between us and the men: not even our closest friends, not even the children who came with us on his "little trips to the country". This was our special secret. I mean we all knew, of course, because we were all doing . . .'

For a moment she was unable to go on. I didn't even try to prompt her. Nothing I could say could possibly be of any use.

'We were all doing the same things,' Schmidt finally said. 'Well, I say that, but I don't know for sure because . . . I suppose that was why Tretow didn't want us talking: so that we would never know . . .'

'What about Mariana? Did she know?'

'Not at first, no. All she knew was that we were getting presents from the men. She was a little jealous. She used to beg Tretow to let her have a nice uncle too, but he said no. She was the precious one, the princess, so he was saving her for a true prince.'

Yes, I thought, a fat, slobbering British politician. Some prince.

'You said, "not at first". So she did find out in the end?'

'We all did. Two of us talked, two boys. They were called Timmi and Marko. You know how some little boys are almost prettier than a girl? Well, that was how Timmi was. He was like a boy version of Mariana. In fact, they were very good friends. Timmi was always playing with us girls. He was very sweet, very gentle, not like the other boys. Marko was the total opposite. He was a little tough guy, not afraid of anybody, always getting into fights, even with the bigger boys. When anyone ever picked on Timmi, Marko always came to his rescue. For some reason, even though they were so different, they were very good friends. They talked about everything. So Timmi was upset by things he had to do, or the way someone had treated him. Then he talked to Marko. Anyway, Marko started telling everyone else, saying he was going to go to Mister Stinky and tell him they wouldn't go with the uncles any more. Tretow found out and he was furious.'

Schmidt's face crumpled. She began to cry, still trying to force the words out: 'He ... He ... Oh God, I am sorry ...'

'That's OK, take your time.'

'He killed them ... hit them again and again ...' Schmidt scrabbled on the table for another cigarette. 'He made us look at their bodies, all covered in blood, and told us that was how we would end up if we told anyone anything at all. And he told us that he could kill us, any of us, and no one would ever care ... and we believed him because he had killed Marko and Timmi and there were no police or anything. Then he cut the bodies into pieces – he did not force us to watch that, thank God – and he put them in garbage sacks and took them to the vegetable garden. He made us dig a deep hole. We had to take it in turns. Then he put the bags into the holes and we had to cover them up again. We even had to take plants from a little greenhouse that he had and plant them in the earth that we had disturbed, so that no one could see what we had done. And then, once again he told us. Do not tell anyone, ever. And to this day, I never have ...'

'Those boys ... had Mariana ... ?'

Schmidt looked me in the eyes and gave a sad little nod of the head. 'She had recruited them, yes. She had such charm, even then, as a little girl. I mean, I knew I was so ugly compared to her, but I didn't mind. She had chosen me to be her friend and that was enough to make me feel a little bit special. I know that must sound stupid ...'

'No, it doesn't, not at all. Believe me, I know exactly how you felt.'

'Then you know she could persuade anyone to do anything for her. But she did not know what would happen, or what Tretow would do to Marko and Timmi. How could she?'

'But once it had happened, and she saw them dead, she must have blamed herself.'

'Yes, I would think so, although she never spoke of it.'

'No . . .'

But the secret shame had been planted deep inside her, covered by layer upon layer of self-protection until, one evening in Yorkshire, a man had come to her house, smelling like Tretow, like Mister Stinky, and then the whole cycle of death and blood had been played out once again. Now I realized why Mariana had said she was guilty, why it was all her fault, why she was a *böses Mädchen*. She hadn't been referring to Andy's death at all. She had no consciousness of that. It was the little girl in her talking and the two boys' deaths for which she blamed herself.

I was lost in my thoughts, so at first I did not feel Heike Schmidt's fingers tapping on my arm . . .

'Herr Crookham . . . Herr Crookham,' she was saying.

'Yes?'

'Are the police going to the garden?'

'Yes, the search is beginning at first light.'

Schmidt glanced out of the kitchen window at the sky just turning from black to a paler grey.

'Then we must get going,' she said. 'I will save them some time. I will show them where to dig.'

50

SIX MONTHS LATER
North Yorkshire

Mariana had planted two large pots of lavender by the entrance to her vegetable garden and there were bumblebees and cabbage-white butterflies buzzing and fluttering among the scented purple flowers in the warmth of the afternoon sun. She was kneeling down, a small weeding fork in her hand, beside a bed she had planted with courgettes. Their large, bristly leaves were interspersed with the vivid orange and yellow of nasturtiums and the scarlet splashes of cherry tomatoes, clambering up a metal frame at the far end of the bed.

I watched as she put the fork down on the grass beside her and knelt there, silently, facing the life that she created. Then I closed the gate behind me. Mariana turned her head at the noise and smiled as she saw me.

'Are you off, then?' she said.

'Soon,' I replied. 'I just came to see how you were.' I

held out the china mug in my hand: 'I brought you a cup of tea.'

Mariana got up, dusted down her bare knees and came towards me. 'Thank you, kind sir,' she said, giving a little mock curtsey as she took the mug.

I looked at her lovely face. It was a little thinner than it had been, frailer, with darker hollows beneath her cheekbones and faint new lines round her eyes and the side of her mouth. The life was back in her tiger-eyes, but there was a new, reflective quality, a gentle melancholy to the way she looked at the world. I leaned forward and gave her a soft, quick kiss.

'You're very welcome.'

'Mmm . . .' she murmured as she took the first sip from her mug. 'Perfect.'

'The tea or the kiss?'

Mariana laughed contentedly: 'Both.'

'You looked like you were a million miles away.'

A shadow of sadness crossed her face: 'I was thinking about my father, how wrong I'd been about him all these years, how cruel I'd been to hate him.'

'You got to see him, though. That was something.'

'Well, to be reconciled at last, that was wonderful . . . but painful too. We had so little time together . . .'

'I know . . . so are you sure you're going to be all right?'

Mariana was five weeks into her phased release from in-patient psychiatric care back into everyday life. Week by week she would be allowed to spend more time at home until she was finally reclassified as an out-patient. Tonight would be her first night alone in the house.

On the basis of the psychiatric evidence, a detailed account of Hans-Peter Tretow's activities provided by the Berlin police and the personal testimony of both Weiss and Heike Schmidt, the judge at Mariana's trial had been as generous in his sentencing as we could have hoped. He had found that she had not been respon-sible for her actions at the time of Andy's death and posed no further threat to society. He therefore placed her in Dr Wray's care, leaving him to decide the appro-priate form and duration of treatment, first at a low-security psychiatric unit and more recently at the private clinic where he also practised. On compassionate grounds she had also been permitted to fly to Berlin to see her father again before he died. His daughter's presence after so many years seemed to give Rainer Wahrmann the closure he needed to depart the world in peace. Mariana and her mother had been at his bedside when he died.

'Yes, I'll be all right,' Mariana answered. 'Thanks to you.'

'You mean, the further away I am, the happier you are?' I teased.

'No,' she draped her arms around my neck and looked

up at me with a gaze that seemed to reach right into my heart and soul. 'Because you saved me.'

I didn't know what to say. I had no easy reply to the depth of feeling in her voice. So I did the English thing and as I put my hands on the back of her hips and drew her body closer to me, I deflected her emotion by self-deprecation.

'No, not really, there were lots of people . . .'

'But it was you who believed in me. You fought for me. You were my knight in shining armour.'

I smiled wryly as I shook my head. 'No, I'm just your husband. That's what I'm supposed to do. And anyway, I love you. I wanted to do it.'

Mariana reached up to stroke my face with the tips of her fingers, looking deep into my eyes as she asked: 'Do you still love me? Can you love me – the madwoman, the killer?'

'Of course.'

She frowned: 'How can you say that, when you know what I have done? When you know the truth about me?'

'It's because I know, that's the whole point. I thought I loved you before, but really I just loved an idea of you, a fantasy. Now, though, after everything that's happened, you're completely real to me. I know the very worst and the very best things about you. And it just makes my feelings even deeper and stronger.'

'I know the truth about you too,' she said, so quietly that it was almost a whisper. 'And I love you more than you can ever know.'

We kissed again, a longer, deeper embrace, and then Mariana pulled away and said, 'Enough of this. Time to go!'

I grabbed her again. 'One more kiss?'

She slapped my chest playfully: 'No, no, no!' and I let go of her with an exaggerated look of despair on my face.

'I must be getting on with my gardening,' Mariana said, all brisk and businesslike now that her need for reassurance had been satisfied. 'And you must start driving if you are going to get there in time for dinner. Vickie will be very cross if you are late for your big reconciliation.'

'All right, all right, I know when I'm not wanted . . .'

'Send her my regards, though I know she will not want them. And Pete . . .' Mariana reached out and took my hand. 'Drive safely. Come back to me safe and sound. I never want to be without you again.'

'I will,' I said and pulled my hand away. But she gripped me tighter.

'There's something I want you to know. I wrote to Doctor Reede. When I get out I am going to see him about my operation. I know it is very, very difficult. But if it is at all possible, I want to have it reversed.'

'That's ... that's wonderful,' I stuttered, trying to control the surge of emotion her words had released in me: a joyous, exultant feeling of hope, combined with a dread that seemed like an echo of the pain that the discovery of Reede's original letter had brought me.

'Can I ask ... I need to know ... why did you do it? I mean, without telling me, or anything?'

Mariana looked at me with anguish in her eyes. 'I don't know. I wish I could give you a good explanation, but I didn't even have one at the time. I think maybe I felt that I didn't deserve children, though I didn't know why. And there was a fear, too ... this terrible black fear ... I thought ...' She was suddenly on the verge of tears, 'I thought I would do them harm – that they would not be safe with me. But I did not understand why ...'

I took her in my arms again and she buried her head against my chest. 'You understand now, though, don't you?' I asked. 'And you know that it wasn't your fault, that you were a victim.'

She nodded, her head still down. I felt her take a deep breath and let it out slowly. Then she raised her head and looked me straight in the eye.

'Yes,' she said. 'I understand. And now I want us to have children.'

51

The churchyard that had been so bare and dead on the day we buried Andy was now filled with reminders of the constant renewal of life. The trees were all in leaf, the trim lawn between the gravestones had the lovely summer smell of new-mown grass and the air was filled with birdsong. The Norman church, which had seemed so bleak on the morning of the funeral, now exuded a comforting sense of permanence. Nine hundred or more years had passed since it was first built. Generation after generation had been baptized and married within its walls then laid to rest in its graveyard, and here it still stood and would stand for countless generations still to come, a place of peace in which to take one's final rest.

I am not a religious man and I cannot believe in a God who knows and cares about me, or a soul that lives forever. But I like the rituals of church, the comforting reassurance of a hymn I have known since my earliest boyhood and that special church scent of dust and old wooden pews. So I went inside and knelt for a minute to gather my thoughts before I walked back out to the place where Andy was buried.

I stood for a moment and looked at his stone, then I got down on my haunches and placed some flowers in a vase at its base. I didn't know what to do next. I felt shy, uncertain, almost embarrassed. But there was no one else in the churchyard and nothing to stop me talking. Alive or dead, he was still there and he was still my brother.

'I know it's been a while, but I had a lot to do,' I said. 'I was trying to make things better … well, as much better as they could be, anyway …

'Oh Christ, I wish you were here with me now, mate. I wish we could go down to the pub, have that pint we were meant to have, you know, that night, and just have a laugh. All the way down in the car, I was wondering what to say, but now I'm here I don't have a clue, except … I'm so sorry, Andy. I'm just so, so sorry …'

And then my shoulders heaved, my breath caught in my throat and for the very first time I wept for my poor, dead brother …

AUTHOR'S NOTE

Not surprisingly, this book could not have been written without the unfailing kindness, generosity and assistance of Germans: three in particular. The London-based consultant psychotherapist Bernd Leygraf was invaluable in explaining the mechanisms by which buried childhood pain can explode into adult violence, and the passing on of the burden of sin or suffering from one generation to another. In Berlin, Matthias Willenbrink, director of the AXOM Group of detective agencies, was a superb guide to the city and its recent history, a fount of great stories about detective work and an insightful observer of the way in which ex-Stasi operatives have transitioned into private detectives. Further thanks go to Jochen Meismann of the Condor detective agency, in particular for his description of German bureaucracy as it applies to birth certificates.

The scenes set in Hohenschönhausen were hugely influenced by the archived testimony of the following survivors of imprisonment by the Stasi: Sigrid Paul, Mario Röllig, Edda Schönherz, Matthias Bath, Horst Jänichen, Herbert Pfaff and Wolfgang Arndt. The account of the Hohenschönhausen tour (which takes place every day, guided by ex-prisoners) was entirely fictionalized, but the descriptions of the various offices, corridors and cells, and the hellish treatment meted out in them are, I hope, a true reflection of the prison and its terrible history.

Anna Funder's book *Stasiland* was an enthralling, wonderfully readable, guide to the mindset of the East German state, its agents and its victims: I strongly recommend it to anyone interested in the subject.

Many thanks, too, to Agatha Rogers of the Priory Hospital, Southampton, for her explanation of the rules governing patient confidentiality, and Marina Cantacuzino of The Forgiveness Project, whose advice about the ways in which we come to terms with loss was never far from my mind. Bob Colover, a lawyer with decades of experience as a barrister, stipendiary magistrate and lecturer in law, was immensely helpful in taking me through the various legal and procedural issues involved in cases of diminished responsibility. I have knowingly taken liberties with some aspects of what Bob told me. Any legal errors, therefore, are entirely my fault, not his.

I would also like to thank my father, David Churchill Thomas, for two things. In the first place, he explained how a man such as Rainer Wahrmann would signal his availability as an asset to Western intelligence (a much fuller account of his defection was written, but did not survive my editing process). And in the second, through a diplomatic career that took our family to Russia and Cuba, contrasted with three years in Washington DC, he unknowingly instilled in me a fascination for and loathing of totalitarian communism.

As I was writing this book, I mentioned to Dad that I'd been watching *The Lives of Others* (*Das Leben der Anderen*), Florian Henckel von Donnersmark's Oscar-winning film about East Germany. Much of it is set in a Berlin apartment bugged by the Stasi. 'You spent the first two years of your life in a flat just like that,' he replied.

It turned out that the Moscow apartment block in which we lived between 1959–61 during my father's posting to the British Embassy had been bugged by the KGB. The various international diplomats who lived there were forbidden from going into the attic on the grounds, they presumed, that the agents listening to them were working there. So my earliest years, like Mariana's, were lived in the shadow of the secret police.

Perhaps all fiction turns out to be autobiography in the end.